He picked up the novel from his desk and hefted it, a heavy book bound in what felt like leather. It looked expensive. According to the checkout dates stamped in the back, Mark was the first one to have taken the book out in a little over seven years. If the note was straight, that meant that for a little more than two years the money had been just sitting in the Moorland High School library, waiting to be found.

A pure piece of luck, and it couldn't have come at a better time. The injury to his knee that had finished him in football in October had also cost him his part-time job at the Giant Eagle Supermarket. Since then, he'd had to depend entirely on his mother for spending money. He hated having to get money from his mother.

And here was a gift of three hundred dollars with no strings attached that he didn't tie himself. It was almost too good to be true.

ANOTHER KIND OF MONDAY

WILLIAM E. COLES, JR.

property of
the Velez
family.

AVON
tempest

AVON BOOKS, INC.
1350 Avenue of the Americas
New York, New York 10019

First Avon Tempest Printing: June 1999

Printed in the U.S.A.

OPM 10 9 8 7 6 5 4

For Janet
My wife and pal

I think that if we examine our lives, we will find that most good has come to us from the few loyalties, and a few discoveries made many generations before we were born, which must always be made anew. These . . . may sometimes appear to come by chance, but in the infinite web of things and events chance must be something different from what we think it to be. To comprehend that is not given to us, and to think of it is to recognize a mystery, and to acknowledge the necessity of faith.

—Edwin Muir, *An Autobiography*

The hundred-dollar bills were so new that Mark had had to pinch them apart. With the eraser at the end of his pencil, he slid one to the top of his desk blotter and centered it. Then he carefully aligned the other two bills seamlessly below the first. Leaning forward over his folded arms, he stared straight down into the mild eyes of each of the Benjamin Franklins. It was then that he noticed the serial numbers on the bills were consecutive.

A sudden gust of December wind rattled sleet against his bedroom window, bringing his head up. Maybe there were more.

The two deliberately stuck-together pages of the library book that had hidden the note and the money had re-sealed. Beginning at that point, Mark went through the last quarter of Dickens's novel, turning one page at a time. Nothing.

He went back to the note. It was typed on very thin paper.

Assignment 1

Greetings and Congratulations.

Though at this writing it has been five years since anyone checked this copy of *Great Expectations* out of your high school library, I knew

1

that sooner or later you were bound to come along. At least I have invested much in that assumption, so without further ado let us begin our conversation.

Pip, the hero of the novel you are reading, singled himself out as a young man worthy of Great Expectations and was then offered the opportunity for an education that would enable him to realize them.

You too are now a young man or a young woman of Great Expectations should you care to define yourself that way, and if you do, you will be given the opportunity for an education that will enable you to prove you merit the distinction. To wit: You are hereby offered a quest, which you must take up and complete satisfactorily if you are to receive what is being held in store for you. Should you decide to elect the quest, you will do so with the understanding that you are forbidden, until otherwise instructed, to say anything of it to anyone. You are also forbidden to make any attempt to discover the identity of your benefactor—namely, myself. A violation of either of these conditions will result in the immediate termination of our conversation. You will signal your willingness to elect the quest by locating Assignment 2 with the verse clue below. The money accompanying this assignment, incidentally, is yours whatever you decide to do.

> Mihal Dobrejcak and his Mary
> Also were led by a star.
> Quester: read their history,
> And decide what your chances are.

By the Number Four Gate of what killed him
Is what came of Mihal's dream.
Look to the steps you're invited to take
To become part of the scheme.

What was this that he'd found—or that in some way
had found him?

It was pure chance that he'd gotten the copy of *Great
Expectations* that he had. His school-issued paperback
copy of the novel, which he was supposed to have finished
by the end of Christmas vacation, he'd lost. At least it
hadn't been in his locker when he'd rummaged through
it the afternoon Moorland was shutting down for the holidays. He'd burst into the school library just as Mrs. Ham-
mersmith was putting on her coat to leave, and the copy
of *Great Expectations* he'd grabbed off the shelf was the
first one to catch his eye.

He picked up the novel from his desk and hefted it, a
heavy book bound in what felt like leather. It looked expensive. According to the checkout dates stamped in the
back, Mark was the first one to have taken the book out
in a little over seven years. If the note was straight, that
meant that for a little more than two years the money
had been just sitting in the Moorland High School library,
waiting to be found.

A pure piece of luck, and it couldn't have come at a
better time. The injury to his knee that had finished him
in football in October had also cost him his part-time job
at the Giant Eagle Supermarket. Since then, he'd had to
depend entirely on his mother for spending money. He
hated having to get money from his mother.

And here was a gift of three hundred dollars with no

strings attached that he didn't tie himself. It was almost too good to be true.

Mark put down the book, picked up the bill closest to him, and rubbed it between his thumb and forefinger. Under the light of his desk lamp, the details of the engraving sprang up sharp and clear. Nothing wrong with the money that he could see—and besides, if the bills were counterfeit, then wouldn't their serial numbers all have been the same?

Was it a joke of some kind, then? A put-on?

But a joke of what kind? Who would put up three hundred dollars of real money just to send somebody they didn't know off on a wild-goose chase. No student at Moorland for sure, weird as some of them were.

A teacher then? "Quest" was sort of a teacher word. And there was all that talk about education.

Or maybe the guy was a lawyer. "To wit." "Hereby." That sounded legal. And he had to do this and he couldn't do that, like with a contract.

Mark bit his lower lip, thinking. He got up from his desk, pushed in his chair, and stood leaning on the back of it looking down at the mat of money he'd made on his desk blotter. He massaged his left knee. It had been almost two months since his operation, but wet weather still made the knee puff and ache.

He picked up the note again and looked at the verse clue. This Mihal Dobrejcak and his Mary—his girlfriend? his wife?—had had a dream of some sort. They were led by a star. But something happened to . . . to their dream? to them? Probably just to him, because something had killed him, something that had a Number Four Gate. A factory? A mill maybe? And right near that Number Four Gate was what Mihal's dream had come to . . . had come down to? had grown into? It was evidently going to invite

Mark to . . . take certain steps? in order that he might then . . . what? Become a part of *what* scheme?

Mark went over to his bed and sat down. Maybe the guy who'd left the money in the Dickens novel had counted on getting some kind of super student to work with—which Mark knew he wasn't. He was a senior at Moorland, and he'd already been accepted into the University of Pittsburgh for the fall. But so had half the senior class; Pitt was no big deal to get into if you lived in the city. In fact, Mark had applied to college mainly because he knew that his girlfriend Merial and his mother expected he would. So if it was some kind of a grind the guy had counted on getting, maybe this quest thing was out of Mark's league.

He went back over to his desk and sat down again, frowning at Assignment 1.

Were Mihal Dobrejcak and his Mary real, like people you could find listed in the phone book, or were they made-up, like characters in plays or stories?

Mark took the Greater Pittsburgh Telephone Directory from his bottom desk drawer and looked up Dobrejcak. There was no such name listed, nor could Information help him—which didn't mean anything either way, of course. There could be a Mihal or Mary Dobrejcak living in Detroit or San Francisco.

But they had to be Pittsburgh people. It'd make no sense to expect a high school student to find some Dobrejcak who lived in Albuquerque.

He glanced at the digital clock at the back of his desk. Almost six, dinnertime Saturday, and since he had to pick up Merial for Barbara Brunkenhoffer's party, too late to look for anything at either a bookstore or library today. Tomorrow then.

But would a bookstore be open Sunday, even in the

malls? Particularly on a Sunday just a couple of days after Christmas?

Damn.

Then it occurred to him. Maybe Merial would know the name Dobrejcak. Her family was Hungarian. He could ask her on the way to the party tonight.

Mark leaned back in his desk chair.

In fact, why not just show Merial the money and the note so that they could work out together how to get to Assignment 2? She was good at school, and there was certainly no way that whoever had set this thing up would be able to know whether he'd talked to her.

Unless he was being watched, of course.

But that was silly. Mark grinned at the image that came into his mind of a guy prowling the streets of Pittsburgh in one of those Sherlock Holmes hats, peering around corners with a magnifying glass. Or perhaps he was someone shuffling through the corridors of Moorland at night by the light of a candle, a stooped old man with porkchop sideburns, pockets stuffed with money. A character right out of Dickens, right out of *Great Ex*—

Mark sat bolt upright in his desk chair.

Suddenly, he saw. This wasn't a joke, someone's idea of a game. Neither was it accidental that the money had been hidden in *Great Expectations,* nor that it had been hidden precisely at the point in the novel it had. What was at stake with the quest was nothing less than a fortune—Mark was sure of it—and Dickens's novel was the key to everything.

The novel was the story of an orphan named Pip, a poor kid who works for a blacksmith way out in the boondocks of England. One day, right out of the blue, a lawyer comes to him and tells the boy he has a secret benefactor—a *benefactor,* which was exactly what the person in the note called himself. Through the lawyer, this secret benefactor pays for Pip to go to London to be educated. One day he's going to inherit a lot of money, he's told, and he has to learn how to handle it.

Mark picked up *Great Expectations* again and flipped quickly to the stuck-together pages.

The money and note had been at the very place in the story where Pip's benefactor comes forward to tell him that *he's* the one responsible for Pip's fortune—he, an escaped convict Pip had once been kind to, but without even remembering it. The guy was someone that Pip would never, never in a million years, have guessed to be the source of his wealth.

And Mark too now had a benefactor—that was the message being given—someone who would see to *his* education, and who would one day give *him* a fortune, provided he could show that he deserved it.

It was crazy, of course, somebody giving away a pile of money to someone they didn't even know. But Mark had heard of people who'd left fortunes to a pet cat or a parakeet, and this was certainly no crazier than that.

And besides, he wasn't being just *given* a pile of money. He was going to have to prove himself worthy of his Great Expectations. And not until he had completed the quest satisfactorily could he expect his benefactor to come forward as Pip's had to say, to say . . . what was it exactly Pip's benefactor had said to him?

There it was right at the bottom of page 345, the last thing he'd read before finding the note and the money: "Yes, Pip, dear boy, I've made a gentleman on you! It's me wot has done it!"

Mark then unstuck page 346 from 347 and looked to the next place the benefactor spoke. What he read there sent a tingling through him, like a small wave of electricity. "Look'y here, Pip. I'm your second father. You're my son—more to me nor any son."

For a while Mark just sat at his desk. Then he got up and went over to his bedroom window. From the glow of the Christmas lights he himself had strung along the sill of the dining room window just below him, he could see the outline of a cedar deck built out from the dining room. Its surface was dark and shiny with sleet.

Mark's father had built the deck. He'd been a line foreman for Duquesne Light Company, and one day, when Mark was about four, he'd simply walked away from everything—his family, his job, Pittsburgh. No one knew where he was, according to Mark's mother. It was as though the earth had swallowed him. "He just couldn't handle having a home" was the most she would say in explanation.

Mark continued for a time just to stare down at the deck below him. Then he went back over to his desk and looked up "quest" in the dictionary just to make sure it meant what he thought it meant. "A journey in search of adventure," he read, "such as those undertaken by knights in medieval times."

Well, he could give it a shot, anyway. And he'd play it by the rules too. What did he have to lose?

2

The sleet had turned to rain by dinnertime, but even that had stopped by the time Mark finished washing the dinner dishes. There was no ice on the roads, so there was no trouble over his getting the car to pick up Merial. They lived within walking distance of each other in a section of Pittsburgh known as Highland Park, but the party they were going to was in Shadyside, a couple of miles away.

"You sure you'll be warm enough in just that parka, now?" he said to Merial, taking her arm for the three concrete steps that led down from her family's row house to the sidewalk. Her coat was open, and Mark could see she had on the hand-knit Irish sweater he'd bought her for Christmas. It had cost him just about every cent he'd saved when he was working. The thought of the three hundred dollars he'd hidden away in the bottom drawer of his desk lifted him like a wave.

She looked up at him amused. "As opposed to *two* parkas, you mean? What are you talking about, warm enough? It's like spring out."

He stiffened slightly, feeling rebuffed. When he dropped her arm to walk to the other side of the car, she caught one side of his open jacket and held him. "I'm sorry," she said. "You were just being nice, weren't you?"

He shrugged. "It was kind of a dumb thing to say, I guess."

"Kiss me, fool."

He did that.

"You'll never guess what I was thinking about this afternoon," she said as he turned off Elgin Avenue onto Negley. On Elgin, the Christmas decorations at house after house blazed like jewels. There was a lighted plastic Santa Claus in a sleigh on a lawn at the corner of Negley, but beyond it the street was dark. "I'll give you a hint. It was nothing seasonal."

"Names," he said without having to think about it.

"You're a genius," she said, sliding over next to him. "Names it was. What do you think of Justin?"

"For a boy?"

"No, for a rabbit. Of course for a boy. Justin. What do you think?"

It was a game they played, talking about what they'd name their children, though Mark played it mainly to please her. She was the youngest in a family of five. Her two brothers and sisters were married.

"How about Rumpelstiltskin?" he said.

She leaned her head against his shoulder, and he put his arm around her and rubbed her forehead with the back of his hand.

"Justin," she said thoughtfully. "Maybe Justin. I still like Jonathan for the *first* boy, though."

"Good solid Hungarian name, Gyp. Jonathan. Your mom and dad'll love it."

Gyp was short for Gypsy, though he was the only one to call her that. Her grandparents on both sides had immigrated to Pittsburgh from Hungary.

"I'll tell them we're going to name the first girl Budapest."

The first girl. The first boy. Mark glanced down at the numbers of the odometer, the last one turning very slightly. She had given him the schedule toward the end of the summer. Four years at the University of Pittsburgh. Then marriage. Then, in two years, the first child. Two years after that . . .

Mark took his arm from around her, hunched forward a little, and put both hands on the wheel. They were going to have to borrow heavily to go to college but that didn't seem to bother Merial. The thought of the money Mark was going to need just for tuition made him feel short of breath.

"Who all do you think'll be there tonight?" he asked. Barbara Brunkenhoffer had advertised her party as a get-together of some Moorland graduates already at the University of Pittsburgh with some students, like Mark and Merial, who were headed there in the fall.

Merial sat up. "Well, Tom Gaylor, but not Mitzie. They broke up. And Betty Donovan. Chip Broughton and Blake, of course. Dom Rinzi. I forget who all else. Barb said a lot of people are out of town for Christmas, though. Dick's in Florida."

"Good for Dick," Mark said tartly. Dick Byrnes, a senior last year, had gone steady with Merial the fall she was a junior. He'd been captain of the basketball team. All last spring, even when Mark started going with her, she'd continued to dance with Dick at parties. It made him sick to have to watch the two of them move together.

Merial said, "And Silk. I think Barb told him how none of us could do without his wit and wisdom."

He looked over at her. "What's that supposed to mean?"

"What?" she asked in mock innocence.

"You know what."

They were speaking of a graduate of Moorland High

School the year before named Aubrey Samuri, nicknamed Silk, in part for his athletic ability, but mainly for his political skills. Silk had founded the Black Action Society at predominately white Moorland, and later was also elected president of the senior class. He was liked by men and liked by women. Though Mark didn't really know Silk, he had played football with him and had always admired him.

"Well," Merial said, "don't you think he lays it on a little thick sometimes—champion of his people and all that?"

They'd stopped at the light on Penn Avenue, just off the edge of the East Liberty Mall. The high-rise projects, looming to their left, spilled all the way down to the deserted-looking shopping center. On the far corner was a bus shelter filled with a number of older black women holding shopping bags on their laps. They were as fixed as though they'd been carved from wood.

"That's a racist thing to say," Mark said without looking at her. "Silk's not like that. He's just like . . . you and me. I don't even think of him as black."

Merial slid next to him quickly. "Oh, come on. I was just putting you on for a minute. You know that."

The light changed, and they moved with traffic down Negley Avenue toward Shadyside. Past Babyland, the Podiatry Hospital, past the old broad-shouldered brick homes, all of them stripped of their stained glass, all of them cut up into cheap apartments. But a block after the turn at Ellsworth they were in a different world. Even old garages in Shadyside, in high demand for renovation into town houses, sold for astronomical prices.

"I still think Silk will be good to talk to about college," Mark said, a bit stiffly.

"Well, he's sure serious about it." It was common knowledge that Silk had turned down a couple of athletic scholarships in order to accept one from Pitt to study political science.

"Maybe he'll—" Mark started, but then he stopped himself.

"Maybe he'll what?"

Mark didn't answer for a moment. "Give us some tips," he said finally—but what he'd been thinking was that maybe Silk would be a better person than Merial to ask about Mihal and Mary Dobrejcak. Whatever Merial knew, she'd also come at him with all kinds of questions.

At Barbara's they moved first as a couple, getting soda, eddying in and out of conversation. In the cleared-out dining room a group of people were moving to a guitar strumming in stereo. Mark knew it was only a matter of time before someone asked Merial to dance. That it turned out to be Blake Kuzinski was just fine with him. Blake was a nice guy, but also sort of geeky looking, lean as a pair of fire tongs. And he and Christine Broughton were practically married.

Mark saw Silk on the far side of the living room, leaning gracefully against the wall talking to, or rather, being talked at by one of Mark's classmates, George Boknovitch. Mark knew Boknovitch from football, too. To one side of them, standing with her arms folded across her chest, was Zeena Curry. Though she was in Mark's English class, he'd never said more than hello to her, but he'd looked at her a lot when he was sure she wouldn't see him doing it. She had dark, slightly slanted eyes, and her straight black hair was cut to hug her head like a helmet. She'd always reminded Mark of a queen—from Africa somewhere maybe, or like that famous one from ancient Egypt with the long neck.

"Marky," George yelled from across the room to him. "Get over here." Mark set his jaw as he walked over.

William E. Coles, Jr. · 13

Boknovitch was an explosive linebacker but had always seemed to Mark to use football as an excuse for hurting people. And Mark hated being called "Marky."

"'S happ'nen, man?" George said jovially as Mark came up.

"George," Mark said, nodding to him. Mechanically, he held out his hand low and palm up and George slapped it. Mark nodded at Zeena. "Hi, Zeena. How's it going, Silk? How's Pitt?"

"He chucked football, is how Pitt is," George broke in. "Can you believe it? Tell him, Silk."

It surprised Mark. "I didn't even know you'd decided to play. I thought you weren't going to."

"Yeah, well . . ." Silk said with a deep sigh. "I let myself get sweet-talked into it. But I quit in October. Incidentally, I heard about your knee. I'm sorry, Mark."

"Yeah," Mark said, flexing his left leg up. "No super loss to Moorland, though. Without you there, I wasn't all that hot anyway."

George guffawed. "That's for sure," he said, punching Mark's shoulder.

The year before, Mark had been only a backup quarterback for Moorland until their regular quarterback got hurt in the game against Ridley Heights. "Keep your eye on me, now," Silk had said to him when Mark was sent in. "I'm going to get open for you. Don't worry. I'm going to be open. Just drift to the right behind Dadvers and Glenn, and make sure you keep your eye on me." It was the best game Mark had ever played. With Silk as his primary receiver, he'd passed Moorland from almost certain defeat to a two-touchdown victory and himself into a starting position his senior year. He'd played only two games as a senior before getting hurt. Moorland had lost them both.

Mark felt himself redden at George's remark, and he

glanced quickly at Zeena, but she was looking off across the room. She whispered something to Silk and then, without saying anything to either George or Mark, went into the dining room.

"You lose your job when you got hurt?" Silk asked, ignoring George in a way that would have crushed Mark.

"What? Oh, yeah," Mark said, flustered at first and then flattered. How had Silk known he had a job? He grinned. "But who likes to work?"

Silk studied him. "I'd have thought you would. You worked in the Giant Eagle, didn't you? Didn't you like it?"

Mark looked down quickly. He'd loved his job, even apart from the financial independence that it gave him. In fact, losing football and his job at the same time had been one of the worst times of his life. For a couple of months, he hadn't felt that he was anybody, that he belonged anywhere.

"Well, to tell you the truth I did like working at the Eagle," Mark said. "And I miss the money."

"Tell him *why* you dropped football, though, man," George prodded Silk. "Wait'll you hear this, Marky. Tell him. Tell him what you told me."

Silk straightened up and shrugged. "Well, I didn't have the time for one thing. Beyond that, it was bad for me. I was just saying to our friend George here that I'm not all that sure football's good for anybody. Do you know anybody you'd say it touches the best in?"

"Can you beat that?" George said to Mark, nudging him, eyes wide behind his scholarly looking horn-rimmed glasses. "Can you beat it? Guy tears up a one-way ticket to the pros because all of a sudden football's no good for people. Make any sense to you, Marky?" He blinked fiercely, first at Mark, then at Silk, then back at Mark again.

"The pros," Silk laughed. "Are you kidding? I'd have about as much chance in the pros as I'd have been Queen of the May. Do you know how many people actually *make* it in the pros?"

It did not seem to be an idea George liked considering. He backed up a step. Then he put a hammy fist on Silk's upper arm and shoved a little. "Guy with your talent doesn't even try? That's a mistake, pal, believe me. Buh-LIEVE me." Then shaking his head he turned away and headed for the buffet.

"What a jerk," Mark said.

Silk smiled. "What's really insulting is how nobody— nobody like our friend George anyway—expects a black to work out that professional sports are a sucker's game. The coach down at Pitt suggested I might want to see a psychiatrist."

Mark too smiled and shook his head knowingly—feeling like a fraud as he did so, feeling sure that Silk understood what he too should have understood but didn't. He looked just to the right of Silk's shoulder at the Christmas tree in the far corner of the room, sprayed white and hung with silver bells, angel hair, and blue lights. The guitar on the stereo had given way to a woman's voice, clean as rain. There was a fire in the fireplace, a table filled with food, people talking, laughing, all of them either in college or college bound, eager, purposeful, whereas he . . .

Like a light the name Dobrejcak came into his mind. Maybe there was another way. Maybe for him there was another way. As he was about to speak to Silk, he felt two arms encircle him from behind. Merial leaned her cheek against his shoulder.

"Hi, Silk," she said cheerily. "How's Pitt—if you don't mind saying it all twice."

"It's good," he said, nodding and smiling back at her. "Really good."

"What are you majoring in, do you know yet?"

"Oh, sure. I'm in political science."

"He got a full scholarship in political science, Merial," Mark said. "That'd probably be his major."

"Not necessarily," Merial said. "People can change their minds. Is it . . . you know, hard? Do you have to study all the time?"

"Well," Silk said, "the more you study the better you do."

"I was afraid that's what you'd say," Merial said with a laugh. She squeezed Mark. "When are you going to dance with me?"

"Merial," Mark said, "we were—"

"No, no. It's fine," Silk broke in. "Go ahead, please. I have to leave anyway. I have to be up early tomorrow." He began looking around the room as Merial took Mark's hand to lead him toward the dancing couples in the dining room. Mark pulled her back.

"Say, Silk," Mark said, "if you're going to be around the next couple of days, maybe we could . . . get together or something."

Silk looked at him with surprise, but then with a broad easy smile he said, "Why sure, Mark. Sure thing."

Mark new he'd never get in touch with Silk—and knew that Silk knew it. And he'd lost the chance to ask him about the Dobrejcaks.

In the car on the way home, Merial tried for some conversation but gave it up in the face of Mark's monosyllabic sullenness.

"Why the pout?" she asked as he pulled up in front of her house. He'd left the engine running, a clear signal to her that the night was over.

"I don't like you trying to teach me how to dance in front of people," he said without looking at her. "I told you that."

"I wasn't *teaching* you how to dance. All I did was put your hands on my shoulders once."

He stared straight out the windshield, both hands on the steering wheel. "And I was in the middle of a conversation with Silk," he went on. "You interrupted."

She flounced back against her door. "I inter*rupted*? At a *party*? Silk didn't act like I interrupted. You didn't either."

He turned to her. "I did too. I kept pulling you back. You were rude."

"*Kept* pulling me back? Come on, Mark. You pulled back once—and I don't like being *pulled*. That's rude too."

He set his jaw and again looked out the windshield. For a time neither of them spoke.

"What was this big conversation you were in the middle of? What were the two of you talking about that was so important?"

He didn't answer. He could feel her staring at him.

"You *afraid* to tell me what you were talking about?"

"If you must know, Merial," he said with exaggerated distinctness, "we were talking about quests."

"Oooo," she said, mockingly. "Quests. Like a pair of knights or something. That sure as hell sounds important to me."

Refusing to look at her, he raced the engine slightly. He hated it when she made him feel like a fool.

"I didn't expect you would understand."

"You haven't explained anything yet."

"And I don't have to either."

"You sound like a five-year-old," she said. "What's the matter with you, anyway? What do you want to fight for?"

"You started it," he said, still not looking at her. He knew what they were at the edge of.

"*I* started it!" she yelped. "*I* did? Oh, boy." She folded her arms over her chest and stared down at the dashboard.

Again, neither of them said anything.

"Is this the way you want to spend Christmas vacation?" she asked, finally.

He could feel her looking at him. He didn't answer, didn't move.

"Well, is it? Answer me."

He didn't. He wouldn't answer. He just couldn't.

She sighed a long sigh of exasperation, opened the car door, and got out. "You're just impossible when you get like this," she said, the door still open. "You really make me sick sometimes." Then she slammed the car door and raced up her front steps.

"Me too," he said to the empty night as he pulled away from the curb. "Me too."

At home in his room, Mark sat at the desk making no move to get into bed. He took out the money and Assignment 1 from under the telephone directory in his bottom desk drawer and an envelope with a snapshot in it that was under the directory as well. He reread Assignment 1. Then he folded the three hundred-dollar bills in half, creased the fold hard several times with his thumbnail, put the money and the assignment in the envelope with the snapshot, and put the envelope back in the drawer. But then he took out just the snapshot again and looked at it.

It was the one picture Mark had of his father, a Polaroid photograph that he'd found lying loose in his mother's high school yearbook. He was sure his mother had forgotten about the picture because all the other photographs of him, of them, of their lives together, she'd burned. In the snapshot, he and his father were sitting together on the cedar deck off the dining room, both in shorts, both squinting and smiling into a summer sun. His father held a steel-shafted hammer in the hand of the arm he had around Mark's shoulders, and there was a red coffee can of heaped-up nails between Mark's crossed legs. Mark looked to himself to be three or four.

Had the picture been taken on the day his father had built the deck? Sometimes Mark seemed to remember things that way. The August heat. The cinnamon smell of the cedar planks. The feel of his father's arm around him. Had there been locusts singing? Iced tea? Sometimes in his head he could hear the rhythm of his father's hammer. Bang, bang, bang, bang, BANG. Bang, bang, bang, bang, BANG. But he couldn't be sure that any of what he thought he remembered was real.

After a while Mark put everything away, turned off his desk lamp, and groped his way in the darkness across the room to the window. There was no light from the dining room, so he couldn't really see the deck below him. But after a while, as his eyes became used to the darkness, he was convinced that he could.

3

Mark came to like a shot, sitting straight up in bed, breathing hard, eyes staring wide into the darkness. The top of his T-shirt was soaked. Had he cried out, or was that only in the dream?

Awful. It had been just awful.

He'd been running for his life down the center aisle of some kind of cathedral, a cathedral so high he couldn't even see the roof of it, and he was running and stumbling and falling and getting up, again and again—whether in pursuit of something or fleeing something, he couldn't remember. For some reason, his life had depended on his getting to . . . it was like an altar up at the end of the church, draped in white and blazing with candles, hundreds of them. But around the altar was a pack of hyenas, with huge grinning jaws, just sitting there watching him, dead quiet, watching and waiting . . .

He shook his head to clear it. The blue numbers of the digital clock on his desk read 6:30 A.M. His mother wouldn't be up for an hour yet. It was Monday, and in a couple of hours Carnegie Library would be open.

Mark dressed quickly, went down to the kitchen, and poured himself a cup of coffee from the timed percolator.

He shook up the orange juice and put a glass of it at his place, another at his mother's.

He felt ready. He'd made it up with Merial the day before, and that afternoon in her basement family room they'd watched the Steelers blow their play-off game. Her father, one of her sisters, and one of her brothers with his two small children had been there with them, but that was okay; Mark liked her family. Besides, it always took him a while to feel right with her after they'd had a fight.

Mark heard his mother in the upstairs hall on her way to the bathroom. He poured another cup of coffee and set it at her place alongside the orange juice. Neither of them ate in the morning.

"This is nice," his mother said, smiling as she sat down across from him at the kitchen table. "A girl could get used to having her breakfast fixed."

He looked down at his coffee. He didn't like it when his mother referred to herself as a girl.

"You're up early, love," she said after finishing her orange juice. "You sleep okay?"

"Fine. Okay if I have the car today? I thought I'd start checking some things for my honors project. Down at Carnegie Library."

He emphasized the word "honors" slightly. Mark had elected the senior honors English course at Moorland only at his mother's insistence—which, from time to time, it could be convenient to remind her of. His mother had not been to college but had heard somewhere that the course was supposed to be invaluable in preparing students for college work. One of its requirements was an individually designed term paper project.

"Hey!" his mother said cheerfully. "Would I stand in the way of education? You'll have to drop me at Northwood, though. We got a deal brewing."

Mark's mother sold real estate for Northwood Homes out of Shadyside, condos and townhouses mostly. "We," he knew, was his mother and Jody Banner, a vulcanized blonde with a wide toothy smile and eyes like knives. She moved property, though. Her greed had made her a fortune selling houses in Pittsburgh.

In the car Mark's mother checked her hair and makeup several times in the rearview mirror on the way to Shadyside, leaning close to him to do it. He could smell her perfume. She'd once told him it was lily of the valley.

"You have a nice day." She smiled at him before getting out of the car. "Good luck with the project. You seeing Merial tonight?"

"I guess," he said.

"Ah," she said knowingly. She ran the tip of her tongue lightly across her upper lip and then smiled at him again. Mark smiled back but felt himself flush. He looked quickly out the windshield.

She got out of her car and leaned down through the open door. "Now remember to put the potatoes in about four."

Mark nodded, still looking out the windshield. "I know. The pork roast is defrosting and is on the timer. You told me already."

"I tell you Guy and I were going to the symphony?"

Mark's mother had been going out with Guy for some time. He was Canadian, from Toronto, and a widower. He taught history at the University of Pittsburgh but wasn't stuffy the way Mark imagined a university professor might be.

Mark turned to her smiling. "Only about four times—and that he isn't coming for dinner."

She stood up and shook her hair back; it shone like black glass in the sun. He'd read a poem in English once with a line describing someone's hair that made him think of his mother's: "Dark as a raven's wing."

"Right," his mother said. "Jody'll drop me fiveish or so. 'Bye, love," she said with a little wave.

The University Branch of Mellon Bank was only a couple of blocks from Carnegie Library. Mark waited in the parking lot until the bank opened at 9:00. At 9:04, he noted the time to the minute on the bank clock, he presented one of the hundred-dollar bills for change. The teller, a sweet-faced black woman, passed the bill easily into her drawer, and after counting out his fives, tens, and twenties, winked at him and wished him a happy holiday. Again, Mark noted the time as he went back out through the revolving door—9:07. Phase one successfully completed, he thought to himself, grinning as he drove down Fifth Avenue. He felt like a character in a movie.

At the Carnegie Library a guard directed Mark to the circulation desk. There were several people at the far end of it putting books on a cart. One man, a sour-looking guy with a beaky nose, was sitting at the counter part of the desk reading. Mark unfolded the slip of paper on which he'd written the name MIHAL DOBREJCAK in block capitals and, fixing his face with what Merial called his little boy grin, held the slip out for the man to see.

"Can you tell me how I can find out who this person is?" he asked.

Keeping his finger pointed down to his place in the open book, the man looked up at Mark. Black thatches of hair sprouted fiercely out of each of his nostrils.

"This isn't a game show," he said, without looking at what Mark had written. "Use the computer—or a reference work."

"I tried both," Mark lied. "There's nothing there. Will you just look at the name, please."

The librarian took the paper from Mark and held it as though he thought it might contaminate him. He read the name, and then let the paper flutter to the desk. "I don't believe you tried both," he said going back to his reading. "And you're probably looking under the wrong heading."

"Well, what heading do I look under, then?" Mark asked, fighting his irritability. On the whole, he hated librarians. They always acted like you were stupid for not knowing things.

"You could try the *right* heading," the man said with a flicker of a smile at his own wit but without looking up.

For a moment Mark just stared at him. Then he reached across the desk and closed the book the man was reading with an audible snap. "I need some information here," he said, raising his voice a bit. "It's important." He knew his face was flushed.

"Is it?" said Thatchbeak in a squeak, sweeping his book up from the desk and standing. "Is it indeed, now? I'll give you some information. I'll have you thrown out of here!" His nose hair quivered with indignation.

A pretty young woman hurried over from the far end of the circulation desk. Her hair was honey blonde, the color of Merial's, but she wore it long, brushed straight down, almost to her waist, from a black velvet bow at her neck. And she was magic. Within fifteen minutes Mark was on his way to the stacks with the call number of a novel, Thomas Bell's *Out of This Furnace,* and less than five minutes after that he was sitting in one of the cell-like carrels by the stacks with a copy of it. He took Assignment 1 out of his pocket and unfolded it so that he could read the verse clue again.

    Mihal Dobrejcak and his Mary
    Also were led by a star.

Quester: read their history,
And decide what your chances are.

By the Number Four Gate of what killed him
Is what came of Mihal's dream.
Look to the steps you're invited to take
To become a part of the scheme.

"Mike Dobrejcak" was the name of a whole section of the novel, one which looked to be about one hundred eighty pages long, and "Mary" was the name of the section right after that.

Within an hour Mark discovered that Mike or Mihal Dobrejcak was a steelworker married to the woman named Mary. He'd been killed in an accident in a mill in Braddock in 1917—a steel mill called the Edgar Thompson Works. Braddock wasn't a made-up name. It was a real town no more than five or ten miles from Pittsburgh, Mark knew, though he'd never been there. It had to be that the mill was real too, and that it had a Number Four Gate.

But Mark could not work out from what he skimmed in Bell's novel what "Mihal's dream" referred to. As a Slovak immigrant, Dobrejcak had had a lot of dreams, all of which centered on making a place for himself and his family in America. He'd dreamed of educating himself. He'd dreamed of a better job, a better place to live, of a future for his kids. And he'd believed in a lot of things, like God, his fellow workers, having a life with dignity. Which dream was being referred to, and what was supposed to have happened to it? And how did all that translate into a hiding place for Assignment 2? The questions made him anxious.

He told himself to slow down and back up, to take

things one step at a time. He'd have to go over to Braddock, find the Number Four Gate of the Edgar Thompson Works, and take things from there. There was a map of greater Pittsburgh he knew in the glove compartment of his mother's car.

On the way down the stairs, however, Mark stopped. The assignment had stipulated that he read the history of Mihal and Mary Dobrejcak and he hadn't. All he'd really looked at in the novel was the section of it called "Mike Dobrejcak," and he'd read that very quickly. He hadn't even returned the novel to the stack shelf. Was he going to be seen as violating the conditions of the quest?

Had there been other people around the circulation desk when he'd had his altercation with Thatchbeak? He couldn't remember.

But he couldn't check the book out and finish reading it at home because he didn't have a card for the Carnegie and getting one would probably take time. And to read the book here—he glanced at his watch; it was past noon—would take him at least the rest of the day. Maybe it would take him tomorrow too, the day of New Year's Eve. What if the Carnegie was closed the day of New Year's Eve? Maybe it would even close for the rest of the week. That meant it would be *next* week before he could even get to Braddock, next week when he'd be back in school and without his mother's car.

It wasn't right that he had to wait that long. Certainly whoever had written the assignment expected him to be resourceful.

Okay, then, here's what he'd do. He'd at least *see* if there was some way he could take Bell's book out today. If there wasn't, he'd buy it—as soon as he got back from Braddock. He'd buy it somewhere and start reading it this very afternoon.

Mark raced back to the carrel for the copy of *Out of This Furnace* he'd left lying there and then headed again for the circulation desk.

From the doorway of the stacks, he looked for the woman with the honey blonde hair, but he didn't see her anywhere. In fact the only person behind the desk was Thatchbeak. He looked up from his reading and noticed Mark, and then, after glancing to both sides, to Mark's surprise beckoned him over. He was smiling, a wide smile with pointy teeth like those of a cat. When Mark got to the desk, Thatchbeak looked around him quickly and then leaned toward Mark, still smiling.

"Just want you to know it's obvious you're a little shit," he hissed. Mark stared at him, incredulous. He then slammed the copy of Bell's book down hard on the desk between them. It made a sound like a shot, and Thatchbeak humped back with a squeal. "Guard!" he cried, "Guard!"

Grinning, Mark gave him a jaunty finger and stepped briskly to the exit turnstile. It wasn't till he was in the car that he realized he'd left *Out of This Furnace* lying on the circulation desk.

4

The Braddock of Bell's novel was red-eyed and violent, a twenty-four-hour-a-day clanging giant, but what Mark drove through was a town being silently throttled by its own decay. Two out of every three stores on the main street were boarded up, their doorways piled with trash. In several of the parking lots on the side streets, Mark could see the hulks of abandoned cars listing crazily over their missing wheels. A small knot of men, the only people visible, huddled hopelessly around a fire burning in an empty oil drum outside a bar. They did not so much as turn their heads when Mark drove slowly by. Most grotesque of all were the chains of black and green Christmas decorations that ran straight down the main street of town to a number of massive buildings and a forest of swollen smokestacks.

Mark could see it was the mill all right as he came up on it, the Edgar Thompson Works, now also called the Mon Valley Works according to the huge faded sign over what looked to be the main gate. A high chain-link fence ran from one side of the gate down a side street. From the other side of the gate the fence ran as far ahead along the road as Mark could see. A few operative cars and trucks were parked just the other side of the main gate, but there were no other signs of life. Mark had already passed the gate before remembering to see whether it was numbered.

For miles he drove alongside the fenced-off buildings, dead weeds sprouting from their rain gutters, and cracks running up and down their enormous brick chimneys. Even after it was clear that he had left town behind him, the mill went on and on, mile after mile of rust and desertion. "Like a dinosaur graveyard," Mark said to himself. He was looking for a place to turn around when he came upon another gate, much smaller than the main one back at the intersection. The gate was closed and locked and topped with barbed wire, but it was plainly marked Number Ten. A sign under the number said that all deliveries were to be made at Gate Four off Eleventh Street.

Gate *Four* off Eleventh Street. "By the Number Four Gate of what killed him." All *right!*

Mark could see no one in the mill, but on the other side of the street were a couple of parked cars and a guy in overalls bent over the engine of a pick-up truck. Leaving the motor of his mother's car running, Mark ran across to him.

"Can you tell me where Eleventh Street is?" he asked. "I have to get to Gate Four."

For a moment Mark thought the man hadn't heard him. He was on the other side of the truck, his head down over the engine, and he kept doing something that made the engine race and roar. It died and the guy stood up.

" 'Sit worth?" he drawled back at Mark. The guy looked to be about fifty and had mean-looking, close-set eyes.

"All I want to know is where Gate Four is," Mark said.

The man picked up a filthy rag from the fender of the truck and wiped his hands. "Piss off," he said, spitting to one side and bending down over the engine again.

Mark backed up a step. "Okay," he said. "For a buck."

The man straightened up and put the rag down. "Let's see it," he said.

All the money Mark had with him was in his side pocket. He knew he had a dollar in change from the Carnegie Library parking lot, but the rest was in the bigger bills he'd been given at the bank. He had no intention of letting the man see how much he had with him.

"It's over in the car."

"Let's go get it," the man replied with a wolfish smile.

Mark turned his back as though to head for the car and at the same time took out the folded bills from his pocket. He snatched the dollar from them and quickly put the rest away.

"Okay," he said, turning back and holding up the bill. "Now where's Gate Four?"

"Money's in the car, huh?" the man said, gliding toward him with one arm extended. He was still smiling and was rubbing his thumb and forefinger together. There was now a wrench in his other hand.

Mark whirled and tore across the road, just ahead of an oncoming car. He heard the screech of tires and a yell. Springing into his mother's car, Mark jammed it into gear, U-turned sharply, spraying stones up onto the chain-link gate, and fishtailed around the screaming bull-faced woman who'd gotten out of the car that had swerved to avoid him.

Mark sped back down the way he'd come, slowing as he came into town. At the intersection of the main gate of the mill, he hung as quick a left as he dared, went down a couple of blocks, and parked. Only then did he become conscious of his shaking hands and the blood still pounding in his neck. He sunk down in the front seat and adjusted the mirror so that he could check anything turning down the street. After five minutes or so when nothing had, he sat up, laughed weakly, and shook his head. Where the hell was he, anyway? What kind of people lived in a place like this? Mark had stopped in front of a stretch of row houses, all of them with their roofs caved in. The Edgar Thompson Works on the other side of the street stretched down for a quarter of a mile or so beyond where he was parked, ending it seemed at a railroad track, but there was a break in the fence about two blocks down, a wide opening. Mark started the car and eased his way slowly down the street. His heart leaped at the sign on the glassed-in guard booth at the opening. "Gate Four," it said. He had turned off the main street onto Eleventh just by chance. He parked again.

The guy inside the guard booth seemed absorbed in polishing his windows, but Mark could feel his watchfulness. He got a spiral notebook and pen from his backpack on the seat beside him, climbed slowly out of the car, and looked deliberately around him. He'd parked almost at a corner in front of a huge apartment building, a great square thing six or seven stories high. It was one of ten or fifteen identical structures he could see stretching down the street that led away from Gate Four. The buildings looked fairly new, but were obviously as abandoned as the collapsed row houses a couple of blocks above them. The first-floor windows of all the buildings were covered by metal plates. Above the first floor, even at the very tops of the buildings, the glass in all the windows had been smashed. "Talbot Towers," read a washed-out sign in front of the building closest to Mark, and in small letters underneath it, "Take Pride."

As he crossed the street, Mark saw the guy inside the booth put his bottle of Windex and a wad of paper towels to one side. He opened a small hinged window as Mark came up to him, giving out a blast of warm ammonia-smelling air. The guy was slight but shrewd looking, with a sharp, darting manner that reminded Mark of a bird.

"Hello, sir," Mark said. "I'm doing some . . . research on the area. For a term paper. Could you . . . could I ask you a couple of questions, please?"

"Research," the man repeated, but not as a question. "For a term paper." He cocked his head to one side and looked amused. "Maybe that's one thing we're still good for around here. What'd you want to know?"

"Well," Mark said half turning back to the apartment building, "why doesn't anybody live here anymore?"

The man crossed his arms on his counter sill, leaned forward nodding, and looked up from Mark to the building behind him. "If you mean in *there*, nobody ever did live in there, really. Not *people*. Animals maybe. And even they got out finally." The man's shirt was snowy white and sharply ironed.

"What do you mean?"

"Well, the Towers was supposed to be for the workers, see. Keep 'em all close to the mill, keep 'em in line. Like slave pens on the plantation. Except that in the sixties and seventies, the slaves was making more than the slave owners, see?"

The man widened his eyes at Mark, in what seemed a request for confirmation of what he'd just said, so Mark nodded. "No workers ever lived in these buildings then?" he asked.

"Not many." The man jerked his head in the direction of the mill to his left. "Would you live right next to a blast furnace if you could live somewheres else?"

"I guess not," Mark said, swiveling to face the ruined apartment buildings again. Off to the side of the one just across the street was a rusty jungle gym. Thick stalks of some kind of spiny weed had pushed up through it almost to the top. Just behind it a short flight of metal stairs led up to a steel door with a plaque beside it that read RENTAL OFFICE. But no one had rented anything anywhere in Talbot Towers for years.

How solid the buildings looked though. How substantial. "They look like nice buildings, though. At least they weren't just . . . rat traps."

The man snorted. "You put people in prison, the interior decoration don't matter all that much. Suppose you was stuck in there just because you couldn't afford to get out. They knifed each other. They shot each other. Pissed down their own stairwells. Broke their own windows. There was cops down here all the time, I mean *all* the time—and this was even before the mill closed. Same thing happened all over the valley, in Clairton, Hazelwood."

The man cocked his head and looked down at Mark good-humoredly.

"You could write all about this in your term paper, maybe. One more dream of the Great Society gone right down the shit chute."

Mihal's dream, Mark thought. Mihal's dream. He ran the final lines of the clue through his head again:

```
By the Number Four Gate of what killed him
Is what came of Mihal's dream.
Look to the steps you're invited to take
To become part of the scheme.
```

Was Talbot Towers what Mihal's dream was supposed to have come down to then? And if that was the point, where were the steps that would lead to such a ruin?

He was going to have to talk to somebody connected with Talbot Towers. "I guess there's nobody in that Rental Office over there, is there?"

The man smiled. "Ghosts maybe. That's all there is here is ghosts—except me of course."

Mark was feeling desperate. "But the people who ran the Towers, would they be around anywhere?"

"Ain't nobody here don't have to be here." The man looked up to his left, up to the dead, black mill that filled the sky. "Nothing really going on here either. All they're doing here is selling off old stuff." He looked back at Mark, cocked his head again, and winked a beady eye. "When they get rid of that, they get rid of me too, you know what I mean? Place be just one great big haunted house then."

Mark, preoccupied, just looked at the man.

"But they don't make *me* a ghost, know why?"

Mark shook his head.

" 'Cause I seen it all coming, is why, and I got me a place with a garden. It's just a little place, but we grow all our own food, me and my family. We got chickens and we got a couple of goats, and—"

A telephone in the booth shrilled and the man jumped. "Hang on," he said, holding up a hand to Mark as he grabbed the receiver off the wall. After listening for a moment, he mouthed the word "sorry" to Mark and pulled the window to the booth closed.

It seemed a long conversation. Mark turned his back on the booth and looked across the street to the steel door into the Rental Office. When he looked back to the booth, he saw the man was still talking into the telephone and going through a lot of papers in one of the trays. Mark headed across the street to Talbot Towers.

At the top of the flight of metal stairs leading to the Rental Office, Mark saw that what he had thought was a door was a steel plate like those covering the first floor windows. There wasn't even a knob. Mark pounded on it

William E. Coles, Jr. · 35

a couple of times, but it was like pounding on a street. He sat down at the top of the stairs, his hands in his parka pockets, feeling everything slipping away from him.

> Look to the steps you're invited to take
> To become a part of the scheme.

Well, he thought despondently, he was doing that. He stamped both feet hard on the stair they were resting on, making them sting and his left knee throb. He was looking at the only goddamn steps he could see and—

And then it struck him. The stairs, these metal stairs. Were *they* the steps? They had to be the steps.

He ran back down to the bottom of them and looked up. The stairs rose out of a concrete pad and seemed to be perfectly ordinary in every way. There wasn't even any writing on them anywhere.

Something under them, maybe?

In a flash Mark was on his back, his head under the stairs. There was broken glass, and the area smelled strongly of urine. He could see the underside of everything except the first step, which was raised only about three inches off the concrete. Mark took off a glove, inched himself more deeply into the alcove, and felt along the shelf of concrete just below the first step. Toward the wall, he felt a lump of something smooth, like plastic. He worked an edge of it loose and tore free a black packet, which he shoved inside his parka. After wriggling back, Mark could see the guy in the booth, still on the telephone, but staring at him. Mark waved his notebook cheerfully and walked quickly back to his mother's car.

His hands were shaking so that he ended up ripping the packet open with his teeth. Inside was a thick piece of cardboard, a white envelope scotch-taped to it containing two brand new hundred-dollar bills, and a second envelope inside of which were two sheets of neatly-folded thin paper:

Assignment 2

Congratulations on your having decided to elect the quest—and in spite of what must be the mixture of your motives. But Dante did not go gentle into the underworld, nor was his guide someone who believed it was simply delightful to be chosen to found a city. And would Beowulf have taken on the dragon, or Siegfried the Nibelungs, without the prospect of a treasure?

We are all of us Children of this World as well as Children of Light.

And what have you concluded so far about this place you live in? Pittsburgh. Western Pennsylvania. What do you think makes a place a place? Have you felt the working of the forces Thomas Bell sees in and under where you are? Forces of decay as well as of generation, of creation and destruction both, embracing one another like Möbius curves, balanced rather than harmonized, and working still, ineluctably.

For me, for instance, it has always been worth the twenty-mile drive to the airport just to be with someone who has never seen the city when they respond to the Genesis 1:3 smash of things at the end of the Fort Pitt Tunnel on the way back into town. Wham. And there, all of a sudden, all of it is, the whole oxymoronic triumph of Pittsburgh all at once: glorious rivers and grinding mills, graft, goodness, grime, blood-forged steel springing into soaring spirey towers, and then back into fold after fold of unhuddled hills, pockets of ethnic brutality, also havens for the ethnic soul.

Amounting to what, would you say, Quester?

Options which were never intended? Variety by default? Manyness born of too much? Democracy for which no one is to blame?

Perhaps. As is the case with the human heart. Perhaps.

But perhaps what really matters is there being a city in consequence that remains unkillable.

Speaking of the human heart, your next task is to find out about someone who was once described as walking through our city like a visitor from the Islands of the Blest. Quite incidentally, he made The Man Who Sold Time, but there was nothing incidental in his testament to what he believed in:

We have loved the stars too fondly
To be fearful of the night.

Here is your clue to Assignment 3:

'Neath the flags before their resting place
Look for the russet stone.
The gateway to the future
For a Quester seeking home.

On his way back into Pittsburgh, Mark stopped at the University Bookstore where he bought a paperback copy of Thomas Bell's *Out of This Furnace*. At home he put the potatoes in the oven and then went up to his room to read.

5

Hillman Library at the University of Pittsburgh had been Merial's suggestion the night before, right after Mark had given her a slightly edited account of his run-in with Thatchbeak. *Now* where was he supposed to go to work on his term paper project? he'd whined. Maybe, she said, Hillman would be open, even the day before New Year's. It wasn't more than a block from the Carnegie, and the people there, she'd heard, were pretty nice about working with Pittsburgh high school kids.

Just outside Hillman, Mark got out the sheet of paper on which he'd printed all the information from Assignment 2 he figured he could share without violating the conditions of the quest:

```
A Visitor from the Islands of the Blest

The Man Who Sold Time

We have loved the stars too fondly
To be fearful of the night
Buried in a grave underneath some flags.
The grave has a red-brown headstone.
```

"Red-brown" was his translation of "russet" from the assignment, one of the many words in it that he'd had to look up in the dictionary. He just had to hope he could find a librarian who would buy his story of being "on a sort of treasure hunt" for his English class and could make sense of what he'd written out. What he needed was someone like the magical young woman he'd met in the Carnegie yesterday.

The reference librarian was hardly what Mark had in mind. She had close-cropped, dark hair, and a broad, squarish face bottoming out in a little pointy chin that made Mark think of home plate.

"These all refer to just *one* person?" she asked, staring down at his sheet of paper. "Someone from *Pittsburgh?*"

"Yes, ma'am," Mark said, trying to sound worried. "I'm afraid so."

The librarian glanced up quickly at him over her glasses and then looked down again. "Not 'ma'am,' if you don't mind," she said, but she smiled as she said it and continued smoothly. "Then why is it 'we' here?" she asked, pointing at the two lines Mark had quoted from Assignment 2. " 'We have loved the stars too fondly'? Is this . . . Man Who Sold Time of yours buried with someone else?"

Mark felt himself redden, and he shifted his weight from one foot to the other. The reference librarian's name was on a little brass stand on the desk: Dana Ossip.

"Ms. Ossip," he said, "I'm not too sure who he's buried with. And . . . see, the guy I want, *he* wasn't the one who sold time. He created him. I should have put that down there, I guess."

Ms. Ossip took off her glasses and tapped her mouth with one of the earpieces as Mark tried to clarify the connections. "Those lines about the stars," she said when he'd finished, "sound like a quotation to me. Try checking the key terms in it in Bartlett's."

Mark did. In Bartlett's *Famous Quotations* he tried looking the lines up under "loved," "stars," "fondly," "fearful," and "night." They weren't listed. He went through several other dictionaries of quotations. Zip. Zilch. Negative. Not a thing.

He got out the copy of Assignment 2 and looked at it again. Maybe the *verse* would be in one of the damn dictionaries:

> 'Neath the flags before their resting place
> Look for the russet stone.
> The gateway to the future
> For a Quester seeking home.

It wasn't—and it was now after 11:00 A.M. and the library was closing at noon because of New Year's Eve. He hurried back up to the reference desk.

Ms. Ossip frowned, thinking. "You know, you might try the Pennsylvania Room over in the Carnegie. They're open till five o'clock today. Maybe Mrs. Harbinger could help you. If the person you want is part of Pittsburgh history, she'd be the one to see. She knows a great deal about Pittsburgh history."

The Carnegie. Lair of Thatchbeak. Mark felt his stomach twist. "Is the Pennsylvania Room . . . near the circulation desk?"

"Oh, no, no. The Pennsylvania Room is all by itself up on the second floor. It's restricted to material having to do with the state only, Pittsburgh in particular, and Mrs. Harbinger runs it. You'll see why when you talk to her."

In less than ten minutes, Mark was taking the stairs up to the second floor of Carnegie Library, two at a time.

The woman Mark saw sitting at the desk in the Pennsylvania Room reminded him of a nurse. She had on an open white sweater over a white dress and wore a single strand of pink pearls. Her hair was white also, bluish white and tightly curled. She was knitting something out of bright orange wool, which she put carefully to one side as Mark approached. She and Mark seemed to be the only ones there.

"Good morning," the woman said pleasantly, "or rather good afternoon. Welcome to the Pennsylvania Room. I'm Mrs. Harbinger. May I help you?"

She wasn't as old as Mark had first thought. Her hands were delicate, the skin on them translucent, but her face was unlined, and her clear grey eyes reminded Mark of Merial's. It was a small sweater she was knitting.

"Good morning," Mark said, grinning his little boy grin and holding his sheet of paper in front of him as though it were a ticket. "Ms. Ossip over at Hillman said you were the one I should see, Mrs. Harbinger"—he'd made it a point to remember both names. "She said that you knew more about Pittsburgh than anybody. I sure hope you can help me."

"Did she *really*," Mrs. Harbinger said, taking his sheet of paper and scanning it. "More than anybody. My, my, my, my." Her voice was very cultured, sort of British. "Well," she said, smiling up at Mark. "I see one thing you're interested in and that's John Brashear. You know my mother met him once when she was a little girl. He came over to her school. He loved teaching children." She looked down at the paper again. "These other things here, do they have to do with Mr. Brashear?"

"You . . . know who this person is, then?" Mark asked her delightedly. "And where's he buried?"

"I know who John Brashear *was*, if that's what you

mean. He's been dead for years and years. And indeed I do know where he's buried. In fact, these lines," she tapped the lines about the stars with her forefinger, "are his epitaph. That is, they're the epitaph of Mr. Brashear and his wife Phoebe. He selected them himself, or did you already know that?"

"Well . . . no," Mark said, "I don't know too much about him, really. He . . . he's buried somewhere with his wife, then? They have a . . . a resting place somewhere with, like flags around it, and a stone marker?"

"Oh, I wouldn't think with any flags, no, and I know there's no headstone to their grave, if that's what you mean. But yes indeed, Mr. Brashear and his wife certainly have a resting place. They're inside the foundation of Allegheny Observatory—their ashes are anyway—and there's a brass plaque there with these lines engraved on it." She tapped the paper again. "Mr. Brashear requested that. He was responsible for the Observatory, you know."

"He was?" Mark responded mechanically. There had to be flags where the guy was buried and some kind of stone marker, some kind of russet stone marker. "Is it . . . this Observatory—is it around here somewhere?"

"Oh, my word, yes," Mrs. Harbinger laughed. "You really don't know much about John Brashear yet, do you?" She picked up Mark's sheet of paper, got up, and came around to the front of the desk. "The Observatory is an important part of Pittsburgh history. It's up in Riverview Park over on the North Side. They have guided tours there." She touched Mark's elbow. "Now let me get you something on John Brashear." She headed toward the back of the Pennsylvania Room. "There are several biographies of course," she said over her shoulder, "but I think we'll try Mr. Brashear himself first. Letting people speak for themselves is always the best place to start, isn't it?"

"Tours, really?" Mark exclaimed. "Can you tell me how to get over to the Observatory?"

"I'm afraid not," Mrs. Harbinger said, "but I'm sure they'll give you directions. You'll have to telephone for an appointment anyway. It's free. That was one of Mr. Brashear's stipulations, that the Observatory be forever free to the people. Wasn't that a nice thought? But you may have to wait a while to get a place in a tour. They get pretty full over the holidays."

Mark glanced up at the clock on the wall. It was quarter past noon. All he could think of was getting to a phone.

Mrs. Harbinger stopped in front of a low bookcase running underneath a window and took out a paperback book, which she handed to Mark. *A Man Who Loved the Stars* it was called, and it was subtitled *The Autobiography of John A. Brashear*.

"Now," Mrs. Harbinger said, handing Mark back his piece of paper, "these other things on there. Do they all have something to do with Mr. Brashear?"

"Well," Mark said. "I think so. They're sort of like clues I got in my English class. See, I was thinking of doing my senior project on—" he looked down at the book— "on something connected with astronomy." And then he asked quickly, "Have you ever been to his grave out there at the Observatory, Mrs. Harbinger?"

"No," she smiled. "I haven't."

Ah ha, Mark thought. Then she can't know for certain about the headstone or the flags.

Mrs. Harbinger touched Mark's elbow again. "Incidentally, Mr. Brashear was *not* an astronomer. That's one of the things that makes him so remarkable."

"He wasn't? I thought you said he built the Observatory."

"He did. He was asked to plan and supervise the construction of it anyway, but he wasn't an astronomer. He was a lens maker who lived in Pittsburgh about the turn of the century. He ground lenses for telescopes, he and his wife. He *knew* all the famous astronomers, mind you, corresponded with all of them. His lenses were in use all over the world."

"A lens maker, then. He sounds like quite a man."

"He was, the more remarkable because he wasn't really trained as a lens maker either. Actually, he was a millwright, a kind of engineer. He had no formal education to speak of, taught himself all he knew, even about his trade. He repaired machinery in the steel mills, worked for Andrew Carnegie as a matter of fact, and started to make lenses as . . . well, as a kind of a hobby, because he loved the stars. He and his wife would work together in their home at night grinding lenses. Not for money either. Mr. Brashear never made any money, really, and he was terrible with it. He ground his lenses for . . . well, for love. One of them took the Brashears seventeen years to finish. You can see it over at the Observatory."

"Wow!" Mark said. "Seventeen years!" Impressed, he leafed through the book. It wasn't long, not even two hundred pages. Maybe he should take it out. "And your mother actually knew this man?"

"Oh, not *knew* him, no. She only met him once. Listened to him I should say. She was a very little girl, quite young, but she never forgot his long white beard and how he called the sky 'the heavens.' Not 'heaven,' but 'the heavens.' He told the children how he'd row across the river after work, so he could climb the slag heaps and get a clear view of—" she laughed—"of the heavens. Pittsburgh was all smoke from the mills in the valley then, day and night, so to see anything you had to get up high where the wind blew. Can you imagine rowing all the way across the river after a ten-or-twelve-hour day in the steel mills, and then climbing up a slag heap just to be able to get a clear view of the stars? And then he went home and ground lenses after that."

She paused a moment and looked off, as though remembering.

"But he always had time for children, John Brashear did, even after he became famous. He used to go around to all the Pittsburgh schools to talk to children. He loved their wonder, I think. He was . . . a holy man in some ways. Quite remarkable."

She looked at Mark. "May I have your card, please?"

It startled him. "My what? My card?"

"Your library card. You want to check the book out, surely. It should help you with those . . . what did you call them, clues?"

"Oh, yes," Mark said, "but I . . . don't have a card. I'm sorry."

"Nothing to be sorry about. I'll give you an application form, which you can fill out and turn in at the main desk downstairs. They'll give you a card right away if you have a driver's license, something with your address on it. I'm assuming you live in the city." She moved back toward her desk.

"Oh, yes," Mark said. "Yes, I live up in Highland Park." The main desk, he thought. Where Thatchbeak was likely to be. "Would it be okay if I read the book right here?" he asked. "I don't think I brought my driver's license."

She smiled. "By all means. I'd enjoy the company." She glanced at the empty library tables around the room. "We're not exactly pressed with customers this afternoon."

Well, Mark thought, riffling through the pages of the book he was holding and then sitting down resignedly with it, there was no chance of his getting out to the Observatory today anyway. Besides, he knew that finding the Brashears' grave wasn't the point really—not for whoever was setting up the quest it wasn't, not any more than the point of having him read a particular novel had been to get him to a short flight of steel steps leading up to the Rental Office of an abandoned apartment complex. It was something else he was supposed to see, something more.

He got a notebook and pen out of his backpack and began reading *A Man Who Loved the Stars*.

6

"Okay," Mark said to Merial just after Federal Street turned into Perrysville Road, "remember that Riverview Avenue runs off to the left. They said we couldn't miss the church at the corner."

"People always say things like that when they give directions."

The road became steeper and Mark dropped his mother's car into second gear. They climbed steadily away from the bar-and-porno sleaze of lower Federal Street but up into an area that felt to Mark in some ways worse. It was as though the empty houses and streets on both sides of them had been destroyed in some kind of a battle and then looted. A great many of the buildings had been stripped of doors and windows. The trash lying around was household stuff, rusted appliances, piles of broken furniture. There was not a light to be seen anywhere.

"I wonder what happened here," Mark said. John Brashear's autobiography had given him to understand that the area was pleasant rolling woodland.

"I'm telling you now, Mark, if it's like this up there, I'm not getting out of the car, research or no research."

He bit his lip. "Research" had been his word for why he had to get to the Observatory. "Don't worry," he said.

"I know it won't be like this. The Observatory's in a park. Riverview Park. They said it was perfectly safe."

Actually, the people at the Observatory hadn't mentioned the area, nor had Mark thought to ask about it. He'd never been in this part of Pittsburgh before, and all he'd asked were directions for getting there from Highland Park.

It was Friday night, more than two weeks past the beginning of the New Year. Mrs. Harbinger had been right about the Observatory tours being filled around the holidays, and January 17 was the first opening Mark had been able to get.

Waiting to get into the Observatory had been an agony of anticipation for him, but he'd used the time to read everything on John Brashear he'd been able to lay his hands on. He'd even bought a book of star charts to locate the planets and major constellations. More and more he was certain that he was being given the opportunity of a lifetime.

"I mean it, Mark," Merial said without looking at him. "This is worse than East Liberty. What if we get a flat up here?"

The road curved sharply to the left. "Hey!" Mark said, swerving suddenly to the side of the road and stopping, "look at that, will you." They were far enough back on the crest of the hill so that the height didn't bother him. Far below in the distance lay the whole of Pittsburgh's center city, glittering with light. At the point where the city's two rivers met to form the Ohio, an illuminated fountain waved like a small silver feather. "That is just great," he declared. "Isn't it just great?" He leaned down to look up over Mount Washington. "That's Cassiopeia's Chair up there," he said, gesturing at the stars. "The lazy *W* they call it."

Merial had put both hands on the dashboard when they stopped. Without moving them, she bent down to glance out the side window. Then she straightened up and glanced right, to the remains of a burned-out building just off the road. "Mark," she said, "let's get out of here. There's broken glass all over the street."

In silence they drove on and eventually back into the world of shops, buses, and streetlights. They turned left at a great black hulk of a church and a couple of blocks later entered Riverview Park. A small green and white sign pointed them first through some woods, and then up a long circular drive, swept on either side by great stretches of lawn. The three domes of the Observatory at the top were clearly silhouetted against the brightly starred sky. They were massive but buoyant, like floating black bubbles.

"Wow!" Mark said, leaning down to see the tops of the domes through the windshield, "they're just like the picture in Brashear's book—and that's where Mr. and Mrs. Brashear are buried, right underneath them in the basement, down in the columbarium." He loved saying the word. It was in the Afterword to *The Man Who Loved the Stars* that Mark had read that the Brashears' cremated ashes were "laid away in the columbarium of the Observatory," which the dictionary defined as a sort of vault with niches for funeral urns.

Six or seven other cars were already parked in a line by the Observatory's entrance, all of them with their lights off, but with their idling engines breathing long spumes of white into the cold winter air. Mark pulled up behind them, turned off the motor, and zipped up his parka.

"Let's have a look around."

Merial glanced at the digital car clock. "The Observatory doesn't open for ten more minutes. That's why everybody's waiting here."

"We can be first in line then," Mark said to her, grinning and getting out of the car. He walked past the other cars to the columned entrance of the Observatory, which stood on the other side of the street at the top of a flight of wide stone stairs. Directly across from the stairs, just the other side of the first parked car, was an observation platform, a small open patio of flagstones built out from the crest of the hill. There was a concrete drinking fountain on one side of it. Mark walked out onto the patio and tried the drinking fountain, but the water was off. Merial joined him, took his arm, and led him to the edge of the platform, where they stood together surrounded by John Brashear's burning stars. The hill fell away sharply from where they were standing, and Mark realized suddenly that he was looking down on the stars, on all three sides of him. He took a quick step backward to anchor himself, catching Merial to him as he did so, shutting his eyes tight and burying his face in her hair. She put her arms around him.

"I'm sorry I was such a drag," she said. "It's beautiful up here. I've never seen the stars like this."

Mark held her until his stomach settled. After a while he heard a car door slam behind them, and then another, and another. Across the street a young woman was leaning against one of the two huge brass doors of the Observatory, holding it open. In less than five minutes about twenty people had been ushered into what felt like a large living room. It was filled with rows of straight-backed chairs, however, and lined with glass cases of photographs and astronomical instruments. People were asked to seat themselves.

"This room was Mr. Brashear's idea," Mark whispered

to Merial. "He wanted the Observatory to be sort of like a home and to be free to the people forever."

Merial nodded.

"Remember now," Mark whispered again, as he helped her off with her coat, "we've got to look sharp when we get down to the columbarium. We'll probably go down there first."

"And we've got to ask about The Man Who Sold Time. I know. You only told me three times."

Mark ran the clue through his head again:

```
'Neath the flags before their resting place
Look for the russet stone.
The gateway to the future
For a Quester seeking home.
```

Down where the Brashears' ashes were buried there had to be some flags and under them a red-brown stone. How he was going to move from there he'd have to wait and see.

Their tour guide identified herself as Miranda Bell, a graduate student doing research in star movement. She was small and to Mark looked a little like Jodie Foster, but she had on a business suit and a manner that fit it. Also, it very quickly became obvious she was a lot more interested in science than she was in history. She spoke of how the stars were photographed, of spectrographic analysis, of sidereal calculation. Mark began to fidget. Finally, however, she led everyone down the hall to a life-size bronze statue of John Brashear that was set in a kind of alcove before a huge, stained-glass window. She explained briefly who Brashear was and concluded by saying that the ashes of the Brashears were sealed in a wall in the basement. Then she told everyone they were going upstairs to see the telescopes.

Upstairs? Mark thought in panic. *Up*stairs!

"I have to talk to her," Mark said in a low voice to Merial. He pushed his way to the front of the crowd following the guide down the hall and touched her arm.

"Aren't we going down to the columbarium to see the Brashears' ashes?" he asked her.

"That's not on the tour," she said, heading up a steep flight of narrow metal stairs. He had to rush to keep up with her.

"But I have to see them. It's for a project I'm doing."

"I'm sorry," she said, flashing him a brief professional smile over one shoulder. "It's just not open to the public."

She swung through a heavy metal door and stepped onto a steel catwalk suspended by rods about twenty feet above a concrete floor and circling the entire inside of the main dome of the Observatory. Mark took a few steps onto it, but at the swaying of the catwalk he stopped and seized the rail with both hands. The tour guide went on in front of him, about halfway around the dome, where she stopped and turned, waiting for people to assemble. She was standing directly under a telescope, which stretched from a control booth on the floor to high above her head. It was an enormous thing, big as a boxcar.

Mark could hear the clank of footsteps on the metal stairs behind him, and then he felt the catwalk sway again as people stepped onto it. His stomach lurched. But he had to get to the guide. Hand over hand, fighting nausea, he worked his way ahead of the crowd around to where the tour guide was standing.

"Look," he said, breathing hard, "Ms. Bell, this is really important. I have this project for English to do. I have to see those graves."

"There's nothing to see," she said. "There *aren't* any graves. The Brashears' ashes are sealed in the wall down there. It's just a small bare room with a plaque on the wall. Nothing else. And you can't go down there. It's not open to the public."

"And flags. There are some flags too, aren't there?"

"Flags? No," she snapped. "Of course not. It's a completely bare room. I told you, sir. There's nothing down there to see."

Mark could see her looking over his shoulder at the group and knew he was about to lose her attention.

"Russet stones?" Mark cried in desperation, letting go of the rail with one hand to take hold of her arm. "I know there has to be a russet stone down there!"

She pulled her arm away quickly and took a step backward. There were small spots of red at her cheekbones.

"Stop it, sir!" she hissed at him. "What's the matter with you?" She took another step backward and in a loud voice asked the group for attention. Glancing warily at Mark from time to time, she began to describe the telescope above them. When she'd finished, she led the group the rest of the way around the catwalk to an exit door close to the one they'd all come through. Mark let everyone pass him and waited for Merial, who was at the end of the crowd. He knew what the set of her mouth meant.

"I just hate it when you do that to me," she said. "You just walk away from me as though I wasn't even there."

Mark nodded grimly. "I'm sorry," he said in a throttled voice, not looking at her. His hands were white on the rail of the catwalk. He still felt sick to his stomach.

Merial took his arm. "Here we go," she said matter-of-factly. "It's not far to that door over there. Ten steps maybe. *Don't* look down. Keep looking at me." With her help Mark managed the rest of the catwalk.

The group was assembled in a room with a second telescope, smaller than the one that filled the dome, but still a huge piece of equipment. Ms. Bell began another lecture. Mark and Merial were standing at the back of the room.

"What'd you say to her, anyway?" Merial whispered to him. "She's still looking daggers."

"All I asked was to see the graves. That's what we came out here for. But she says nobody's allowed down there."

"Well, maybe nobody is. Besides you're not doing your project on *graves,* are you? You don't *have* to see them."

"Yes," he said, "I do." He said it more loudly than he'd intended. "It's part of my research." Several people glanced back at them.

"Keep your voice down," she whispered, giving his arm a shake. "What'd she say about The Man Who Sold Time?"

He shook his head. "I never asked her," he said mournfully. "She never gave me the chance."

Maybe there really *weren't* any flags down in the vault, it suddenly struck him. No flags. No russet stone. Maybe he'd got something wrong, or *done* something wrong. It didn't matter which. The quest was over for him either way.

Sunk in himself, miserable, Mark tuned out the rest of the tour. He even refused his turn to look at Saturn through the smaller telescope. To hell with it, he thought. To hell with John Brashear and his Observatory and his lousy blazing heavens too. Finally, the group was led down another flight of stairs and shown back to the entrance where Ms. Bell held the brass door open for people to file out. She deliberately looked away when Mark passed her, which made him feel like swinging his elbow into her stomach.

"Excuse me, Ms. Bell," he heard Merial say behind him as he started down the steps, "but can you tell me whether there was anyone connected with John Brashear who was called The Man Who Sold Time?"

He stopped and looked back up to the top of the steps. Ms. Bell was smiling.

"Well," she said to Merial, "you really know your history, don't you? Indeed there was. That was Samuel Langley, the astronomer, one of John Brashear's patrons. There wasn't any real need for accurate time, you see, until the railroads got big. Then, it mattered a lot whether, say, Pittsburgh was five minutes slower or faster in schedule than Philadelphia. There were wrecks. So Langley kept time here in the Observatory, solar time not sidereal, though he kept both, and he literally sold the *right* time to the railroads. That's where his name came from. How'd you hear about Langley?"

Oh, swell, Mark thought, walking stiffly down the rest of the steps hearing Merial and the guide laughing and chatting behind him. So Samuel Whoozis was The Man Who Sold Time. So that was going to help him a lot.

He wound his way between the departing cars and went back to the edge of the flagstone observation patio.

"Got him," Merial said perkily as she came up behind him, "or did you hear? The Man Who Sold Time was an astronomer named Samuel Langley. He—"

"I heard," Mark interrupted stonily. "Great. Wonderful."

For a moment she said nothing. "Come on, Mark," she said after a time. "We got most of what you came out here for, didn't we?"

He shook his head. "You don't understand."

"*What* don't I understand? Why *do* you need to see those graves?" She cupped his chin with one hand to turn his face up to her. He wouldn't move his head at first, but then he did.

He took a deep breath and stuffed his hands in his parka pockets. "Okay," he said. "There are flags down there, see? And a russet stone. At least I think there are. They're an important clue to something . . . I have to find."

She chewed her lower lip looking at him. "What do you mean flags?" she asked finally. "Waving, or like these?" She stamped her foot.

"What?"

"Do you mean waving flags, like on a flagpole, or flag*stones*, like what we're standing on?"

At first he just stared back at her. Then he looked down at the stones of the observation patio.

```
'Neath the flags before their resting place
Look for the russet stone.
```

Of course, he thought. Flag*stones*. Flagstones in front of the Brashears' resting place, in front of the Observatory where they were buried. Of *course*. And one of them, though he couldn't tell which one without daylight, one of them had to be red-brown. And it was under *it* that—

"Oh, Gyp," he said, pulling her to him. "You are something else, you know that? What a dope I am. I *don't* need to see those graves, no. You're right." He raised a hand to the sky over her head in a kind of salute. "And roll on up there, Mr. Heavens," he called out. "Roll on forever. And three cheers for Mr. John Brashear."

7

Waiting at the kitchen table for his mother to come down to breakfast the next morning, Mark ran through what it was likely he was going to need to raise the flagstone of the observation platform. A hammer for sure, maybe even a sledgehammer in case the stone had been laid in cement. Chisels? A shovel? Pry bar?

He poured his mother's coffee when he heard the toilet flush. Her step on the stairs, a few minutes later, told him she had on her high heels. Good. That meant she and Jody had selling appointments, which, since Jody always insisted on driving, meant he could get the car. Busing out to the Observatory with a backpack full of tools would have been a real pain.

"Morning, Mom," he said, grinning his little boy grin. "Bet you got a deal brewing."

She nodded and smiled automatically, but without speaking and without looking at him. He could see the tightness at the corners of her eyes under her makeup. A headache. She'd had a fight with Guy probably. She hadn't been home when Mark came in the night before.

Mark cleared his throat. "Can I . . . ah . . . drop you at Northwood?" If she had had a fight with Guy, he did not want to hear about it.

She started to nod, but then looked off. "No, come to think of it, I better take the car. I have some cleaning to pick up."

"I can do that," Mark said quickly. "For you. You may not get there on time. Doesn't Footers always close early on Saturday?"

"No, as a matter of fact they're open until nine o'clock. I was going to stop on the way over, anyway."

"Oh, you don't want stuff sitting around in the car all day, do you?"

She looked up at him, amused. "You wouldn't be planning to pick up Merial or anything like that, would you, love?"

"I was planning to go down to the Carnegie for some books and stuff," he said archly. "The car would have made it easier, that's all."

For a moment she didn't speak, and then she said, "I'm sorry, Mark, I didn't mean . . ." She shook her head slightly without finishing. "I guess I just have a one-track mind this morning. Just drop me at Northwood."

"You sure it's okay?" Mark said quickly.

She nodded. "But try to get back by lunch, okay? It's supposed to snow this afternoon."

He thanked her and went to get his coat.

"And, oh, Mark," she called after him. "*If* I can't get home by three—I'll call you—could you start dinner? It's just stew. Everything's in the fridge. Guy's coming." And then she paused and added, "At least that was the plan last night."

"Fine," he said from the front hall, more cheerfully than he felt. He liked it when Guy ate with them and didn't really mind doing kitchen stuff, but stew meant peeling things—onions, carrots, potatoes—and since they always ate in the dining room when Guy came, that meant setting the table too. It was time he was afraid he was going to be pushed for.

After dropping his mother at Northwood, Mark got the cleaning, hung it in the hall closet, and then went straight down to his father's workroom. His father had made the room, sectioning off a corner of the cellar with studs and wallboard. It was small but very efficiently laid out. Under the single small basement window opposite the doorway, there was a narrow workbench equipped with a vise. Across the back of the bench was a row of plastic cases filled with delicate looking hardware, tiny nails and screws, fuses, brightly-colored electrical connectors. Mark could remember thinking once that the connectors were pieces of candy. There was a peg-board mounted on the concrete wall with different-size saws and hammers hanging from it. Under the peg-board were shelves of power tools, none of which Mark knew how to use. Just to the right of the fluorescent light, above the workbench, was a pin-up of Marilyn Monroe lying naked on a rug.

Mark didn't like going into the workroom. Once, when he'd been younger, in grade school, he'd been alone in the house and had gone into his mother's bedroom, where he'd opened the drawers of her bureau one by one. He'd found Tampax, though he hadn't know then what it was, and in another drawer, a small one, under a lot of handkerchiefs, there were several pairs of see-through black lace panties and a manila envelope full of what looked to be old letters. He'd run downstairs then and outside to the open air. Going into his father's workroom always made him remember that time.

"Okay," Mark said, pulling the string to turn on the fluorescent light, "now let's see what we got here."

He dropped the tools he thought might be useful into his backpack. A couple of big screwdrivers, some chisels, a hammer, a small pry bar. Under his free arm he tucked a short-handled spade. And he also brought the sledge-hammer. Half an hour later he had passed through downtown Pittsburgh and was climbing Perrysville Road.

At the top of the hill, Mark stopped the car and looked back down on the city for a moment, but the magic of the night before was gone. A low-bellied drift of clouds had cut off the top of the Mellon Bank Building. The fountain at the intersection of the rivers was off, and the rivers themselves were the color of lead.

Snow for sure, but that wouldn't stop him. The Observatory was no more than fifteen minutes away.

Mark expected the circular drive that ran in front of the entrance to the Observatory building to be empty, but three cars were there parked alongside the flagged observation platform. He pulled up behind them.

The first thing was to find the russet stone.

The flags of the patio he saw were cemented together and were mostly of a uniform slate-grey color, but near the drinking fountain were two brownish slabs of stone, and at the far corner a reddish one about two by three feet. He'd start with the one at the corner. It was the most obviously red, and as a corner stone would have been the easiest one for somebody to take up and then replace.

Mark strolled over to the far corner of the patio as though to see something in the distance more clearly. There was no trouble with his stomach. In the daytime the view was quite tame. The cement on the two inside edges of the red stone he noticed was a little different in color from that along the edges of the other stones in the platform. Did that mean it was newer? Mark stood on the flag and rocked his body, but the stone felt firm. He stamped on the outside corner of it, but the stone didn't move.

Mark looked casually around him, first back up at the Observatory, which was fronted with windows, and then down the slope of lawn that ran off three sides of the platform to a circle of trees at the bottom of the hill. He was in full view of anyone who happened to glance out of one of the Observatory's windows or look up from the bottom of the hill. To use either the sledgehammer or the shovel was out of the question.

It started to snow, just a few large downy flakes. He went back to the car and transferred two chisels and one of the large screwdrivers from his backpack to his parka pockets. The hammer and short pry bar he slipped inside his belt, covering them with his coat. Then he went back onto the patio and sat down on it cross-legged, his back to the Observatory, the red flagstone just in front of him. The tools he placed between his legs.

The snow was coming down faster, but melting on the flagstones, leaving wet spots the size of quarters.

In two blows with the hammer, Mark drove the big screwdriver three inches into the earth at one of the cemented edges of the flagstone. Very good. The cement of the two joints, new or not, broke out in chunks easily. Then, using the stone he'd been sitting on as a fulcrum, Mark got to his knees and tried to lever the red flagstone up with the big screwdriver. He felt it move slightly, but the stone was far too heavy to lift with the screwdriver alone. As he was trying to work the pry bar down into the crack, he heard the door of the Observatory open behind him. Quickly, he reseated himself and put his tools back between his crossed legs. He glanced over his shoulder to see a man joking with two women as he locked the Observatory door. All three people looked to be in their twenties, graduate students he guessed, just like Ms. Ding Dong Bell. Mark kept his back to them and sat up with exaggerated straightness, as though he were at attention. He heard the people fall silent and knew it was because they were looking at him.

"You okay, fella?" the man called over to him.

Mark thought he could hear them walking down the steps. Without turning around, he raised both hands high over his head with both thumbs up.

The air was filled now with snow and Mark could see the grass on the slopes in front of him beginning to whiten. He felt the blood throb in his neck. What if these idiots just stood there and watched him—or if the guy came over?

Mark couldn't hear anything. Had the people gone to their cars?

"You sure you're all right?" one of the women called out. "There's a storm coming, you know."

Mark turned his head part way in the direction of their voices but without moving his legs. "My business is with prayer and thanksgiving," he said in a booming voice. "Leave me to my meditations." He then looked down the slope and, holding his elbows high, pressed the palms of his hands together as he had seen Asians do in the movies.

He heard whispering behind him, and then one of the women giggled. "Well," the man said, "I'm out of here, ladies." A car door opened and shut. After a moment Mark heard the door of another car open and close. But that still left the third car. He didn't lower his arms until he saw both cars disappear into the trees at the bottom of the hill. The second held two people. What should he do? Suppose whoever owned the third car came out of the Observatory while he was working to raise the russet stone.

The snow was coming down harder, and the flakes were no longer melting on the flagstones.

He'd simply have to chance being caught. He went back to work with the pry bar.

It was too thick to work down between the two stones where the cement had been. And though Mark could get the bar under the stone from either of its outside edges, the ground was too soft to provide him with any leverage for lifting. The stone was a monster, three or four inches thick. It looked to weigh at least a hundred pounds.

What Mark needed was something firm to lever up from. He tried using the screwdriver set crossways under the pry bar, but he still couldn't get enough lift. Then he tried putting the two chisels and the screwdriver together under the pry bar. He got the stone up about a quarter of an inch before pressing the tools into the soft ground, but no more than that. Damn to hell.

The shovel would have been ideal of course, or he could have tried breaking up the flag with the sledgehammer, but given the car still parked behind him, Mark didn't want to risk using either one.

Something wide and flat was what he needed, something that wouldn't press down into the ground when he put pressure on it, like a brick, or better, a flat rock, like a small flagstone, or . . . like a *piece* of a flagstone.

He walked quickly along the outside edge of the patio, scraping the flags free of snow with his shoe as he went. Nothing. Halfway down the side that ran back to the Observatory driveway, however, was a flagstone broken into three pieces. He rammed the pry bar under one of them and it came up immediately, a piece of slate about the size of a small plate, three inches or so thick. Mark raced back to the red stone and using the piece of flag as a fulcrum for the pry bar, managed to lever the stone up several inches. Pressing down with his left hand and knee on the bar, he groped as far back under the stone as he could reach, about to the heel of his hand. He could feel nothing but damp, packed earth. He then raised the other outside edge of the stone and searched again, but this time felt something at the very ends of his fingers, something smooth, about the thickness of a wallet that he couldn't quite get hold of.

He needed more of a fulcrum, another piece of flagstone to put on top of the first. He ran back over and dug out another piece of the broken flagstone, and three minutes later had extracted what looked exactly like the packet he had taken from Talbot Towers. In the car he opened it with one of the chisels. Again there were two plain white envelopes, one of them scotch-taped to a stiff piece of cardboard. Inside the loose envelope was:

Assignment 3

At this stage of your education, and even before beginning your work on this Assignment, you must select a companion with whom to continue the quest, one who will agree to abide by all its conditions as stipulated in Assignment 1, and who will agree also to work with you on all of your future research and excursions. This person is to be a different sex from your own, a member of your same class at Moorland, but may not be a friend of yours at present.

Since this person is to share in your Great Expectations, he or she may share also in all that you know, or think you know, of the quest so far.

Choose your companion with care, for you may

ask only one person, and ask him or her only once, to be your fellow traveler. If for any reason he or she should refuse to be your chosen companion, or fails to abide by the conditions of the quest as I have already explained them to you, my relationship with the two of you will be immediately terminated.

Now and then, it was said of John Brashear, a man stands before the stars as he stands before his family or his fellow men or his enemies, with the circle of his integrity drawn, and with all his ghosts inside him, working for him and not against him. But most of the time, some of one's ghosts work one way and some another, making it difficult to determine not just what stars one stands before, but what is involved in following them.
As the case of a Pittsburgh woman may be said to demonstrate.

In leading them from the Way of Sorrows,
In leading them past the Bridge of Sighs,
Her action still the question poses
What she revered and what defied.

Was it all for love, or sickness rampant,
Or something somewhere in between,
That led this prison warden's wife
To dream the act and act the dream?

right eye/throat/nose/nose/right breast/mouth
right ear/right hip/forehead/left wrist/mouth

Find the Star.

Inside the second envelope were four hundred-dollar bills, again brand-new, and with consecutive serial numbers running straight up from those of the bills accompanying Assignments 1 and 2.

8

"I'm certainly no authority on Pittsburgh history—Ev, may I have the biscuits please? They're lovely—but I'm sure the woman you mean is Katherine Soffel. A pretty historical problem, the Soffel case."

"Hey!" Mark exclaimed. "All *right!* Who was she exactly? What'd she do?"

Mark's mother handed the last two biscuits across the table to Guy. Both the honey and butter were already in front of him. Outside the small dining room's picture window the snow was falling steadily, the flakes glowing with color as they fell through the glare of the Christmas lights Mark hadn't yet removed from the outside sill. It looked like a serious snow, the first of the winter. The forty-five-minute trip back across town from the Observatory had taken Mark about two hours.

Guy buttered one of the biscuits. "Who was she exactly? Well, that of course is the problem—though what she did, or most of what she did, seems clear enough. She was, as you just said, the wife of a prison warden, the warden of Allegheny County Prison to be exact, back around the turn of the century."

Guy dribbled honey over his biscuit, quite a lot of it, from a plastic container in the shape of a bear. He leaned forward over his empty stew plate quickly, being careful of his beard, and bit the biscuit in half. Several thin strings of honey stretched down from the uneaten portion even so.

"Okay," Mark said, "so what'd she do?"

Guy looked up sideways at Mark and held up a finger while he chewed and swallowed. His face was broad and ruddy, as though he worked outside. Guy had always looked to Mark more like a lumberjack than a college professor.

"She helped a couple of condemned murderers escape from the jail. Two brothers. The Biddle boys. Smuggled them in some saws and a gun. After they cut their way out, the three of them went off together. In the snow too. Zero degree weather. And on foot, heading north. On foot at first, anyway. They stole a horse and sleigh later."

"Really!" Mark said delightedly. "*Really!* They crashed out of her *hus*band's jail? What happened? They get away?"

Guy popped the rest of the biscuit in his mouth and shook his head. "Oh, no," he said, as soon as he could speak. "They were hunted down by a posse. Up around Butler someplace, as I remember. They shot the boys to pieces. It was an act of real butchery. Even killed the horse that was pulling the sleigh. Katherine was shot too. Maybe by the Biddles. Maybe by the posse. Maybe she shot herself. Nobody really knows. But she lived—and was sent to prison eventually, ironically, to the same prison, her husband's, that she'd helped the Biddles escape from. The case was quite a sensation. It was reported all over the world."

"They made a movie about this," Mark's mother said, pointing her finger at Guy.

"They did indeed," Guy said, offering the last biscuit

on the plate first to Mark and then to his mother, both of whom shook their heads. "Made the film right here in Pittsburgh a while back. *Mrs. Soffel* with Diane Keaton and . . . who?"

"Mel Gibson," Mark's mother said. "Dreamboat Mel. I never saw the movie, but I heard about it. She fell for one of the brothers, right."

"Well," Guy said, preparing his biscuit, "that's the point of view of the film anyway."

"Listen, Guy," Mark said, leaning toward him intently, did the Biddles and Mrs. Soffel have, like, any kind of secret code they used, do you know?"

It was Mark's guess that the parts of the body strung together as they were at the end of Assignment 3 had to be some sort of code.

Guy wiped his fingers on his paper napkin and frowned. "Code? What do you mean code?"

"Oh," Mark said, gesturing, "you know where they use objects or something like that to stand for words and letters."

Guy shook his head slowly. "Not that I know of," he said. "I don't remember there being any code in the film, but films, you know—"

"*You* went to see the *movie!*" Mark's mother exclaimed, laughing. "I can *never* get you to the movies. Whatever made you? Diane Keaton?"

"Ev, my dear, please. It was the students, the flap they made about whether the film was true or not. You simply cannot break them of thinking of history that way. Very curious. 'Facts' they keep saying. The 'facts' of history when actually—"

"Okay," Mark broke in, having heard Guy on the nature of history before, "so you mean the movie changed around what really happened?"

Guy raised both hands. "Mark, you're as bad as the students. What really happened indeed. What I'm saying is that the Soffel case is a fine example of what we can never know for sure about history, or for that matter about anything else. I never did any research on the case myself, you understand, but Jack Cates, fellow in my department did, and I heard him talk about it. The love angle, overpowering romantic love, that was the point of view of the film. But that's a *today* point of view, you see, when it's generally believed *all* institutions are corrupt, that we're *all* victimized by the culture, or our childhoods—"

"But didn't Mel Gibson write her love letters?" Mark's mother interrupted.

"To be sure, to be sure," Guy said, "and the Biddles themselves were both very good-looking boys, by all accounts, very dashing—the courtroom was filled with swooning women when they were sentenced to death, though that happened a lot in courtroom trials back then. And he also wrote poetry for Katherine, that is Ed Biddle did, Mel Gibson. Awful stuff, really, but maybe she was moved by it. Love letters and love poetry don't mean love though, Ev, on either side. Those boys were going to swing, remember. It's to be expected they'd make the most of their chances."

"If the guy looked like Mel Gibson," Mark's mother put in, "I'll bet she really did fall for him."

"But how'd they get to talk to Katherine if they were in prison?" Mark asked. "They know each other before?"

"No, no. That was what made the case such a sensation. They were complete strangers. She got to know the Biddles because she read them the Bible. They did that then, groups of women called Gospel Ladies. They'd go into the jails and read to prisoners through the bars. To save their souls, you know."

"Wow!" Mark said.

"And she smuggled these guys saws and a gun? She took saws and a gun into her *husband's* jail? She had to have been in love," Mark's mother declared. "Why else would she have done it?"

Guy shrugged. "Could have been conviction. She could have been convinced the Biddles were innocent. Plenty of people were. They were convicted of murder on the testimony of someone who'd turned state's evidence. Right up to the end, the Biddles claimed *he'd* been the one to do the murder, and that he'd lied to save his own skin. A lot of people believed them."

Mark's mother smiled and shook her head. "Sorry, but women just don't work that way—and I don't care what the modern point of view is. Besides, if it were just conviction, what'd she go off with them for? Why didn't she just let them escape by themselves?"

Again Guy shrugged. "Maybe she lost her nerve at the last minute, didn't want to stick around for the consequences. It was, after all, her husband's jail remember. Or maybe she hated her husband and used the Biddles to humiliate him."

"That's pretty far-fetched, don't you think?" Mark's mother said.

Guy cocked his head. "No more far-fetched than to say she was in love with Ed Biddle. And if she was in love, why take the second brother on the honeymoon with them?"

"Maybe they kidnapped her," Mark said. "You know, for a hostage."

"I don't think so," Guy said. "Nobody ever suggested such a thing—which they certainly would have had there been any way to make it wash. Would have saved her honor, you know."

"What did she say when they caught her?" Mark's mother asked.

"Nothing really. She wouldn't say anything to explain why she did what she did—though she may have and they may have suppressed what she said. It was a highly political event."

"It was love then," Mark's mother said firmly, rising from the table and picking up her plate. "I'll get dessert."

"She never said *anything?*" Mark asked incredulously. "Not a word?"

"Not in explanation of *why* she did what she did, no. All she'd say was that she was a bad woman and deserved to go to prison. And when she was asked about Ed Biddle, all she'd say was that she loved only her children."

"Children!" Mark's mother exclaimed, turning around at the doorway to the kitchen. "This woman had *children?*"

"Oh, yes, indeed. Little too. Dependent children. Three or four of them."

For a moment Mark's mother just stood there holding her dinner plate, staring at Guy. Then she shook her head and disappeared into the kitchen. "She must have been crazy," she called out.

Guy nodded. "That, of course, is a distinct possibility— and predictably it was what was most stressed then. It's always the easiest solution to things, however, and I'm suspicious of it."

"What do you mean?" Mark asked him.

Guy crossed his arms on the table and leaned forward on them. "Well, what the woman did, you see, struck at the very foundations of society as people understood it then. Ideals of marriage and motherhood. The institutions of law and religion. It called into question everything people take for granted as normal and right. Secondly, Katherine Soffel was a woman with a position. She wasn't an aristocrat, but she was solidly upper middle class. She even had an education of sorts. Now, if someone like that can do what she did, then how could you be sure of anyone? So the easiest thing always to do with otherwise solid citizens who call essential things into question is to see them as crazy. It's like calling Hitler insane."

"Wasn't he?"

"My point is that that way of thinking about him is a way to stop thinking about him. And that's dangerous."

"So Mrs. Soffel *wasn't* insane."

Guy raised one hand with a gesture of smiling uncertainty. "All I'm talking about is how she was represented. She was seen as a kind of monster, a lunatic monster, and the events of her life made it easy for them to represent her as a lunatic. She had a history of mental instability, Jack told me—or what they called that. She'd been in and out of asylums, anyway. And there were other things they used against her."

"Like what?"

"Wait a minute," Mark's mother called in from the kitchen. "Guy, don't answer yet. I want to hear this. Mark, bring the other plates out, will you please, and help me with dessert?"

In a few moments Mark and his mother were back in the dining room.

"Chocolate mouse!" Guy said jovially, rubbing his hands over the dish of mousse Mark had plunked down in front of him. It was a joke he always made. Like Mark's, Guy's dessert was mounded with Cool Whip.

"Okay," Mark's mother said, sitting down. "What else did they use against her?"

"At her arraignment, Jack told me, the prosecution claimed she'd had five or six lovers while she was married to Soffel."

"No kidding," Mark said. "Is that true?"

"There you go," Guy said, waggling his dessert spoon at him. "I've told you, Mark—"

"That there's no truth in history that way. I know, I know. I mean was there any *evidence* that she . . . you know, slept around?"

Again Guy shrugged. "The prosecution named names, produced some of the men to testify, Jack said. The defense denied it all, of course, claimed the men had been paid to slander her."

"And she never said anything even about *that?*" Mark's mother said.

"Oh, *that* she denied, sure. She also denied that she'd slept with Ed Biddle, but of course it didn't matter."

"What do you mean it didn't matter?" Mark's mother asked sharply. "Maybe she didn't."

"I mean whether she'd actually slept with Biddle or not was strictly academic. She'd spent a night on the road with him, and this was the turn of the century, remember. All her husband had to do for a divorce was show opportunity."

"So it was just taken for granted she was lying because that's how he could most easily get rid of her, is that it?"

"Well, he did divorce her in any case."

"Why not?" Mark said. "I would've too."

Mark's mother put her fork down and looked at him. Then she looked back at Guy.

"I see," she said. "She claimed she was innocent, but that's just academic. I suppose he took her children away from her too."

For a moment Guy didn't respond. Then he nodded. "He was awarded custody of them, yes. He moved out of state with them when she was in prison."

Mark's mother looked down at her dessert again and

for a moment didn't speak. "Sure," she said in a hard voice. "That figures. I don't suppose he ever had to pay her a cent either, right?"

"Hey, come on, Mom," Mark said. "She did help two guys break out of her husband's jail, you know. Maybe she did play around."

Mark's mother looked out the picture window at the steadily falling snow. Her lips were tightly compressed. Then she looked at Mark. "And of course what she *said* doesn't matter, does it?" she said sarcastically. She shook her head and looked down. "Didn't anybody even imagine she was telling the truth?"

Guy cleared his throat. "I'm sure some people did. Maybe even her husband. He could have divorced her for . . . other reasons."

"What a wonderful guy that husband of hers must have been," Mark's mother went on. "What'd he beat her only on weekends, or something? Nothing really serious?"

"Hey, Mom, come on," Mark tried. "This lady doesn't sound like the Good Housekeeping Mother of the Year, exactly."

"He was apparently a model husband, Evelyn."

"Sure," Mark's mother nodded, picking up her spoon and stabbing it savagely into her dessert. "I'll bet he was a model husband. Is that what your friend told you? I suppose she never saw her kids again. What, she die in prison?"

"No, she didn't. She got out in five or six years and became a seamstress. Over on the North Side somewhere, I think."

"A seamstress? Wonderful. What about her children?"

"I don't know. Nobody seems to know much about her after she got out of prison. She didn't live all that long. Nobody even knows where she's buried."

For a while no one said anything.

"Well, I'll lay you odds they never let her see her children again," Mark's mother said without looking up.

Mark and Guy glanced at each other. What was she making such a big deal about? Mark wondered.

"How'd you get interested in Mrs. Soffel, anyway?" Guy asked Mark.

"Oh . . . I'm looking around for a project for my English class. We have to do this senior project, you know? I was just sort of poking around in the Pennsylvania Room and . . . I heard about her."

"From Mrs. Harbinger, yes?"

"You know her?"

Guy laughed. "I know of her. She owns western Pennsylvania, historically speaking."

"She sure knows a lot. Nice lady too."

Again, there was a silence. Mark's mother had not raised her head. Guy leaned forward, put his elbows on the table, and rested his chin on his clasped hand. "Ev," he said gently, "would you care to join us in the present here? You know what a terrible tendency we historians have to get stuck in the past."

She smiled briefly to acknowledge the joke, looked quickly up at Guy, and then looked down again. But Mark had seen her eyes flash. Tears? Was she angry? What was going on? *Something* was going on.

"Stay in the present. Good advice," Mark's mother said in a businesslike voice.

Whatever, Mark thought, it was between the two of them. He rose from the table and picked up Guy's empty dessert dish as well as his own. "Think I'll go call Merial, if that's okay," he said.

Actually, he had talked to Merial just before dinner.

What he really wanted was to think some more about what he was going to say to Zeena Curry. He'd known from the moment he'd read Assignment 3 that she was the one he was going to ask to be his chosen companion.

9

Zeena read through the Xeroxed copies of the three assignments carefully, turning back from time to time to read some passages twice. When she'd finished she tapped the pages into a neat rectangle and lay them face up on the table of the booth between them. She crossed her forearms and leaned forward on them, looking not at Mark but out the plate glass window of King's Restaurant at a small snowplow that was tidying up the parking lot of the mall. Her skin looked apricot-colored against her brown uniform, more like the skin of someone Asian than black.

"So . . . what do you think?" Mark asked her with feigned casualness. He took a sip of coffee.

It was Saturday, early afternoon. Zeena, who worked as a part-time waitress at King's in the Waterworks Mall, hadn't yet started her shift. Mark had arranged the meeting five days earlier, just at the end of Hunter's honors English class, when, face flaming, he'd told her he had to talk with her about something important, please, and that he needed to sit down to talk with her about it alone, please. She was different up close from across a classroom. She was taller for one thing, a good two inches taller than he was, and her face, so queenly-looking in profile, up close was as oddly angled as the head of an insect.

"What do I *think*?" Zeena answered still looking out the window, "or will I be your . . ." she turned her head back and nodded down at the papers on the booth table, "your chosen companion and fellow traveler?"

It sounded mocking to Mark. "Look," he said, "this isn't my idea you know—to talk to you that way, I mean."

Sitting across from her at King's, he'd told her the whole of it about the quest, the whole of what he knew for sure, anyway. In one great excited rush he'd told it, right from how he'd found the money in the Dickens novel to his getting Assignment 3 from under the flagstone at Allegheny Observatory. He'd even showed her the money he'd brought to give her. Half. Four hundred and fifty dollars.

Maybe that was the problem, though, his having shown her the money. Maybe she thought he was trying to hustle her.

He picked up the papers on the booth table nervously. "This isn't a con, you know," he said. "Not by me it isn't."

"Oh, I know," she said, smiling slightly. "Don't you wonder what it is though? Whose idea it is; what they really want?"

"Sure I do," Mark said. "Of course I wonder." Was she in or not? That's what he really wondered. He finished his coffee at a gulp and set his cup down somewhat harder in the saucer than he'd intended. Zeena moved it from in front of him to the window end of the booth table.

"I accept the quest," she said, "if that's what you're asking. With all its conditions."

"You do?" Mark grinned, in spite of himself.

"Sure I do," she said. "Who wouldn't—and I *don't* want any of the money you've got so far, by the way."

"Come on, Zeena. Half's fair."

She shook her head. "Half from here on's what's fair."

"Don't be silly," he said, reaching to his pocket.

She caught his arm quickly but just as quickly dropped it. She had his full attention. "Would you take half if you were me?"

So dark were her eyes that the pupils and irises seemed to have melted together. What surprised Mark about her question was that he'd never even thought to put it to himself.

"Okay," he said, nodding. And then he leaned toward her grinning again. "I think I see what we're going to be working on to get the next assignment."

"Sure," Zeena said, picking up the sheaf of assignments again and frowning down at them. "We're supposed to go find out about Mrs. Soffel." She paused. "I still wonder what's really going on here, though."

It deflated him the way she sounded as though she already knew all about Mrs. Soffel.

"I mean what's this person *after*?" Zeena went on musingly. "What do they *want*?"

"It could be just what the guy says, couldn't it—that he wants to be a . . . a benefactor to somebody? The right somebody? The right some*bodies*? There are people like that, who set up scholarships and things. We could be in for a lot of money here. I mean a *lot* of money— like Pip in *Great Expectations*."

Zeena shuffled the page she'd been looking at to the bottom of the sheaf of assignments and continued to read. "Pip didn't end up getting any money at all though, remember?" She said it without looking up at him. "And how do you know a guy's doing this? How do you know it's a he?"

Mark stared at her for a moment. "Do you think it's a woman?"

Zeena read on for a bit and then put down the assignments and looked out the plate glass window. "No," she said. "As a matter of fact I don't. It all sounds like . . . some man's idea." She glanced at him and then looked quickly away again. "All this . . . proving yourself talk. All those orders and conditions. You don't by any chance smoke, do you?"

Oh, great, Mark thought. A man-hater. And hooked on cigarettes, too. Just what he needed to work with.

"No, I don't smoke. Women can talk that way too, you know."

Zeena shrugged concessively. "It's an easy tone to fake. In fact, a lot of the stuff in here could be faked—right down to the time frame."

"What do you mean the time frame?"

Zeena picked out Assignment 1 and slid it around on the booth so that both of them could see to read it. Her hair smelled faintly of cinnamon.

"Here," she said, tapping with her forefinger, "where he says it's been five years since anyone checked the Dickens novel out of the library? And you said it was, what, seven years since the book had been taken out? Okay. But that doesn't mean the *money's* been in the book that long. It could have been put there the same day your book was stolen."

Mark nodded. "I thought of that. But I told you, my book *wasn't* stolen. I found it under my sweatshirt on the floor of my locker. It was the first thing I checked after vacation."

"It could have been put there after you got the copy out of the library."

That possibility too had occurred to him. "It could have,

yeah. But even if somebody stole my book to set me up that way, how could they be sure I'd go to the school library? And even if I did, how could they be sure I'd pick the right copy of *Great Expectations*?"

Zeena leaned back in the booth and looked at him. "You think you found the money just by chance, then? That you were," she moved her hands like ribbons fluttering, "just lucky?"

The image of his father sitting on the cedar deck flashed across his mind. "I don't see how it could be any other way, do you? There are no," he waved a hand dismissively, "escaped convicts in my life that I've helped out or anything like that."

She nodded and then picked up the assignments again and studied them. "I just don't like feeling manipulated, if you know what I mean. What's 'oxymoronic' mean, do you know?"

Mark had looked it up. "It's like a contradiction in terms. Like saying fair is foul or sweet bitterness."

"How about 'Möbius curves'?"

Mark had looked it up as well.

"And what was the name of the novel again, the one that got you over to Talbot Towers?" She'd known all about Talbot Towers. "Not *Blood on the Forge*. What?"

"*Out of This Furnace*. It's about this Slavic family over in Braddock, three generations of people, who all work at the mill. It's about how they get a labor union going and . . . try to come up in the world."

"Talbot Towers is the way they try to come up in the world?"

"No, no, no. All that was later, way after the story in the novel. I bought the book. I'll bring it to school for you Monday. What's *Blood on the Forge*?"

"Oh," she said offhandedly. "It's a novel about the steel

mills in Pittsburgh too. But it's about a black family. And it's by a black."

It was, he felt, a pointed remark, but he decided to let it slide. He cleared his throat slightly and held out his hand for the pages he'd given her. "Okay if we talk about Assignment Three now?"

"Sure."

He extracted it, put it on the booth table between them, and tapped the final lines.

```
right eye/throat/nose/nose/right breast/mouth
right ear/right hip/forehead/left wrist/mouth
Find the Star
```

"Anything you know about Mrs. Soffel help with this?" Mark asked. "It has to be code."

"Absolutely," Zeena said, nodding. "Parts of the body used for letters. And see that 'nose/nose' in the first line. That's got to be a double letter, right? And there are only two letters in front of it." She looked up at him. "Do you see?"

Mark stared down at the lines, feeling stupid.

"How do you spell 'Soffel'?" Zeena asked.

"Heeeey," Mark said after a moment, smiling up at her.

"And that means that the next word ends in *l* too, yes?" Zeena went on. " 'Mouth' is *l*."

"So we want a five-letter word ending in *l*—"

"Uh-huh—a five-letter word that *doesn't* use the letters *s* or *o* or *f* or *e,* because the code words for those letters aren't repeated in the second line."

"Probably a place. 'Soffel porch,' or something like that," Mark said. "The guy has to put Assignment Four somewhere."

"Only it can't be 'porch,' of course."

No kidding, he thought to himself. As if he couldn't work out that "porch" doesn't end with an *l*. What a know-it-all she was.

"Maybe the answer's in the movie," he said. "Did you know there was a movie made about Mrs. Soffel? Right downtown at the jail where everything happened?"

"There wasn't anything in the movie about a code, though. I saw it twice."

"Okay," he said, leaning back in the booth, "then our next step is the Pennsylvania Room, unless you can think of something better."

At that Zeena did look up. At least there was *something* she didn't claim to know already.

"Who's Guy?" Zeena asked after Mark had finished telling her about the Pennsylvania Room and Guy's recommendation of Mrs. Harbinger.

"Oh," Mark said offhandedly, "he's this professor I know. He teaches history down at Pitt."

Zeena nodded but didn't comment. She looked out the window again. "Why me?" she asked after a time. "What made you pick me?"

It was a question Mark had prepared himself for. He knew Zeena wrote for the school newspaper. He'd heard that she'd once published a poem.

"Books and poetry are real important to this guy obviously, and you know a lot about stuff like that. I thought we might . . . make a good team."

But out loud "good team" sounded phony to Mark the moment he heard it.

"I see," Zeena said with a cold smile. She picked up the assignments and again tapped them into a neat rectangle. "So you think I can talk as good as Oprah Winfrey. Silk Samuri wouldn't have anything to do with your picking me, would he?"

It stung him. He was also dumbfounded. "Silk!" he exclaimed. "No, of course not. What makes you think that? And I didn't say anything about Oprah Winfrey."

At first Zeena didn't answer. Then she said, "Silk believes in things like . . . like quests. 'Journeys,' he calls them. He's big on people having journeys." She put the assignments down on the booth table and tapped them. "He just might engineer something like this."

Mark stared at her incredulously. "You mean you think he came to me about setting you up? You don't really think that, do you?"

She shrugged without looking at him. "So it's not even possible?"

He couldn't be sure of her tone, but then he decided he didn't care what it was. "No," he said with conviction, "it isn't. Silk gives me nine hundred dollars to take you on some kind of journey? Does that make any sense to you?"

But then it struck Mark that maybe that wasn't what she'd meant.

"Or," he went on, "are you saying I told Silk all about the assignments and that we decided *together* you'd be the one I ought to work with? For the sake of your soul or something."

"It was just a thought."

Like hell it was, he thought to himself. It was more than a thought.

"Look, Zeena, I don't even know Silk, really," Mark said, "and I haven't talked to anyone about this quest except you."

"Okay," she said again without looking at him.

For a while neither of them spoke.

"So . . ." Mark said, "how do you want to move here with Mrs. Soffel? Can you come down to the Pennsylvania Room with me after school Monday?"

"Not Monday this coming week. It'll have to be Tuesday or Wednesday. Also, you better know now that I have to work here Thursdays and Fridays after school and weekends."

Swell, Mark thought. That gave them three whole afternoons a week to work together—provided, of course, she didn't have Mondays regularly tied up, too. He pushed down his irritation and nodded. "Okay, Tuesday, then. I can meet you out at the bus stop."

There was a bus stop practically at the front door of Moorland High School. It was always jammed when school let out.

Zeena stared straight into his eyes for a moment and then looked down. "I better meet you down at the Carnegie," she said. "I . . . I'm going to be held up for a while Tuesday."

"That's okay. I'll wait for you."

"No," Zeena said. "You go on. I'll come later."

"Really, Zeena. I don't mind waiting for you."

"I don't want you to wait," she said sharply. "I don't want to get on the bus with you at Moorland. I catch enough flack already."

The heat with which she spoke astonished him. For several moments they just stared at each other. Then she looked away and then back. She made a shrugging gesture with her hands. "Look," she said, "my father's white, my mother's black, in case you don't know. They're divorced. I live with my mother in East Liberty. She's . . . kind of a radical, if you know what I mean. That's how I heard about Talbot Towers."

Mark nodded slowly. "My mother's divorced, too," he said. "I don't know where my father is. He just walked out on us and kept right on going." He paused for a moment before going on. "The professor I said I know? He's really my mother's boyfriend."

There was a small flash at the back of Zeena's eyes, as though from a bit of foil. Her expression hadn't changed but something had. She dropped her eyes.

Mark got up from the booth. "Okay then," he said. "I'll wait for you down at the Carnegie on Tuesday." And then he left the restaurant.

10

"Well," Merial said flouncing up from the couch and going over to the TV set, "that was one sick lady, if you ask me."

He and Merial, together with her mother and father, had just finished watching *Mrs. Soffel,* the Diane Keaton, Mel Gibson film Mark had bought that same afternoon at the Waterworks Mall, right after his conversation with Zeena. So far as Merial and her parents were concerned, the film was part of Mark's research for his senior English project. They were all sitting together in the Nagys' basement family room. The film had stunned Mark; "sick lady" seemed to him worse than insensitive.

Merial stopped the videotape in the middle of rolling credits and pushed the rewind control of the VCR. A car chase came loudly on the TV screen. Shutting off the sound, she came back to sit beside Mark on the couch. Her father sighed audibly from his armchair and shook his head.

"The poor thing," Merial's mother said from the armchair on the other side of the couch.

It was Mark and Merial's habit on either Friday or Saturday night to watch TV with her parents. Often, some of the families of Merial's brothers and sisters, all of whom still lived in Pittsburgh, would watch with them.

For the most part, these were good times for Mark. He liked being around the Nagys' friendliness, their easy irony, the warmth with which they made him part of everything. And always he and Merial were left alone at the end of the evening—though with the understanding that it was for no more than an hour. He hated it, however, when Merial used the cover of her family, as she sometimes did, to bully him.

"What are you going to do with her, anyway?" Merial asked Mark, nestling up against him. "Are you going to use her and Brass Ears both?"

"Brass Ears?" Merial's mother echoed. "What in the world?" Merial's father chuckled.

"It's Brashear, Mrs. Nagy," Mark said stiffening his arm and shoulder against Merial. "Merial's just being a smart mouth again. He was an astronomer who lived in Pittsburgh a long time ago."

"Not *so* long ago," Merial said, "and he made lenses for telescopes; he wasn't an astronomer."

Mark bit down hard on his lower lip. "Actually," he said, "he was both, all right?"

"They didn't say he was both out at the Observatory," Merial said breezily, "but it's all right with me. So how are you going to use Brass Ears and Soffel the Sickie both?"

"I don't know how yet, okay?" Mark said archly. "I'm still . . . gathering data. That's what research is, you know."

"Oh, is *that* what research is," Merial said, laughing. "That's good to know."

Mark clenched his teeth and looked down at the pad he'd brought to take notes on. So absorbed had he been by the story of the film that he'd written almost nothing. He'd been especially taken by the scene toward the end of the movie where the two fleeing lovers, Katherine and

Ed, pledged their lives to each other. Katherine even made Ed promise to shoot her if it looked like they were to be apprehended. No wonder Zeena had seen the film twice. Mark closed his notepad and turned it over on his lap.

"I think the poor woman went crazy," Merial's mother said. "Leaving her children and going off in the snow like that."

"Maybe she never really planned to leave," Merial's father said deadpan. "Remember how she was throwing snowballs with those fellas right after she let them out of prison? Maybe all she wanted was to make a snowman." He came out of his chair easily. "I'm going to get another beer," he said, at the foot of the stairs up to the kitchen. "Anybody want anything?"

No one responded.

"Yep," Merial went on when her father had gone. "She was crazy all right. A real sickie."

Mark stared at the silent TV screen. A car plunged off a cliff, crashed noiselessly, and burst into flames. "I think maybe there was a little more to her than that," he said without looking at either Merial or her mother.

"Boy, I'd like to know what," Merial chortled. "She leaves four young kids to go off with some guy she doesn't even know just because he writes her some soppy love poem—"

"People who were *murderers*, Merial," her mother interrupted. "That was the really awful thing. They were both convicted murderers."

"But we don't know they were murderers, Mrs. Nagy," Mark said, leaning forward so that Merial couldn't miss he was ignoring her. "Not for sure. Remember how it said at the beginning that a lot of people thought the Biddles were innocent? And when they were talking just to each other, you even heard them say that they hadn't shot that guy."

"We heard them tell *her* they were innocent, sure," Merial said. "What'd you expect them to say when they were trying to use her, that they were really happy about the guy they'd blown away?"

"I was talking about their talk with each *other*," Mark said. And then he sniffed. "*Use* her." He folded his arms on his chest and stared straight in front of him.

"Yes, Mark, *use* her," Merial shot back. "That guy Ed, the big poet, even said to his brother that that's what he was doing, that he was *using* her. That was his very word."

Merial's father came down the stairs holding a bottle of Miller's.

"I still can't see how she could leave her family to go off in the snow like that with a pair of *murderers*," Merial's mother repeated. "All she had on was her nightgown. What did she expect her husband to think?"

"What I don't see is why he didn't kill her," Merial's father said, sitting down in his armchair again. "That's what he should have done."

"He seemed a nice man, John," Merial's mother said. "Maybe he realized she'd gone crazy."

"Of course we don't know for sure that the husband really *was* such a nice man, do we?" Mark said. "Maybe he—"

"Mark, come on!" Merial exclaimed, pointing at the silently running TV. "We all know what we just *saw*. Her husband takes care of her for months while she lies in bed with sick headaches—and when she finally decides to get up, she *still* won't sleep in the same room with him. Suppose we were married. How would you like it if I—"

"Now, that's enough, dear," Merial's mother interrupted. "We get your point."

"And it's *not* the point anyway, Merial," Mark said. "It's just *not* the point."

"Oh? Then tell me what the point is."

Merial's father clinked his beer bottle down on the tile floor beside his chair. "For my money the only real man in the picture was Biddle's brother," he said. Everyone looked at him. "I mean it," he went on. "The guy could have got away if he'd gone off on his own, but he stuck with his brother. That's starch. The guy had starch."

Merial's mother nodded. "Blood's thicker than water," she said. "You're certainly right about that, John."

"I still want to know what you think the point is," Merial said turning back to Mark.

Mark could feel all three of the Nagys looking at him. "Well," he said, "it's sort of like what you were saying, Mr. Nagy. It's . . . it's like a tragedy."

For a moment no one spoke. Mark heard the rewinding tape click off in the VCR.

"That isn't what Daddy said," Merial said. "What do you mean it's like a tragedy? What's like a tragedy?"

Mark hunched forward and rested his forearms on his knees. Damn her anyway.

"It *was* tragic that the poor thing went crazy the way she did," Merial's mother offered. "You're right, Mark. It's a terrible thing for families when something like that happens."

"But Mark doesn't mean tragedy that way, do you?" Merial said. "You think she *wasn't* just crazy, right? That she *wasn't* just sick." And then she added, "Or just dumb."

"She was lucky to get out of the whole thing alive, if you ask me," Merial's father put in.

"What do you mean by tragedy, then?" Merial went on,

giving his shoulder a little push. Mark just glared at her. It served her right that he'd been staring at Zeena in his honors English class the way he had. It served her right that he'd been with her that afternoon too.

"Give up?" Merial asked, grinning.

"Wait a minute now," he said. "I think it's . . . it's like a love tragedy, like in Shakespeare. I don't think Ed Biddle just *used* her. Maybe it started out that way, but . . . their love was so strong that it . . . it just overcame them both, do you see?"

Again, no one said anything.

"Well," Merial said after a time, tossing her head dismissively, "I get that part all right, but I don't see anything . . ." she fished the air with one hand, "*noble* about the kind of love that makes a woman leave her children to go off with somebody she doesn't even know."

"And a *murderer,* remember," Merial's mother put in.

"Oh, I could understand going off with a murderer," Merial said easily, "but not one I didn't know. She didn't know anything about those two guys, really. That's what's so sick."

Merial's father turned in his armchair and gave his daughter a sharp look. "You run off with a murderer," he said, "you better be ready to deal with another one."

"Oh, don't worry, Daddy," Merial laughed. "I'll make sure my guy's a better shot than hers was."

"You better," her father answered, turning back to the muted TV.

"I wonder what that woman did when she got out of prison, poor thing," said Merial's mother. "Did she ever see her children again, do you suppose?"

"No," Mark said, even though he didn't know for sure whether she had or hadn't. "She didn't. She ended up alone on the North Side somewhere and just died."

"Good riddance," said Merial's father.

Mark was too annoyed with Merial to speak. He slid into his parka, went over to the VCR where he punched out the rewound tape, and while fitting it in its sleeve moved toward the stairs. Merial came up behind him. He half turned in her direction but deliberately avoided meeting her eyes. "I better be getting home," he said with false politeness. "I have a lot of work to do."

"Come on," Merial said jauntily. "It's Saturday night."

Merial's father had switched the sound of the TV set back on and began flipping through channels.

"I'm sorry," he said, "but I really do have work to do. I have a lot here I have to sort out." He waved his notepad with seeming casualness, but she had to step back to avoid being hit with it. Good, he thought grimly. That served her right too. "Thanks a lot for the evening, Mr. and Mrs. Nagy," he called.

"Mark, come on," Merial tried again, this time putting a hand on his arm. "I was only teasing." But her shook off her hand with a coldness he knew her parents couldn't see.

"Really," he said pointedly. "I want to write this up. I don't just want to forget it all."

Her mouth tightened. "All right, go ahead and go then," she said.

From the stairs, Mark raised the video of *Mrs. Soffel* to the Nagys in a kind of ironic salute. "Thanks again, folks," he said. And then he left.

11

It was Friday afternoon, grey, cold, cheerless. Valentine's Day, irony of ironies. Mark and Zeena were in his mother's car on their way to Calvary Cemetery, a big Catholic cemetery in a section of Pittsburgh known as Hazelwood. She was squeezed as far away from him in the front seat as she could get, but at least they'd solved the riddle of Assignment 3. Finally they'd solved it, and the quest was what mattered.

It was almost three weeks from the time Mark had asked Zeena to be what Assignment 3 called his chosen companion, though companionable was the last thing in the world she'd turned out to be. There was her stupid job at King's for one thing, which left her free to work at the Carnegie only on Mondays, Tuesdays, and Wednesdays after school, and on Saturday mornings. She was supposed to have Friday afternoons off, too, but twice she'd been called into work anyway. Also because she wouldn't ride the same bus with him from Moorland into Oakland, that cut into their working time even more.

Then there was the *way* she worked with what they had to go over. The key to everything, the only way Mark and Zeena had of getting to Assignment 4, was the meaning of the coded clue from Assignment 3:

```
right eye/throat/nose/nose/right breast/mouth
right ear/right hip/forehead/left wrist/mouth
```

It came out of something connected with the Soffel case obviously, but out of what? There was no book that could help because according to the Carnegie Library computer catalog, there wasn't one on Mrs. Soffel and the Biddle brothers. The only thing left to try was a newspaper search.

But there had been seven newspapers published in Pittsburgh in 1902, a couple of them in foreign languages, and something, it seemed, had been written about the case every day in each of them from the time of the Biddles' escape in January to the sentencing of Mrs. Soffel some six months later. "Keep in mind what we *need*," Mark said to Zeena. "Look for a *drawing* or a chart of some kind." But again and again he'd glance up from his microfilm-viewing machine to see her at hers reading through some article, line by line.

"How many days have you covered so far today?" he'd asked her one afternoon, knowing she'd been on the same article since they'd begun work.

Zeena leaned back from her machine and crossed her arms over her chest. "I cannot *believe* the way they talk about her," she said, shaking her head.

"Yeah, well, that's not going to get us the key to the code."

"Just listen to this," she said, leaning toward her machine again. " 'A cold-blooded degenerate,' 'monstrous,' 'depraved.' "

"Forget it," he said going back to his own machine. "Look for a picture."

For a moment she didn't respond. When she did, her

voice had an edge. "The picture I see is one that none of these sexist creeps even got close to."

He looked over to her. "What's that supposed to mean?"

She shrugged without answering.

"What do you mean?" he asked again. "Tell me what you mean."

She turned to look at him. "Okay, tell me why *you* think she did it? What do you think she went off with that Biddle jerk for?"

The phrase "Biddle Jerk" felt as insensitive to him as Merial's "Soffel the Sickie." What do you mean 'jerk'? You don't know he was a jerk. Maybe they really did love each other. Maybe—"

She cut him off. "That's the movie, right? How he starts out by using her, but then they develop this undying love for each other? Well, what if it wasn't Biddle using *her*? What if she was using *him*—and right from beginning to end? Did you ever think of that as a possibility?"

He hadn't. "No," he said, "I didn't. How do you figure, though?"

She turned her head away from him without answering, her arms still folded against her chest. Merial sat the same way when she was irritated with him.

"Are you going to tell me what you mean or not?"

"Doesn't it seem a little strange to you that *nobody* in all this," she jerked her chin dismissively at the microfilm machine, "even imagined that she knew *exactly* what she was doing by going away with Biddle? That she *knew* they didn't have a chance, that she *expected* to die, *wanted* to die?"

"Why—" Mark started but again she interrupted him.

"Because she was dead already and she knew it, that's why. She was trapped in a life that . . . that all women were trapped in then. At least if she died publicly, she could say something with her death."

"*Say* something? Say what?"

"Say that when you repress people, nothing works. The system kills everything. Prisons don't work, the Bible doesn't work, marriage doesn't work, not even the family works."

"Well," he said, "Guy said that's a very popular way to look at things these days, how we're all victimized by the culture, but could we—"

"Popular!" she broke in. "It's not just popular. It's the reason she killed herself—and it's what she died to say." She looked back at her machine and folded her arms across her chest again. "See?" she said with a small knowing smile. "I knew you wouldn't understand."

For a moment he just stared at her. She looks like some kind of bug, he thought. Like a praying mantis, or something. She looks just like a goddamn praying mantis.

"Oh I under*stand*," he said. "She gave up her life just to say that women are victims. She didn't love her husband, or her kids, or Ed Biddle, or anybody else. I under*stand*. I just don't buy it."

She glanced at him contemptuously. "Of course you don't. You probably think Brashear's wife just loved grinding all those lenses too—and that it was the *men* mill workers who were the real heroes of Bell's novel."

"What's Brashear's *wife* got to do with anything?" he cried, conscious, but not caring, that they'd caught the attention of the two other people in the room.

"She has to do with how you look at things. You never even noticed that . . . that Brashear's wife did just as much work grinding those lenses as he did. She gave up her whole life for him, and how did he see her? She was nothing but 'Ma' for him. He never called her anything else. He never wanted anything else. No wonder she ended up weighing three hundred pounds, eating herself to death."

He went back to the screen of his microfilm machine shaking his head. Then he turned back to her. "Okay then," he said. "If Katherine Soffel's big message was how all women are victims, then how come nobody got it?"

She snorted a laugh. "Plenty of people got it."

"Oh yeah? Then how come nobody says so in any of the newspapers?"

"The newspapers were all written by men obviously."

"The film was done by a woman. How come *she* didn't show things that way?"

She shook her head smiling. The same smug smile. "The film's just an interpretation. There're a lot of things changed in it. Besides the message *was* in the film if you know how to look at it."

"Yeah, sure. The message wasn't in the film, but was in the film if you know how to look at it. So tell me how I'm supposed to look at it."

She didn't respond, didn't look at him.

"Tell me," he jeered, and when she continued to sit in silence, he pushed her shoulder. In one motion she sprang to her feet and whirled on him.

"Don't you touch me," she hissed down at him, eyes narrowed, one hand balled into a fist. "White—" she stopped herself. "Don't you *ever* touch me."

Then he too came up out of his chair. "You can't answer me, can you? You got this big thing you see that nobody else sees, but you can't even explain it."

"Hey, you two," a woman working just down from them said. "Take it easy." But neither Mark nor Zeena paid her any attention.

"I told you, you wouldn't understand," she said. "And you just keep your hands off me."

She strode away, leaving her notebook and backpack at her machine.

He sat down again, furious. The movie was just an interpretation, but the real message was in there if you knew how to see it. And she knew the real message. She alone. It was her utter *selfishness* that burned him up so. How different it would have been working with Merial. And worst of all he was *stuck* with Zeena. He'd stuck himself with her, and there wasn't a thing he could do about it.

In less than an hour, from behind him, a slim brown hand held a slip of paper up against his microfilm screen:

Arthur Forrest. *The Biddle Boys and Mrs. Soffel.*
Phoenix Publishing Company: Baltimore, Md., 1902.
    128 pp.

"That's a penny dreadful," Zeena said from behind his shoulder before he could say anything. "Mrs. Harbinger just ordered it for us from the Library of Congress. If the code's anywhere, she said, it's in there. We ought to have the book by next week."

He took the paper, careful not to touch her hand and without turning around. "What's a penny dreadful?"

"They were . . . like *The National Enquirer,* only they were booklets. People used to put them out to make a quick buck on things, like the killing of Billy the Kid or when the James gang was captured. It was hack stuff mainly, Mrs. Harbinger said. They were written fast, sold cheap, and they aren't very accurate, but they're filled with information."

"How'd you find out about it?" he asked, turning around

to look up at her. "Why wasn't the book in the card catalog?"

She shrugged. "No library in Pittsburgh has a copy. They're only in special collections."

"Yeah, so how'd you find out about it?"

She dropped her eyes and flushed slightly. "I . . . was checking reviews of the movie. It turns out that the movie was made from Forrest's book."

Mark turned away from her and stared down at the slip of paper again. He smiled to himself. She'd been checking reviews of the movie to see whether anybody else had seen what she'd seen. Obviously, nobody had. Catch her admitting that though. Catch Zeena Curry *admitting* she'd been wrong about anything—as he saw proven again the day they sat down to read *The Biddle Boys and Mrs. Soffel*. On page 53 was a crude woodcut of a woman standing with clasped hands, her body covered with letters. The page was headed "The Soffel-Biddle Alphabetical Code" and under the woodcut was the explanation:

A cipher code found in Mrs. Soffel's room showed that by her pointing to her forehead, Ed Biddle, in his cell opposite her window, knew she was spelling the letter A. Pointing to each of her eyes meant B and C, the tip of her nose was D, and so on.

"Hey," Mark said, pointing to the first line of the coded clue. " 'Right eye/throat/nose/nose/right breast/mouth': that's not 'Soffel.' "

"It's 'Biddle,' " Zeena said, "and the second word is 'grave.' "

" 'Biddle grave'!" Mark said, jumping to his feet. "I know where it is, too."

She looked up at him, eyes wide with surprise. "You do?"

"You bet I do. I remember reading that they were buried in Calvary Cemetery over in Hazelwood, about five miles from here. Merial's family has a . . . what do you call them, some plots out there. We had to go out and put some flowers on her grandmother's grave once."

But all Zeena said in response was that it was too late for them to get over to Hazelwood that day. She never even mentioned her mistake, how sure she'd been that the first word of the code was "Soffel."

At the cemetery, Mark assumed Zeena was going to leave it to him to find the exact location of the Biddles' grave, but she was out of the car and into the office before he was. A fish-faced woman behind a counter ogled the two of them. After hearing what they wanted, she sighed, pushed her glasses up into her hair, and taking the top copy of a great pile of dittoed maps, put it on the counter. "Right there," she said, tapping a section of the map with her pencil and then drawing a circle around it. "You'll see the new stone those Hollywood people set up down there," she said. "Only new stone on the hill."

"A new headstone you mean? The people who made the movie here in Pittsburgh bought it?"

"Money down the drain, if you ask me," she said contemptuously. "We've got a lot of good people out here. Those Biddles were just trash."

Mark stepped back from the counter and drew himself up. "I'm a Biddle, ma'am," he said to her coldly. "I wish you wouldn't talk about my people that way." Then he turned and stalked from the office.

At the car he caught Zeena looking over the roof at him. "What?"

She smiled slightly and shook her head. "Nothing really.

I was just thinking of . . . the different ways we deal with the world."

"What do you mean?"

She gestured with her head. "Like in there, like the man in the library—"

"Thatchbeak?" he said, grinning.

She too smiled. "Yeah. Him."

Mark had told Zeena of his confrontation with Thatchbeak. The first time the two of them had gone down to use the computer catalog, he'd been on duty at the circulation desk. Mark strode directly over to him and before the man could speak said, "Just wanted you to know we're here to do some research. And you're here to help. Any trouble with you, I mean *any trouble with you,* and Mrs. Harbinger told us to report you to the Director immediately." Then he turned away, winked at Zeena, and marched to the computers. The man had gone white with rage, but that was all that had happened.

"How different?" Mark asked.

For a time she didn't answer. And then she smiled at him. "Just different," she said. Her smile, the openness of it, sent prickles through him.

When they got to where the Biddles were buried, Mark checked the location several times against the map because it didn't look as though the place were even part of the cemetery. A slope of maybe fifty feet fell almost vertically from the road down to a hollow bordered with a clump of woods, where a single dead oak tree stood out from the rest. So thick was the slope with weeds and patches of snow that the seven or eight widely separated headstones, all of them on the hill rather than at the bottom of it, were almost invisible. None of the stones looked new.

Mark glanced over his shoulder at the neatly groomed,

regularly spaced graves on the far side of the asphalt road-way. "Boy. They sure didn't want the Biddles contaminating their good people, did they?" He walked over to the edge of the slope. There was no path down the hillside from the road. "They didn't plan on their having many visitors either." He got his backpack of tools out of the car trunk, almost the same assortment of tools he'd taken with him to the Observatory. "Let's find the grave first, and then work from there." He pointed, "Why don't you walk down to that little bend in the road there, so you can try those graves in the corner. I'll go down here and work my way over to you." It had begun to rain, a soft, but chilling February rain.

"How are we supposed to get down there?" she asked.

Without answering he walked back to the edge of the hill, crouched down, and inched himself forward. No sooner had he come to the edge of the grass slope, however, than his feet went straight out from under him. He slid down twenty feet or so of the wet snowy slope on one thigh. From there he worked his way over to the headstone nearest him. "Be careful," he called up to Zeena. "It's really slippery."

"Abraham Tutton" was the name on the first stone he looked at. Ten feet or so away was a marker for someone named Sievers. Then he found a headstone that read simply "Baby Louise." The next two headstones he crawled down to had weathered into illegibility. Zeena had slid down the far side of the slope and was about two hundred yards away from him. They worked toward each other at the lowest part of the hill.

"Here, Mark!" Zeena cried. "I've got it!"

He half ran, half crawled, down and over to her. It was a simple grey stone with a highly polished and obviously new face. It had the Biddle brothers' dates and a verse beneath them:

```
And soon this little token,
Wrapped in hand so neat,
Lies quietly in a grave,
O'er which a true heart does beat.
```

For some reason, Mark thought of the photograph of his father. "That's the poem Ed wrote about the violet," he said. "He wrote it for her."

Zeena shook her head. "That's just the movie. Actually, he wrote it for the daughter of a minister he knew. And it's not the whole poem. It's just the last stanza."

They stood looking down at the grey stone together.

After a time Zeena glanced around her and moistened her lips. "It's . . . getting dark."

There was no star on the Biddles' grave marker, and nothing on the ground immediately around it that Mark could see. The nearest headstones were about ten yards away, one off to the left, the other in the opposite direction. Both were higher up on the slope.

"There's got to be a star here somewhere—I hope not covered by snow or weeds. How about you check that stone over there?" he said, pointing off to their left. "I'll catch the one up above."

The markings on the stone he climbed to were illegible.

"What about it?" he called over to her when she'd reached the other grave. He watched her look first at one side of it and then the other. "Is there a carving? Anything?" She shook her head and started toward him. Then she fell forward heavily and for a moment didn't move.

"You okay?" he yelled. She didn't answer. He clambered over to her. "Zeena," he cried. "Are you hurt?"

She came up slowly on one elbow and turned around, brushing the ground behind her free of wet snow. When he reached her on his hands and knees, she was sitting cross-legged on the slope and smiling.

"Look what I tripped on," she said gesturing.

It was a slab of what looked like plain grey cement in the shape of a star. There were no markings on it of any kind.

"All *right*," Mark said. "I bet the assignment's under this stone just like out at the Observatory. Help me lift."

Zeena came up on her knees beside him. "You don't want to be robbing a grave, Mark."

Mark cleared off the surface of the stone. "I'm not robbing any grave. This isn't a gravestone. There's no name on it." He kneeled on one of the points of the star and the slab wiggled slightly. "It's loose too," he said. "I won't even need any tools." He half slid, half pushed himself up the slope to a position above the stone. Then he stripped off his gloves and worked his fingers under the point of the star that lay highest on the hill. "It doesn't feel too thick either," he said, lifting. The point raised, but only about an inch. "Grab that other point over there," he said, nodding his head at it, "and help me lift." She didn't move. Her face was a mask.

"Zeena," Mark said sharply. "I need your help."

She crawled forward, but she didn't touch the stone.

Mark dropped his hold, stood up, and turned around so that he faced up the slope. Then he straddled the slab of stone and went down into a crouch. Grasping the high end of the star, he pushed himself to his feet. The star was heavy, but it tipped up toward him easily as he rose, like a trapdoor opening. Lying in a scooped out hollow in the dirt beneath was a packet sealed in black plastic.

"Grab it," Mark grunted, and Zeena did.

Back in the car they opened the packet. There were four hundred-dollar bills in it and with them:

Assignment 4

Congratulations, Children of Light.

First Child: please add the enclosed to the twelve hundred dollars you have already earned—and that I hope you have decided to share with your chosen companion.

But I intrude, for I am sure your partnership has been arranged democratically and to the satisfaction of you both.

This is America, children. You are America.

And such a lot of stars in the firmament of America, so many to choose from, so many paths it is possible to follow. Stars fixed and in motion, dwarfs and giants, dark stars, bright ones, stars binary or optically doubled, stars clustered galactically, globularly, and all of them colored—red and white and true blue, of course, but yellow too, and black and bluish-white and red-yellow. Perhaps there are wild stars too, as Thoreau found wildness in certain books, stars erratic of orbit, chameleon-hued, collapsing categories, dissolving laws. The untamed, Thoreau called it, something natural and primitive, mysterious, marvelous, ambrosial, fertile as a fungus or a lichen—and speaking, he claimed, in some measure to muskrats and skunk-cabbages as well as to men.

Witness he who entered Pittsburgh like the Fifth Angel, a star fallen from heaven onto the earth. Witness he who sought to pour the bowl of wrath on the throne of the Beast and plunge his

kingdom into darkness, he who saw himself preparing for the burning of Babylon, for the bind-
ing of Satan and his many false prophets, and for
their final casting into the lake of fire.

In the place where The Coke King pondered
His expedient use of force:
That's where he proposed to kill the Beast
(For Justice and Truth of course).

What warmed him there (I mean the King,
Not the one who would killer play)
Now hides what the questers must locate
To continue on the way.

12

That same night, just before Mark was to leave to see Merial, the telephone on his desk rang.

"Mark, this is Zeena. Can you meet me tomorrow morning at about nine up at Highland Park Reservoir? By the main steps, you know?"

He was dumbfounded. Zeena Curry was calling *him* on the telephone? "Sure," he said automatically. "Something wrong?"

"I just need to talk to you before I go over to King's. It won't take long. And thanks."

And then she hung up.

Something was wrong all right, but it wasn't until later that same night, not until Mark reread Assignment 4 after getting home from Merial's, that he saw what it was. *Twelve* hundred dollars the guy was claiming he'd given Mark, not the nine hundred he actually had. And though Mark may have missed this out at the cemetery, Zeena hadn't. What made things even worse was Mark's certainty that it wasn't just a mistake; the guy was deliberately lying. That's what all that sarcastic talk of the democracy of the partnership he was supposed to have worked out with Zeena was doing in the assignment. He'd been set up. Betrayed. He'd played everything connected with the quest just the way the guy had told him to, and he'd been stabbed in the back anyway.

For most of the night Mark tossed and turned with fragments of the same dream. There'd been an old, high-turreted Victorian house, the rooms completely bare, but thick with dust. Moonlight streamed through a set of windows with sills set at the level of the floor. At the center of the house was a great sweeping stairway, which at the second floor led him only to more flights of stairs, going off every which way, leading up, leading down, and then he was climbing a flight of stairs, climbing them first, but then he was being drawn up them, by someone or something, faster and faster, the stairs growing steeper, becoming narrower, angling more and more crazily upward. And then the banister fell away and the wall he hugged grew crumbly, showering down plaster and lath wherever he touched it, until there was no more wall, just rough black studs standing against cold starry space and now he was being thrust up, pushed from behind until the studs too were gone, and there was nothing but himself in the middle of an endless empty darkness.

Mark had been sitting at the kitchen table for almost an hour when his mother came downstairs. She poured herself a mug of coffee and a glass of orange juice. Mark saw her glance up at the clock on the wall behind her. A little after eight o'clock.

"You're up early for a Saturday, love," she said, sitting down. "Got something special on?"

He'd forgotten to set anything out for her. "Just stuff for school," he said, forcing a smile. "Sorry about your coffee."

Mark's mother dismissed his apology with a wave of her hand. "I drink too much of the damn stuff as it is," she said. "You're turning into quite a student these days.

Are you going to be working on . . . that project you're doing with the Curry girl?"

Mark hunched over his place and nodded, wishing he'd gone back up to his room. The week before, Merial had asked him about his being down at the Carnegie with Zeena. How she'd found out he didn't know. She'd asked quite matter-of-factly, quite casually, but in front of his mother. Flustered, he'd lied. He said that he and Zeena had been assigned a project to work on by Ms. Hunter, their honors English teacher.

"You can have the car if you need it. You'll have to drop me at Northwood first, though."

"Okay," he said without looking up. And then he did look up. "I mean thanks. Sure. I'll drop you."

For a while neither Mark nor his mother spoke.

"Not very conversational this morning, are we?" she asked after a time.

"I guess not."

"You and Merial wouldn't have had . . . a bit of a tiff, would you?"

She said it teasingly, but her tone irritated him. He shifted his position slightly. "We're fine."

"You know," Mark's mother said as if incidentally, "Guy met the Curry girl's father at the university. He's a math professor."

Mark looked up at her with narrowed eyes. The way she referred to Zeena sounded to him like a put-down. "She's not 'the Curry girl,' okay? Her name's Zeena, Mother. And how come you were talking to Guy about her?"

"I *wasn't* talking to Guy about her. I merely mentioned her name. I didn't know whether you knew her father had worked at Pitt, that's all."

"Of course I knew," Mark said exasperatedly—though

he hadn't. "And you don't need to tell me that her mother and father are divorced or that her father's white and her mother's black either. It was *Hunter* who assigned us to work together, by the way. If you and Guy have a problem with that, maybe you better talk to her."

"Mark, that's not fair. I don't see what's so wrong with my having mentioned to Guy that you and . . . Zeena are working on a history project together. That's Guy's field. And all he said was that her father was a good teacher— and a nice guy. I just thought you might like to know. He knows her mother too."

For a moment he didn't speak. "What about Zeena's mother?"

"Nothing, for heaven's sake. All Guy said was that he'd met her once, worked on some kind of committee with her."

Again there was silence.

"Well, come on," Mark asked brusquely after a time. "What kind of committee? What'd Guy say about her?"

"He didn't say anything, really. I see I shouldn't have mentioned it."

"Oh, for God's sake, Mother," Mark said angrily. "Guy said *something*. What'd he say?"

"I don't like you talking that way."

Mark bit down hard on his lower lip.

His mother sighed. "All he said was that"—she spread the fingers of one hand, palm up, and gestured—"well, Guy called . . . referred to, Zeena's mother as an 'activist.' She's very big in the East Liberty Black Action Coalition, he said. Very good organizer. Very smart."

The East Liberty Black Action Coalition, Mark knew, had sponsored the Black Action Society at Moorland, which had been founded by Silk Samuri. So Zeena's connection with Silk was also a family affair.

"Is there something wrong with a black woman being smart?"

"Look, Mark," his mother said, crossing her arms on her place mat and leaning toward him, "I've got nothing against this young woman. I've never even met her. And you know I'm not prejudiced. Neither is Guy."

"Then how come you can't even say her name without . . . flinching or something?"

For a moment they just looked at one another. Then Mark sighed heavily. He ran a hand through his hair and massaged the back of his neck. What was he defending Zeena for, given what he knew he was in for with her in less than an hour? That day in the library, what was it she'd been about to call him? White *trash*, maybe? White *boy*? And what was her name for him going to be now?

"I guess I'm just touchy this morning," he said. "I'm sorry."

There was an uncomfortable silence.

"Is . . . is Merial upset about the two of you working together? Is that it?"

Mark puffed his cheeks out and let out a long breath. If his mother wanted to think that was the trouble, then maybe that's what he ought to let her think. "Maybe," he said. "Maybe so."

His mother seemed about to speak, but she didn't. She reached across the table and smoothed his hair up from his forehead. "I can see how she might be upset," she said. "You can too, can't you?"

Mark moved back slightly from her hand. "You know, the ironic thing is that Zeena doesn't like me all that much—and she . . . can be a real pain to work with."

"Couldn't you ask your teacher to assign you to work with somebody else?"

Mark leaned back in his chair. "Well, you can see what that might look like, can't you? And we're almost done."

Mark could feel his mother watching him.

"Merial's a nice girl, Mark," his mother said.

"I know," he said.

His mother looked down at her place mat and smoothed it along the edge closest to her. She drank about half her orange juice.

"I have an idea," she said brightly, putting down her glass. She took up the purse that was hanging by its strap from the top of her chair and took two twenty-dollar bills out of her wallet.

"What do you say to you and . . . and your lady fair having dinner together at a nice restaurant on me?" She smoothed the two twenties out on the place mat alongside his coffee cup. "My treat, three weeks from today. You can have the car the whole weekend. Guy's giving a paper at a conference in Toronto, you see, and he's invited me along, so I've decided to drive up with him. I want you and Merial both to let me . . . spring for dinner."

For a moment Mark just stared at her. "Spring for dinner" wasn't his mother's way of talking. "You're going to Toronto for the *weekend*?" he repeated incredulously. "With Guy?" She'd never gone on a weekend that way before, not with Guy, not with anyone.

"Well, I'm *driving* up with Guy, yes," she said, looking off from him and tossing her hair back. "I'll be staying with some friends of his, though. It's the first Saturday in March he gives his paper. But it isn't really for a *weekend* we'll be away, exactly. We'll leave Friday and be home early Sunday. It's more like just the day."

It was like hearing the guy who'd done the assignments try to make him into a liar and a thief.

"See, Guy will be giving his paper Saturday morning,"

his mother went on, her smile wide and brilliant. "I'm really looking forward to hearing him. I've never heard him . . . do anything like that before." She laughed self-consciously. "Of course I'll probably stick out like a sore thumb in the middle of all those intellectuals, but in the afternoon we'll sightsee. Guy really knows Toronto and he says it's a wonderful town to sightsee in. It can be like spring in Toronto the first weekend in March, Guy says. And we'll head for Pittsburgh early the next morning. We should be back home before dinner." She patted the twenty-dollar bills lying in front of Mark. "I know this girl can use a holiday," she said, winking at him. "Maybe we can both use a holiday."

Again, for a time Mark just stared at his mother. He smiled bitterly, shook his head, and then looked directly into his mother's eyes. "You're all the same, aren't you? Why can't you tell the truth?"

She recoiled as though from a blow. "What?" she said dazedly. "What did you say?"

"I said you're all liars is what I said." And then he leaned forward. "Tell me why my father left here really."

Her face twitched with fear. "What?" she asked him again, and again he repeated himself, not knowing why he'd asked her what he had. The two of them just looked at each other.

"Well," Mark's mother said stiffly, getting up and taking her orange juice glass to the sink. "I'm sure I don't know what you expect me to say. I've already told you everything I know."

"Right," Mark said, getting up from the money lying in front of him. "Sure you have." He went to the hall closet where he got his parka.

"Mark!" he heard his mother call out to him from the kitchen. He shrugged on his parka and went quickly to the front door. "Mark!" he heard again, from just behind him this time. "Mark, what are you doing? What's the matter with you?" But he strode away.

He walked the six blocks from his house up to the reservoir without feeling anything other than surprise at the fact it was no longer important to him what Zeena thought. She was already there he saw from across the street, even though he was early. She was leaning against one wall of the wide stone staircase that led up to the water, her head down and her hands jammed deep into her parka pockets. She didn't notice him until he was standing in front of her. She started when she did.

"You look like you're going to kill somebody," she said. "What's up?"

She stared at him for a moment, took a deep breath, and looked off. "I want you to know that I'm sorry for . . . the way I've been with you."

He just looked at her.

"And I want to be better . . . a better companion for the quest."

He had no idea what to say. "That's why you wanted me to meet you?" he asked her finally.

"I was afraid if I didn't say it now, today, I wouldn't say it."

All of a sudden Mark was aware that they were standing together in the middle of a brilliant blue February day, a day that looked warm even if it was not warm. He touched Zeena's arm and pointed up the steps. "Let's take a turn around the water, okay?"

The Highland Park Reservoir, which supplied the whole East End of Pittsburgh, was in effect the hollowed out top of a small mountain. It was about a mile in circumference and circled by a macadam path. The slopes of the mountain were wooded and laced with trails and picnic areas. On one lower slope was the Pittsburgh Zoo. Close as the park was to where Mark lived, he'd only been up to it a half dozen times or so, always in the summer. At one time the park had been a popular family recreation area, but it had developed a reputation for being dangerous. There'd been some gang fights there, muggings, drug deals.

It surprised Mark to see the macadam path dotted with joggers and a number of strolling couples, many of them with young children. The frozen reservoir was a blinding sheet of white in the sunshine. They walked in silence for a time, which Mark broke by thanking her for what she'd said—and by confessing to her what he had thought she was going to say.

Zeena laughed, the first time Mark had heard her laugh. "Oh, I noticed the difference in the amounts, all right, but I knew that was him, not you."

"How'd you know that?"

She laughed again. "Shoot, baby," she said, "that kind of cheat just ain't your style."

It made him smile. It warmed him deep in his belly, the way she called him "baby."

All of a sudden he wanted things clean between them. He told her about Merial's question and what he'd said to her and his mother about Hunter's assigning them to work together. "I was trying to protect the quest," he finished. "I'm sorry I lied."

Zeena didn't respond right away. When she did, she kept her eyes down on the macadam path. "In front of your mother Merial asked you what you were doing at the Carnegie with me?"

"Yeah."

Zeena looked off across the frozen water. "Wonder how she knew," she said. She took a deep breath and then audibly breathed it out again. "I guess if it had been me I'd have lied too," she went on. And then, after another pause, she asked him a question. "You're not saying you want to tell Merial, Merial and your mother, about the quest, are you?"

"No," he said immediately, shaking his head. "No, I'm not." And then, "How about you? You want to tell Silk?"

"Oh, no," she said as quickly as he had. "but I don't go with Silk the way you go with Merial."

"What do you mean?"

She shrugged. "He's not my boyfriend. I'm not his girlfriend."

Mark nodded without trusting himself to say or ask anything more.

She went over to the rail that ran around the reservoir and stood looking out over the ice. He followed her but stood with his back turned to the water, both elbows up on the rail.

"Silk and I go back with each other, you know?" Zeena said.

"I figured."

"In fact it was up here I got to know him. I mean, I *knew* him before, but . . ." she trailed off.

"I know what you mean."

"He's the only other person from Moorland I ever saw up here. I used to come here to run."

"I didn't know you ran."

She shook her head. "I don't. Not that way." She hunched over the rail and looked down at the ice directly beneath her. "I used to come up here and run when my mom and dad were splitting. This was a year ago—well, over a year ago now. I felt . . . safe up here." She paused. "Not safe exactly, but . . . something. Maybe that's why I wanted to meet you here today."

A jogger, huffing like an engine, swept by them on the outside rim of the path. Then another, a black guy in spandex tights running in the opposite direction, passed them soundlessly, his legs shining like oil in the morning sun.

" 'Course I was smoking a pack of cigarettes a day at the same time I was running, not the greatest of combinations." She looked over at him and smiled. "I don't smoke anymore, by the way. I just feel like it sometimes."

Zeena stood up straight and shaded her eyes to look out over the gleaming ice. "You know I even got an idea for a poem when I was up here with Silk once."

"You did?"

Zeena pointed across the water. "When I was on that stretch of path over there. When I heard the tigers."

"When you heard what?"

"Tigers roaring. The zoo's at the bottom of the hill over there, and in the late afternoon, before they get fed, you can hear them from up here sometimes, if the wind's right."

"No kidding!" Mark exclaimed.

Zeena swung away from the rail and began walking again. Mark fell in beside her.

"I'd like to see your poem sometime," Mark said after they'd walked a while. She glanced over at him quickly but then just as quickly looked away again. "I mean," he added, "if that's okay."

She nodded, but concessively it seemed to him, without really meaning it. "It's . . . it's not finished yet."

"Well," Mark said, "show me where you heard the tigers roar, then."

13

Zeena snapped off the power to her microfilm-viewing machine, crossed her arms over her chest, and sat staring into the dead screen. "We've missed something. We're on the wrong track."

"Again," Mark nodded glumly. "Let's go back to the clue," he said, getting his copy of Assignment 4 out of his notebook and putting it on the table between them:

```
In the place where The Coke King pondered
His expedient use of force:
That's where he proposed to kill the Beast
(For Justice and Truth of course).

What warmed him there (I mean the King,
Not the one who would killer play)
Now hides what the questers must locate
To continue on the way.
```

The research problem had not at first looked all that difficult. Somebody—a Pittsburgh somebody?—had either planned to take out, or had actually succeeded in taking out, some kind of drug czar, also from Pittsburgh presumably, known as The Coke King. But nothing Mark and

Zeena read on the problem of drugs in Pittsburgh, and later in the whole of western Pennsylvania, turned up anybody with such a nickname. But this was just their first dead end with the assignment, and getting to it took them almost a week.

A suggestion from Mrs. Harbinger—finally a suggestion from Mrs. Harbinger, who had a rule against helping students find in the library what she believed they could find for themselves—headed them in what they were sure was the right direction. Perhaps The Coke King was a reference to the Pittsburgh industrialist Henry Clay Frick, a man of great sovereign power, who at the beginning of the century had made his money in coke and steel. Yes, Mark and Zeena found out quickly, Frick was the man being referred to all right. Several encyclopedia entries gave "The King of Coke" as his newspaper nickname, and all of them described the event in Frick's life that the verse clue had to be alluding to.

In Homestead, a town just outside Pittsburgh, Frick managed a steel plant for another big industrialist, Andrew Carnegie. In 1892, there was a strike at the plant, the Homestead steel strike, which all the encyclopedias referred to as one of the most bitterly fought industrial disputes in United States labor history. It lasted nearly five months and ended in a terrible defeat for labor. In order to protect the property of the plant and the non-union men he had hired to work in it, Frick brought in about three hundred Pinkerton men, private detectives from outside Pittsburgh ("his expedient use of force"). A battle broke out between the Pinkertons and the strikers, in which a number of people on both sides were killed, and the governor of Pennsylvania called out the National Guard to restore order. Under its protection, Frick was able to keep his non-union men at work, scabs they were called, and that broke the strike. It also broke the back of organized labor in the mills of Pittsburgh. For over forty years, there was no steel union in the city.

The man "who would killer play" was a Russian-born anarchist named Alexander Berkman who believed he could build popular support for the cause of working people by assassinating Frick. Right after the strikers' battle with the Pinkertons, therefore, Berkman took a train to Pittsburgh from new York, walked coolly into Frick's office inthe Chronicle-Telegraph Building, and shot him several times at point-blank range, wounding him in the ear and neck. Berkman was immediately overpowered, jailed, and eventually sentenced to serve twenty-two years in a Pittsburgh prison.

Very good. All Mark and Zeena had to do then was find Frick's original office in the old Chronicle-Telegraph Building and in it something that might have "warmed" him, like a stove maybe, or a fireplace, or even a liquor cabinet—inside which or around which would be Assignment 5. They'd finished their library research that day in excellent spirits and in less than an hour.

The next day, however, they discovered that the Chronicle-Telegraph Building had been demolished years before. Maybe Frick had more than one office, or maybe he'd done his "pondering" at home, and Berkman had planned to shoot him there. Or, if "pondered" meant talking things over, as well it might, maybe Frick had done that in someone else's office—like the governor's. Maybe Berkman had planned originally to assassinate both Frick and the governor at the same time.

A detailed account of Frick's life, a biography, was what Mark and Zeena needed.

But none of the many books they consulted helped.

Their last resort was the microfilm room, the newspaper

reports of Berkman's trial. Perhaps the way Berkman had altered his plan for killing Frick had come out in court.

Except that if there had been any questioning of Berkman at all in open court, none of the newspapers had reported it.

Mark sighed, shook his head, and threw his ballpoint pen down onto the assignment. "I thought for sure Berkman would talk at his trial," he said. "Wasn't publicity what he wanted?"

"That's probably just why they kept him muzzled. Crazies like Berkman scare the hell out of the Establishment. They're not going to give them a chance to talk if they can help it."

She looked at him with an unpleasant smile.

"And besides," she went on, "he wouldn't have said anything that would help us anyway. I've heard guys like Berkman talk before. They're all the same. It's always slogans. You remember all that stuff in the assignment about how Berkman thought he was The Fifth Angel out of the Book of Revelation? Well, on this T.V. show about the Manson cult it said Charles Manson thought he was The Fifth Angel too."

"I don't know," Mark said, "Berkman was a writer, remember, who—" He stopped himself and looked at Zeena. "Maybe Berkman *wrote* something about what he did. I never looked him up as an author."

"I didn't either," Zeena said.

Alexander Berkman, it turned out, who had served fourteen years of his twenty-two-year sentence for his attempt on the life of Henry Clay Frick, who shortly after his release from prison was deported from the United States to the Soviet Union, and who was then in turn exiled from Russia to the continent, where, in Nice in 1936, he took his own life, had written a great deal about what he had done in Pittsburgh and what had happened to him as a result of it. He had written an entire book as a matter of fact, *The Prison Memoirs of an Anarchist,* which Mark checked out of the Carnegie that same afternoon.

It was a strange experience for Mark reading Berkman that night and thinking of him and John Brashear and Mrs. Soffel and the Biddle brothers in Pittsburgh at the same time, all following, as that guy making the assignments might have put it, such different stars. Mark saw immediately what Zeena meant by Berkman's use of slogans. Frick was no more than a "beast" to him, a "monster," a "vampire." "Removing" him was simply a way of raising the consciousness of the working class and of no more consequence in itself than was Berkman's sacrifice of his life to bring it about. Indeed, Berkman had never intended to survive his trial. After making a speech in court, he'd planned to blow himself up with a cartridge of nitroglycerin he'd sewn into his coat, but the prison guards had foiled him by taking his clothes. No wonder what Zeena called "the Establishment" refused to give such a man his hour in court.

But Berkman in prison, interacting with other people, was something else again. On the one hand, he claimed to have nothing but contempt for his fellow prisoners; "animals" he called them, "creatures." And yet on one occasion he took a terrible risk to smuggle food to a man who had been reduced by beatings and solitary confinement to bleating on all fours like a goat. Another time Berkman deliberately mutilated his own hand to be sent to the prison hospital so that he could comfort a friend of his, a young boy, who was in the hospital dying. And when Berkman himself was serving a stretch in solitary confinement, reduced to one meal a day for weeks, he nevertheless reserved a portion of his food to feed some baby birds that had fallen from their nest just outside his cell. Most touching of all to Mark was Berkman's account of his release from prison. So grateful was he to the woman who'd met him, that on their train ride back to New York City, he ate the bouquet of flowers she'd brought him, petal by petal. In the midst of details like these, Mark almost missed what he was looking for in Berkman's book—almost but not quite, and he was on the telephone with Zeena less than half an hour after he'd found it.

"Got it!" he said excitedly. "Originally, Berkman was going to kill Frick at his *home,* not at his office!"

"Wow! You're sure?"

"Listen to this. Berkman's in prison thinking about how he blew his chance to get Frick. 'It might have been different,' he says, 'had I gone to *Frick's residence*. It was my original intention too. But the house in the East End was guarded.'" Mark paused dramatically. "And guess where that house in the East End is?"

"Where?"

"About a mile from us right now, just off Penn Avenue on Homewood in Point Breeze. And you know what else? The whole estate's a museum now, called Clayton House. They run tours through it."

"Tours? How'd you find that out?"

"From a phone message. When I read about Frick's house being in the East End, I looked him up in the phone book and that's how I got Clayton House."

She laughed. "Any idea of where we go once we're inside?"

"No, but Frick must have had a study or something like that in there. I haven't finished the book yet. It's . . . some book. I'll let you know in school tomorrow if I find anything else."

From school the next day Mark was able to reserve two places in a tour of Clayton House that started at 9:00 A.M. Saturday morning. Since the person he talked to had said the tour lasted only about an hour, there'd be plenty of time after it for him to drive Zeena across the river to her job. It was the weekend Mark's mother was in Toronto with Guy, so he had her car.

The remarkable thing for Mark in going through Clayton House was his sense of the place as a home, as something that a family had lived in. Right along with the displays of wealth—in the intricately detailed reaches of stained glass, the parquet floors and ceilings, the marble statues, the diamond-cut crystal—were odd reminders of the Fricks' daily life. Bells for servants. A checkbook. Mrs. Frick's ledgers of household accounts. But what most impressed Mark was the Fricks' relation to their children. One daughter's room was painted in lovely soft colors, and with clouds and birds drifting across the ceiling. Another daughter, who had died at about age eight, neither parent seemed able to forget. To the end of Mrs. Frick's life, the guide said, she surrounded herself with photographs of the dead child, and a life-size statue of her holding a rose quietly dominated the Fricks' reception room.

After doing the whole downstairs of the house, the tour moved directly to Mr. Frick's private bedroom and study on the second floor. It was here, the guide told the assembled group, that Frick made all his important decisions, and he went on to speak of the Homestead steel strike and of Berkman's attempt on Frick's life.

"He was truly," the guide said, "a most remarkable man. Right after the capture of Berkman, Mr. Frick's people tried to get him to go to the hospital—he'd been hit by bullets in the neck and also in the ear—but he would not leave. 'It might show weakness to the strikers,' he said.

He refused anesthetic for the treatment of his wounds. 'Without the ether,' he told the doctor, 'I'll be able to tell you when you've found the bullets.' And then, *then*, after being patched up, Mr. Frick stayed at his office to do a full day's work, walked unassisted to his carriage for the ride home, and after having dinner with his wife and children in order not to worry them, came up here and collapsed." The guide pointed to the far end of the room. "Right there in that bed."

Mark felt Zeena nudge him, and he followed her eyes to a screened-in fireplace beside Mr. Frick's bed. A wide brass plate ran across the bottom of it.

"Has to be," he whispered in confirmation. "Make sure you stay with that guide. Do what you can to distract him."

Mark waited until Zeena had slipped to the front of the small group of people and then worked his way over to the fireplace. Standing with his back to it, he dropped one of his gloves behind him. Zeena was talking to the guide who, at that moment, was leading the tour into a hall to Mrs. Frick's bedroom. Just as the last person was leaving the room, Mark turned, stooped, and while picking up his glove with one hand, with a quick sweep of the other retrieved the envelope that had been stuck up under the brass fender of the fireplace. He stood up and turned to stare straight into the cold eyes of a female security guard, standing in the room's main doorway.

"Thought I'd lost my notes," Mark mumbled with his little boy grin. He waved the envelope at her, quickly crossed the room, stepped through the hall, and caught up with everyone else in Mrs. Frick's bedroom. He flashed the envelope he'd just retrieved at Zeena and then put it inside his coat.

Outside Clayton House, standing beside Mark's mother's car in the parking lot, they opened the envelope containing Assignment 5 and four brand-new, consecutively numbered hundred-dollar bills. Like Assignment 4, 5 had a lot to say about the stars, how unpredictable they could be, how dangerously explosive, but what Mark and Zeena focused on was the verse clue:

```
Hooded Grief in the Gypsy's Mural
Shows the sweet that now is mute.
The middle brick there of the north side embrasures
Restarts the music with a different lute.
```

"Mean anything to you?" Mark asked.

She shook her head. "We've got to find some embrasures somewhere with a brick . . . in between them, is it? but that's all I see right now. How about you?"

Mark laughed. "Are you kidding? I don't even know what embrasures are."

Zeena leaned up against the car and looked at him. "You'll find out what they are, though, won't you? You'll look them up. Even if I tell you what they are you'll *still* look them up—and not because you don't . . . trust me either."

He just stared at her, not being sure what she was getting at.

"Didn't you finish Berkman's book?"

"Yeah," he said, glancing into the back seat of the car. "It's—"

She put a hand on his arm, stopping him. "Same way you finished *Out of This Furnace* when you didn't have to. And you read *Blood on the Forge,* too, didn't you, after I mentioned it that first day we talked?"

"How did you know?" he asked her, feeling himself redden.

William E. Coles, Jr. · 129

"I saw it in the trunk of the car the day we were out at Calvary Cemetery."

He nodded.

It was a warm March day, springlike. Zeena's coat was open and Mark was suddenly conscious of her lean, hard body. He swallowed and looked down. He was about to say something, but she had already gone around to her side of the car. Mark got in and started the engine. He took the Berkman book from the backseat and handed it to Zeena as she was buckling her seatbelt. "You've got to read this. He's not just a crazy. And he's more than . . . just slogans. You'll see."

At the corner of Fifth and Penn, Mark turned to head down the long hill to the Allegheny River. He had almost a full tank of gas, he noticed. Tonight was the night he was to take Merial to dinner at Jimmy T'sang's, but what if he drove away with Zeena instead, across the river and then north to Erie, to the Great Lakes, to Canada, driving all night, just the two of them? Would she do that with him? Would she be with him that way?

"I brought you something too," Zeena said, gesturing with the Berkman.

"Really? What?"

"The poem you said you wanted to see, but it isn't finished yet remember."

"Hey, great!" Mark said, not daring to look at her. "Thank you. I really mean thank you."

She didn't speak, didn't move for a while. "You said you wanted to see it," she said finally.

"Absolutely. I really do. Do you want me to read it now?"

"You don't have to read it *right* now, no."

And then for a time, neither of them spoke.

"Listen," Zeena said as they turned off the Highland Park Bridge toward the Waterworks Mall. "My father's coming in for a visit two weeks from today. I'm taking off work that Saturday. We'll probably go to the zoo—Dad and me and Robbie. He's my little brother."

At this Mark did glance over at her, but she was looking straight ahead. He thought she was going to go on, but instead she rolled down her window.

"I hope it will be . . . a good time for you," he said after a bit. "I hope you enjoy it."

She looked off through her open window over the river.

God, he thought to himself, everything he said to her sounded so obvious, so stupid.

At King's restaurant Zeena got out of the car, but then turned back and leaned down to look in at Mark through the window she'd opened. "You want to come?" she asked him.

He looked at her, puzzled. "Come where?"

"To the zoo. With me and Robbie."

"And your dad?"

"And my father, yes."

"You sure I won't be in the way?"

She dropped her eyes, shook her head and smiled slightly, but not at him. Then she looked up again quickly, not smiling. "You want to come or not?"

"Yes," he said just as quickly. "I do."

She nodded, hanging down from the top of the car with one hand. "Thanks for the ride," she said to him, smiling briefly—something she'd never said to him before.

As she started walking toward the restaurant he leaned across the seat and called to her. "Hey. You forgot the poem."

She came back to the car, took a folded sheet of paper from her pocket, and handed it to him.

"Remember—" she started.

"That it isn't finished yet. I'll remember."

WILLIAM E. COLES, JR. · 131

14

"Your menus, sir," the waiter said, after taking their orders. Mark handed up first his and then Merial's menu of Chinese specialties. The napkins in front of them were of heavy, pink cloth, folded into the shapes of swans, and there was a candle on the table. Mark had on a tie and jacket.

"It's really nice your mother and Guy could get away together, isn't it?" Merial smiled at him.

Mark had made peace with his mother about her trip to Toronto. At least he'd accepted the money she'd offered him to take Merial out to dinner the same weekend. But it chafed him that Merial's attitude toward the trip—it had been the same since he'd told her of it—was that it was perfectly okay for his mother to do with Guy what he knew Merial would never even consider doing with him.

"Yeah," Mark said, forcing himself to smile back. "It is."

"And that she treated us to dinner—that was nice too."

Mark nodded, wishing he hadn't told Merial he'd taken the money from his mother.

"They've been going together for, what, almost two years now is it?"

"Well . . . no. Not that long. Only about a year, I think."

"Oh, Mark." Merial laughed. "They'd been going to-

gether for more than a year when *we* started to go together—and that was almost a year ago."

He fiddled with his water glass, turning it round and
round in place. "Really? I didn't realize it was that long."

She nodded and then asked, "And how long has it been
since Guy's wife was killed?"

Guy's wife, Cindy, had been killed in an automobile
accident in Toronto some years before he came to teach
at the University of Pittsburgh.

"Eight years ago, I think," he said. "Maybe ten."

Merial looked down again, nodding. Then she looked
up, smiling. "Think they'll get married?"

"Come on, Gyp," Mark said, shifting his position.
"What a question." He drank some of his water. Merial
was looking at him expectantly. "How would I know a
thing like that?" he replied crossly.

She cocked her head slightly. "I thought you might have
asked. It's a natural question, isn't it?"

"No," he said. "It isn't. I don't think it's any of my
business."

Merial picked up her fork and dragged it across the
tablecloth in front of her. "I don't see why," she said,
keeping her eyes on the tracks it had made, "you *both*
need to go back to the Frick place. Why can't she go
back just by herself?"

Why was it, Mark thought ruefully to himself for the
thousandth time, that all the real trouble between Merial
and himself seemed to come as a result of his attempts
to prevent it? On the way to dinner, he'd told Merial of
the tour of Clayton House he'd taken with Zeena that
morning, enumerating all the things he thought she'd be
interested in—especially the Fricks' children, but also the
richly framed pictures and expanses of oriental rugs, the
sweeping staircase and gold leaf carvings, the luxury of

Mrs. Frick's dressing room. But when he'd mentioned casually that he and Zeena were probably going to have to go back to the Frick mansion next Saturday, and maybe even the Saturday following, Merial fell silent in a way that made him aware he was foolish to have said such a thing.

"I told you," he said, "we both have to take some more notes."

"Notes on what?"

"Well, me on Frick's finances," Mark said airily. "I'm not sure what kind of line Zeena's taking."

"You're not, huh? And just how are you going to find out about Frick's finances by looking at his house? In fact, I don't see where Frick comes into your project at all. I thought you were working on those other two people, Brass Ears and Soffel the Sickie."

He looked at her, his face hard. "Do you want to pick a fight? Is that why we came here?"

"I want you to answer my question. What's Frick got to do with what you're doing?"

"They all lived in Pittsburgh about the same time, Merial," he said stiffly. "There are connections between them."

"What connections?"

"Look, I don't know yet. That's . . . what we're doing research on."

The waiter arrived with two steaming bowls of hot and sour soup. Mark looked at Merial's bowed head, shining gold in the candlelight, and felt a stab in his chest. "Gyp," he said, "what do you want me to do here?"

She looked up quickly. "You could start to—" she began angrily, but then she stopped herself. She leaned toward him. "Look, Mark. How would you like it if I did *research* every afternoon with Dick Byrnes? Would you like that?"

"We don't do research *every afternoon*. We only work together two days a week."

"Oh really? It was three or four days this last week counting today. So how many days will it be next week and the week after that?"

"Come on, Gyp. I never *went* with Zeena the way you did with Byrnes. And you dance with him every chance you get. How do you think that makes me feel?"

"I wouldn't dance with him if you'd dance with me—and you know that dancing is *all* I'm doing with Dick."

"Meaning what?"

"You know what."

He shook his head dismissively. "It's just not true," he said. "Zeena doesn't like white people much. I don't think she likes men very much either."

"What are you working together for, then?"

"I told you," he said. "It was Hunter's idea, not mine."

"There's nobody *else* in the class that's been assigned to work together."

He knew she was guessing. "That's not true," he said.

"Oh yeah? Who else then?"

"Why don't you ask Hunter?" he blustered.

Merial picked up her spoon and began silently to sip her soup.

"I can prove it to you how she feels about . . . men and things like that. She gave me this poem she's working on."

The sound of the paper he extracted from the pocket of his jacket brought her head up as though from a blow. Her mouth tightened, and she seemed about to say something. Then she looked down again and continued deliberately with her soup, ignoring the paper he was holding out to her.

He put it down next to her silverware. "Aren't you even going to look at it?"

"I'm eating right now," she said coldly.

They finished the soup in silence. She wouldn't meet his eyes. The waiter removed their bowls and put an egg roll in front of each of them.

"Gyp," Mark said. "Please let's not fight, okay? I . . . wanted this to be a good time." He reached across the table and squeezed her hand. "Come on, honey. There's nothing between Zeena and me. There really isn't. Honestly. Will you just read what I gave you? You'll see what I mean when you do."

"You just carry her poem next to your heart in the name of research, is that it?" she said, still not looking up at him.

"I brought it with me because I wanted you to see how . . . Zeena and I live in two different worlds. It's written about Silk. She told me that. Just read it, will you please?" He squeezed her hand.

She opened the folded paper and read:

Longings

When I run the reservoir alone and round and round,
The sounds of the unfed tigers,
Bengals, Siberians,
Will rise from the zoo sometimes to splinter
The light of frosty afternoons
And heat me to charity
Like the voices of black men
Sweet with loving lies,
World-rolling with need.

Deeper than Africa,
Older than salt,
Serious as money,
And sadder than a coronet out of Preservation Hall.

In that fractured rolling world, I am not always sure
There is more than kept and keeper,
Another kind of Monday,
Anything past the hardness of
One divided by two,
When I run the reservoir alone and round and round.

When she had finished reading, Merial tossed the poem to one side of her place, sat up straight, and folded her arms across her chest. Mark had broken open his egg roll and was spooning duck sauce over it. "You see what I'm saying?" he asked.

For a moment she just stared at him. Then she looked off and shook her head slowly. "God, you're such a baby sometimes."

He stared at her, incredulous, indignant. "What's that supposed to mean?"

"Mark," she said, putting her hands on each side of her plate and leaning toward him, "that's a love poem she gave you—or rather, it's a sex poem. What the hell is the matter with you?"

He snatched up the poem and stared at it. "A *sex* poem? 'The voices of black men' are 'sweet with loving lies'? Doesn't sound very sexy to me. I told you she wrote it for Silk when her mother and father were getting divorced."

"She tell you that too?"

He didn't answer. That she'd written it *for* Silk wasn't quite what Zeena had said.

Merial cut a small piece of her egg roll. Then she laid her knife and fork down on her plate. "I think you've done enough research with Zeena Curry—if you're really committed to me."

He stared at her. "Meaning?"

Her face twitched. Her tone shifted. "Meaning this girl is trouble, Mark. Can't you see that? And I'm not the only one saying so."

"Gyp, if you think we got something going, I'm telling you, you're crazy."

She didn't answer.

"Look," he said after a time. "I asked Zeena to show the poem to me. She didn't just volunteer it or anything. If I was wrong to do that I was wrong. I'm sorry."

"How'd you find out about it? She tell you?"

"Hunter mentioned it in class."

Merial slowly shook her head.

"Gyp, I swear to God it's a project we're working on together, and that's all. All I want is to get through the damn thing, and that's all she wants too."

"You don't know what she wants," Merial said. "*She* doesn't know what she wants either. That's why she's dangerous."

Mark watched her break off a piece of egg roll with her fingers and put it in her mouth.

"What do you mean you're not the only one saying so?" he asked her. "Other people been telling you we're . . . burning up for each other, or something?"

She shrugged. "I've had a couple of questions."

"From who? What kinds of questions?"

"*And* I've seen the way people look at the two of you."

"Well, I can't help the way people look."

"That's not the point, Mark," Merial said vehemently, pushing her plate back. "*We're* the ones going together. We're supposed to be anyway. I'm . . . just not sure we really are anymore."

She dropped her gaze, but he'd seen the gleam of tears in her eyes and it bothered him. Damn all the secrecy, all the lies he had to tell. None of it was *his* idea. He reached across the table and took her hand.

"Gyp, listen," he said fervently, "if I pulled out of the project now I'd look like a racist or some damn thing. And we'll be done soon, honestly. No more than . . . than a couple of weeks at the most."

A couple of weeks at the most? The thought that exactly two weeks ago he'd told his mother that his project with Zeena was almost finished scratched at the base of his spine for acknowledgement. He shoved it away.

"Will you just hang with me till then? *Nothing* is going on with her and me. *You're* my lady, Gyp. You're the one."

She looked at him sideways, her mouth quivering slightly.

"Really," he said, "I mean that." And he did mean it. Saying it, looking straight into her glistening grey eyes, pressing her hand, made him sure he meant it. "You're my lady," he repeated. "You're the one."

And as the waiter moved their half-eaten egg rolls to one side of their places, and then began arranging a series of metal-covered serving dishes on their table, lifting lid after lid, filling the air with spicy steam, and as Merial smiled first at her food and then at him, her eyes shining with life in the candlelight, and as he smiled back at her in love and gratitude and pride, he thought of his mother's car just outside the restaurant, of Guy and his mother in Toronto, and of his house empty for the weekend, his room, his bed that Merial had never seen, and then of Zeena and her prism face and quick brown hands and her lean, hard body, and of himself, sweet with loving lies and world-rolling with need, world-rolling with need.

15

Mark and Zeena could find nothing to help with the verse clue of Assignment 5 in either the Carnegie or the Hillman Libraries:

```
Hooded Grief in the Gypsy's Mural
Shows the sweet that now is mute.
The middle brick there of the north side embrasures
Restarts the music with a different lute.
```

On Monday of the week following they took a sheet of paper to Mrs. Harbinger:

1. Is there now, or has there ever been, in Pittsburgh or in the Pittsburgh area, an artist, a painter, or perhaps a sculptor, known as "the Gypsy"?
2. Is there in Pittsburgh or in the Pittsburgh area, or was there ever, a painting or sculpture known as "the Gypsy's Mural"?
3. Who or what is "Hooded Grief" in the Mural done by "the Gypsy"?

"My, my, my, my, my," Mrs. Harbinger said with amusement. "This really is quite a hunt you're on in that

English class of yours, isn't it? There's *nothing,* you say, on any of this in either the catalogs or the periodical guides?"

"Not a thing, Mrs. Harbinger," Mark said with conviction. He and Zeena both knew her rules about students and research.

"I just wonder," Mrs. Harbinger said, tapping the tops of her lower teeth with her pencil, "if maybe you're not dealing with . . . another nickname of some sort here."

Mark and Zeena stared at her.

"Put your heads together," Mrs. Harbinger said, smiling and handing Mark back the list, "and see what you can come up with."

Mark and Zeena went out onto the front steps of the library to talk.

"She knows more than she's telling us," Mark said irritably.

"Obviously."

"Yeah. Well, so what do we do now?"

She shrugged. "Think about nicknames, I guess."

He looked over at her sharply. She'd been flippant with him the same way all week, keeping him at arm's length it seemed to him. Was she sorry that she'd shown him her poem? Did she wish she hadn't asked him to meet her father?

"What is it with you, anyway?" he asked her. "I thought we were . . . friends."

Her mouth twisted, and she turned her head away from him. When she looked back she was smiling, but it seemed forced to Mark. "I did promise to do better, didn't I? I'm sorry. I've just been in a bad mood lately."

At least she hadn't pretended she didn't know what he was talking about.

"And maybe I have an idea," she went on. She pointed across the quadrangle fronting of the Carnegie Library.

"See that stone building over there behind the fountain? That's the Frick Fine Arts Building," she said. "I did a research paper on Salvador Dali last year, and the people in there helped a lot. Let's go ask them about the Gypsy."

The man in charge of the small reading room in the Frick had just locked up to leave for the day, but from him Mark and Zeena learned that "The Gypsy's Mural" referred almost certainly to a huge surrealistic painting—it filled a whole wall in a church in the East End of Pittsburgh—done by a Hungarian refugee named Stefan Vlastos. Hungarian like Merial, Mark thought. The Gypsy. Of course. "Hooded Grief?" The man from the reading room smiled and shook his head.

"You'll see the problem with trying to identify things in the mural that way as soon as you start reading about Vlastos. It's an incredible story, really."

It was, as the next day in the Carnegie Mark and Zeena discovered. Stefan Vlastos had come to the United States in 1957 as a refugee during Russia's brutal repression of the Hungarian Revolution. Shortly after his arrival in Pittsburgh, however, Vlastos had been denounced from Hungary as a criminal, as an art forger and thief, and his extradition was demanded by *both* the Russians and the revolutionists. Vlastos claimed that the charges against him were trumped up, and that if he were returned to Hungary, it would mean his immediate execution.

In the midst of the highly publicized controversy over the case (Vlastos was an artist of international reputation), the painter took up residence in an East End church, St. Anastasius, and demanded sanctuary—aware, of course, that such a claim has no legal force in the United States, but depending on the government's reluctance to take him by force from a place of worship. It was a clever move. While Emigration worked to sort things out, Vlastos lived in a room behind the altar at the bottom of the church's bell tower and passed the time by working on his gigantic mural. He kept what he had done draped, a secret from the public, telling reporters that his picture was to be an expression of his gratitude for the faith that had sheltered and sustained him but that it had to be finished before it could be judged.

Emigration decided finally to deport Vlastos. The artist received the news with no show of emotion, but that same night he very quietly made his way to the top of the bell tower and threw himself from it to his death.

The parish of St. Anastasius, already sharply divided over the question of Vlastos' criminality, was absolutely torn to pieces over how his unfinished mural was to be understood. There were those who saw the painting as the heroic attempt of a visionary to vindicate God's demands on humanity. Others saw in his bizarre images the final despairing statement of a man who had lost faith in everything. There was a riot in the church at the mural's official unveiling, and later that night it was defaced with black paint. The day following, the church was firebombed, badly damaging its interior and completely gutting the bell tower. In no more than two days, the parish of St. Anastasius had virtually wiped itself out. The church had been boarded up for years.

The only photographs of Vlastos' work that Mark and Zeena could find had been taken after its defacement. In examining them, they could see why the man from the reading room had smiled at their questions about the location of Hooded Grief. There were swarms of figures in the mural, a number of which seemed to have on hats or hoods; any one of them could have been the figure being referred to in the verse clue.

In an article done on Vlastos for *Pittsburgh Magazine*,

however, Zeena found a key sentence. "Seated at the lower left," Ms. Martha Formsby, an art critic, had written of the mural, "allegorical Sorrow, muffled in a cloak, indicts with pointing finger the hypocrisy of organized religion." Mark looked hard at the lower left corner of the photograph in the article and shook his head. He could make out a seated figure with a hood cast over its face pointing at something, but in the photograph the something was no more than a smudge.

"We'll just have to find a way into that church then," he said. "We can bus down tomorrow."

Zeena shook her head. "We don't want to be busing down to Albatross Street. I'll have my mom's car tomorrow, though."

"Don't you work Friday?"

"Not tomorrow. I took off Friday *and* Saturday this week because my dad's coming."

The following afternoon in Zeena's mother's car, Mark saw what she'd meant about not busing to Albatross Street. It was in a section of the city known as Larchmont, no more than two or three miles from where Mark lived in Highland Park, though he'd never been in it. Larchmont was gang territory, deceptively deserted he felt as Zeena cruised slowly down Lincoln Avenue.

Except for its tower, St. Anastasius looked more like an old warehouse than a church. It was black as a slag heap, ugly as the butt of a chewed cigar. Zeena edged the car slowly up off the street onto the church's littered parking lot. The only sign of life in the area was a small red neon sign above a fronting of dirty glass brick just across the street: BAR. The doors and windows of the church had been covered with steel plates, and in the fading light of late afternoon it looked as impenetrable as a fort.

"Jeeze—"Mark began, leaning forward over the dashboard to see to the top of the church's bell tower, but a shout from across the street just outside the bar cut him off. A small, hunched black man, all arms and legs, was headed toward them. He had a queer, wobbly way of walking and a voice like a bull horn that came straight through the closed car windows.

"Hey!" the man cried. "Ho! Ho!" and in another instant he was rapping on Zeena's window. "Wachall want?" He demanded. "Wachall want here?"

To Mark's amazement, Zeena laughed and rolled down her window. "Shoot now, Mr. Arnold," she said. "Don't take on so. It's me. Zeena Curry." She turned to Mark smiling. "He lives near me on Rural Street. I'll talk to him."

While Mark watched from the front seat of the car, Zeena and Mr. Arnold walked slowly across the parking lot to the church building. He saw her gesture and make some kind of shape in the air with her hands. Then she pointed to the back of the church and up to its stubby bell tower while Mr. Arnold followed her arm and finger. He shook his head and looked off, but Zeena took his arm and talked some more. And then Mr. Arnold pointed, first toward the back of the church as Zeena had, but then to the front of it. Mark zipped up his parka and rolled up the window Zeena had rolled down. After a while Mark saw Mr. Arnold hobble back across the street. Zeena slipped jauntily into the front seat of the car beside him.

"Bingo," she said with a grin. "He's the custodian. He's got keys. I told him we needed to get some pictures of the mural for a project we're doing."

"Super! He's going to let us in, then?"

"Oh, sure," she said, starting the car and turning on

the windshield wipers. It had begun to snow, big pillowy flakes of it. "There's going to be an admission fee, though."

"Fair enough. When?"

"I'll know tonight when I call him. I told him it had to be early next week. I'll be by for you tomorrow morning at nine o'clock, by the way. Then we'll pick up my dad. Be out front, okay?"

16

At ten minutes of nine Mark looked out the picture window of his living room to see Zeena parked in front of his house. She was sitting rigidly, looking through the windshield, both hands on the wheel as though she were still driving. A small boy, his head almost obliterated by a black and yellow Pittsburgh Steelers stocking cap, knelt on the front seat beside her. Her brother Robbie. He was rocking rhythmically and looking out the rear window. About four inches of snow had fallen in the night. It had already turned soggy in the bright March sun.

Mark tried the front car door on Robbie's side, but it was locked. Zeena reached over the front seat and unlocked the rear door for him. "Sorry I wasn't out front," he said to her, sliding into the back seat. "You're early. Hi, Robbie, I'm Mark. That's a great hat."

Robbie looked owlishly at Mark over the back of the front seat. He had Zeena's high cheekbones and her same apricot-colored skin. "My dad's taking us to the zoo," he announced. "We're going to cheer up the animals. They get lonely in the winter."

"Oh," Mark said. "Well, that's a great way to think of it."

"My dad said that," Robbie explained as Zeena turned him around, sat him down, and buckled his seat belt.

"Yeah, well actually we're taking *him* to the zoo, Robbie," Zeena said, reaching behind her to lock the back door. "And it isn't winter anymore either. Yesterday was the first day of spring."

She pulled smoothly onto Highland Avenue from which almost all the snow had already melted and headed toward Oakland.

"You talk to Mr. Arnold?" Mark asked.

She nodded briefly.

"Well?" he said, leaning on the top of the front seat. "Are we on for next week?"

She hitched herself forward slightly. "Yeah," she said. "We are. I don't know what day yet, or how much. I'll have to let you know."

Zeena's father was waiting for them at the curb just outside the University Holiday Inn. She stopped to one side of him and unlocked the back door again. He had on new white sneakers, jeans, a navy blue bombardier jacket, and was carrying a plastic shopping bag.

"Hey, hey, guys!" he said, almost, but not quite, making it to the car in a long step over the flooded gutter. He got into the back seat alongside Mark, his one sneaker squishing, and then bent almost double over the front seat to hug Robbie. "I missed you, Tiger," he said. "You're my man, you know."

Zeena hadn't turned around. Her father reached over, briefly touched her hair, and then rubbed the back of her shoulder. "Thanks for getting me, Princess," he said. "I missed you."

"Hi, Daddy," Zeena said into the rearview mirror. "Good to see you again."

Good to see you again? It sounded formal to Mark, as though she were talking to someone she didn't know.

Zeena's father sat back in the seat. "You must be Mark,"

he said, holding out his hand. "I'm Zeena and Robbie's father." And then he laughed self-consciously. "I guess you worked that out."

He was a half head taller than Mark sitting down, but slight, and looked younger than Mark had thought he would. His clothes and manner, in fact, made him seem quite boyish, even with his thinning hair. Mark had trouble thinking of him as a math professor.

"Yes, I'm Mark, Mr. Curry," Mark said, shaking hands. "Mark Bettors. It's nice to meet you."

"Thank you. Glad you could come with us today. Sorry about the snow."

"Oh, for heaven's sake, Dad," Zeena said. "Mark knows you're not personally responsible for the snow."

"Weeel," Zeena's father said, cocking his head and grinning. He looked down at his one soaked Reebok and laughed the same self-conscious laugh. "Who'd have thought snow in the spring. Yesterday was the first day of spring, you know."

"I know," Zeena said, making the turn onto Fifth Avenue past the Cathedral of Learning, a soaring, blunting truncated Gothic structure, center of the University of Pittsburgh.

"Zeena tells me you're very good friends," her father said, smiling at Mark.

"I said we were working together, Dad."

"Well, that's friends, isn't it?" he said, winking at Mark.

Mark tried to catch Zeena's eyes in the rearview mirror, but she kept hers on the road in front of her.

Suddenly, Zeena's father leaned forward and tweaked the yellow pom-pom on the top of his son's cap. "Hey, Robbie," he said. "What animals do you want to cheer up today especially? Still like the elephants? Remember them last fall? The peanuts? Zeena always liked the elephants, eh, Princess?" He put his forearm across the top of the front seat and leaned his chin on it, his face close to his daughter's shoulder. "Boy, I missed you guys," he said.

Zeena glanced to her right and started slightly at her father's head so close to her. She hunched forward over the steering wheel, peering out of the windshield.

"Look at these damn students," she said, jerking a thumb. A laughing group of young men and women throwing snowballs had spilled down from the campus lawn onto Forbes Avenue. "Worth your life to come into Oakland on Saturday."

"It's spring, Princess, snow or no snow. Spring and the exuberance of youth. Daffodils in three weeks. You watch. You heard it here."

"Lions," Robbie said. "Monkeys."

"Monkeys and lions, you bet!" Zeena's father exclaimed. "You're a cinch for monkeys. Lions and tigers and bears, oh my. Well get them all some peanuts."

"I don't think they'll let you feed the monkeys," Zeena said. She jerked her chin at the front windshield. "We'll probably get soaked walking around in all this."

"Well, we don't have to go to the zoo, if you don't want to," her father said. "Maybe you guys would like to do something else. The day is yours. Whatever you want."

"I want to go to the zoo and cheer up the animals," Robbie said.

"Then the animals it is—if that's okay with you, Zeen."

Zeena didn't respond. Jesus, Mark thought, feeling his stomach tighten. Give him an inch, won't you?

"Hey, Robbie," Zeena's father said just after she left Oakland. "Come on in the back seat with me." He picked up the plastic bag from the floor of the car and put it on the seat between him and Mark. "Excuse me, Mark. I got presents for you guys. Want to see?"

Robbie started to climb from under the seat belt, but Zeena stopped him with a hand on his shoulder.

"You have to stay in your seat belt, Robbie," she said. "It's a law." And then over her shoulder she said, "Actually, you two should have on your seat belts too."

Robbie slapped at his sister's hand. "I want to go back with Dad."

"No, Robbie," Zeena's father said to him. "Zeena's right. I'll give you your present up there. Wait a minute." He fumbled in the corner of the back seat, dug out his seat belt and attached it. He smiled at Mark. "Guess we better get legal, right, Mark?" Mark too attached his seat belt. Then, from the plastic shopping bag, Zeena's father took out a package wrapped in gaily striped paper tied with scarlet ribbon and handed it over the front seat. "Here, Robbie. Hope you like them."

"Pretty," Zeena said glancing sideways. "Corrine wrap it?"

"Oh sure," her father said with a self-deprecating smile at Mark. "You know my wrapping. But I bought them. I mean I picked them out. They're from us both though, Robbie." He took the other package from the bag, obviously a book, a large one, wrapped in green and silver, and touched Zeena's shoulder with it. "And this is for you, Princess, with love from both of us."

"Nice, Dad," she said, barely turning her head. "Put it on the front floor there, will you, Robbie? I don't trust these streets with this snow."

They were on Shady Avenue now, in East Liberty, headed back toward Highland Park. The gutters ran with water, but the streets were almost dry.

"You can open yours now if you want to, Robbie," Zeena's father said.

WILLIAM E. COLES, Jr. · 151

There was a sound of tearing paper and then of a box being opened.

"Hey," Robbie said. "Sneakers. Look, Zeena." He thrust one snow-white sneaker up and almost against his sister's cheek. She ducked her head to the left keeping her eyes on the road.

"Not while I'm driving, Robbie," she said sharply. But then she glanced to her right. "They're nifty though. Did you remember to say thank you?"

"They're Reeboks," Zeena's father said.

"Thanks, Dad," Robbie said. "Thanks a *lot*." He took out the other sneaker and held them both up together. Then he put them like ears against the sides of his head.

"Now you've got new Nikes and Reeboks too," Zeena said.

"What?" her father said leaning forward. "I didn't know you had a new pair of Nikes, Robbie. Your mother didn't tell me that."

"My Nikes are old, Dad. They're gross. These are really neat."

"I can exchange them, you know. Let me exchange them, Robbie. I can get you something else." He bit his lip and shook his head. "I don't know why your mother didn't tell me about your Nikes when I asked about the size."

"Are they sixes? I wear sixes now."

"Sixes they are. I got something right, anyway. But let me exchange them, Rob. I was stupid not to—"

"For heaven's sake, Daddy," Zeena said, smacking one hand on the steering wheel. "Let it alone, will you? They're fine. Robbie loves them."

"Yeah," Robbie said, turning around under his seat belt and kneeling on the front seat to look back at his father. "My Nikes aren't new. They're gross."

"Besides," Mark put in, "Michael Jordan wears Reeboks, Robbie. You've heard of him, haven't you? Air Jordan they call him because it's like he can walk on air. They put his picture on the Wheaties box once. He's the greatest basketball player in the world. The greatest that ever lived. You'll walk on air with these Reeboks, just the way he does. Let me see one, will you?"

Mark could feel Zeena's eyes on him in the rearview mirror. Deliberately, he didn't meet them. He turned over the shoe Robbie handed him, flexed it professionally, peered inside it, smelled it. "Yes, sir," he said. "These are Air Jordan specials, all right. The best." He glanced down at Zeena's father's new sneakers. "Just like yours, aren't they, Mr. Curry?"

Zeena's father looked down at his feet and smiled the same smile he'd used with Mark earlier. "Well . . . yeah, they are." He leaned forward quickly, put an arm around Robbie and kissed him on the forehead. "See when I bought the sneakers, I—"

"I thought it was Nikes Michael Jordan advertises," Zeena interrupted. "Isn't it Nikes? Or Adidas?"

For a moment there was silence in the car.

"No," Mark said firmly. "It's Reeboks. These." He held up Robbie's sneaker and locked eyes with Zeena in the mirror. "Just like these, Zeena. Exactly like these."

Robbie stood up on the front seat to look down at his father's sneakers, and Zeena immediately grabbed a handful of the back of his coat and pulled him down hard, almost banging the back of his head on the dashboard. "Will you *please* stay in your seat belt."

Robbie hit her on the arm with the sneaker he was holding, and she shoved him back so hard his head hit against the car door. "You quit it, Zeena," he yelled and he started to cry. "Oreo," he spat at her. "Nasty ass."

"Robbie!" Zeena's father said sharply. "The two of you. Now, that's enough."

"Then tell him to stay in his seat belt. This is a bad hill." Zeena was picking her way carefully along the road that wound down from the Highland Park Reservoir to the zoo. It was a wooded area with neither curbs nor sidewalks. They crept by several cars parked just off the asphalt.

"Zeena's right, Robbie," her father said. "We're almost there, anyway. You can park up in here this time of year you know, Princess. You don't have to go all the way down to the lot."

She slowed the car and pulled gingerly off the road behind a red Camaro. Then looking at her father in the rearview mirror, she said, "Okay, but you pay the ticket if I'm tagged."

"Absolutely. But you won't be. I parked here a lot this time of year and we were never tagged, remember?"

"I want to wear my Reeboks," Robbie said as they were getting out of the car.

"No, Robbie," Zeena said. "It's wet. Keep your boots on."

"Dad has his Reeboks on," Robbie said. "Can I, Dad?"

"Got a better idea," Zeena's father said, scooping up Robbie and putting him on his shoulders. "How about a ride down to the zoo?" He held a hand above his head. "Gimme five first though, guy." Robbie smacked his hand. Zeena's father then gripped each of his son's ankles firmly and started down the path that ran alongside the road.

Zeena hung back, both hands jammed into her parka pockets. Her face was tight and angry. Mark took hold of her by one elbow.

"What the *hell* is the matter with you, anyway?" he asked in a sharp whisper. "Why are you acting like this?"

She shook off his arm and backed up a step. "Me?" she exclaimed in a fierce undertone. "What's the matter with ME? You're the one!"

"What are you talking about? What did *I* do?"

"You know Michael Jordan doesn't advertise Reeboks! You *know* that!" She backed up another step, her eyes stabbing. "It's *Nikes* he advertises," she hissed. "You *know* that! What'd you say Reeboks for?"

"Zeena, for God's sake."

"What's the matter with me," she mimicked viciously, cutting him off. "With ME!" She backed up still further and then whirled to walk down the path behind her father.

For a moment all Mark could do was watch her. Beyond her, down the hill, the figure of her father had dropped out of sight. Only the upper half of Robbie was visible. His hands were outstretched on either side of his body, the yellow pom-pom of his Steelers cap nodding, as though he were riding on wind, walking on air.

17

Mark waited at the bus stop outside Moorland until he'd seen Zeena pay her fare, and then, in deliberate violation of their agreement, climbed onto the same Lincoln-Larchmont bus she was already on. He dropped into the empty seat beside her, taking his backpack onto his lap as he did so. It clinked slightly with the tools in it. Mark was one of only three or four whites on the bus.

Zeena had spoken to him only once since the trip to the zoo with her father. It was over the telephone when she called him Monday evening.

"We're on for Wednesday," she'd said without even saying hello. "He'll meet us at the church at four o'clock he said and we're going to have to give him a hundred dollars, so you bring your half. If you can't get your car, by the way, we'll have to bus down, because I can't get ours."

It was said all at once, as though she were reading it. "Okay," he said automatically.

"Okay what? Can you get your car or not?"

"I don't think so."

"We'll have to bus then," she said abruptly and hung up. She didn't even say good-bye.

The hell with her he thought, climbing on the bus behind her. He was finished playing by her rules.

"Here's the money I owe you," he said, making no attempt to keep his voice down. He reached out two twenties and a ten to her and when she didn't respond he tucked them inside her arms folded in front of her chest. She gave him a withering look but slipped the bills quickly into her jacket. Then she turned from him to stare pointedly out the window.

"How's your little brother, Robbie?" Mark asked, his voice slightly raised. "My pal."

Zeena didn't move, didn't acknowledge him.

"That sure was a nice trip we took to the zoo Saturday, wasn't it? You and me and Robbie and your father?" He was as conscious as he knew she was that they were the center of silent attention.

Zeena did her best to behave as though he were not there. As they approached Albatross Street, she got up, and, without meeting his eyes, kneed his thigh sharply to make him let her out. He rose elaborately and fell in behind her. "Oh yeaaaah!" he said in a geeky voice as he leaned down to see the street sign. "Albatross Street. I almost forgot that's where we get off. I sure hope your mom has something good for dinner, don't you, honey?" No one even looked in their direction, but he could feel that everyone was watching them.

The bus stopped not at Albatross Street but at the block past it. They were the only ones to get off. Zeena whirled on him savagely as soon as it left. "You smart-ass sonofabitch. What do you think you're doing?"

"I just figured some of the brothers and sisters might want to know we're an item," he said. "Nothing wrong with that, is there?"

She stood in front of him sunk into one hip, both fists balled, swaying slightly. A fighting stance.

"Go ahead," he said. "Take a punch at me, why not?"

He glanced around him. "Then I'll punch you back. Make us look like everything else around here."

They were standing in the skeletal remains of a bus shelter. All the glass in it had been smashed out. The floor was littered with cigarette butts and trash, and there were a couple of condom rings near the carved-up wooden bench. In one corner lay a headless plastic doll.

"Yeah," Zeena sneered. "My people can really run down an area, can't they? So don't tempt me, baby. Just don't tempt me."

They stood maybe six feet apart, both of them breathing hard.

"I never should have had anything to *do* with a racist like you," she spat at him.

"Me!" he cried. "*Me*? *You're* the racist. With me. With your dad too. You were just mean on Saturday. Nasty. You were just plain nasty."

"Okay, I'm out of here," she said, spreading her hands, turning and starting to walk across the street.

"I thought you said you wanted another kind of Monday," he called out to her back. "Is this it?" It was the line in her poem that had stayed with him, even if he wasn't altogether sure of what she meant.

It stopped her. She turned from the middle of the street, eyes narrowed, and seemed about to speak, but something behind him caught her attention and then she was walking back to him. He glanced over his shoulder. Three black men outside a cigar store about halfway down the block were focused on the two of them and had begun to saunter their way.

"Mark," she said to him in a low voice, "do exactly what I tell you. Just walk toward me." Her tone was urgent, enough to push him into motion. When they'd reached each other, she brayed a laugh, linked her arm in his, and bobbing with cheerfulness led him back across the street.

"You should have seen his face!" she cried when they'd reached the sidewalk, bending almost double with high-pitched laughter. Out of the corner of his eye, Mark could see that the men on the far side of the street had stopped walking. St. Anastasius was about half a block down the way he and Zeena were headed. Aside from the men behind them, there was no one else around.

"What'd you want to save a racist for?" he asked her, after they'd gone on together.

"We got a job to do," she said.

He stopped walking and took her arm from his. "Oh no, we don't," he said to her. "Not this way. Not anymore. I'm not going to go on with you when you're . . . when you're nasty like this."

For a moment they just stood looking at each other. Then she dropped her eyes, but he was surprised to see a small smile flicker at her mouth. "You sound like Robbie," she said. "He calls me . . . he calls me nasty ass sometimes."

"I know. I heard him. He's right too. You are." And then, touched by her half smile, he added, "at least when you act like this you are."

For a moment she didn't move. Then, head still down, she nodded briefly. "I know," she said. And then she said it again. "I know."

He swallowed, not sure where to take things. "And I'm *not* a racist," he said defiantly.

"No," she said, looking directly at him. "Not the way I said. You're not."

For a while neither of them said anything.

"What was the book your father gave you?"

"It was a book of art prints. Salvador Dali."

"Well then," he said after a time, gesturing. "Want to be friends then?" It sounded so silly to him that it made him smile. Then she smiled with him. "You know what I mean," he said.

She nodded. "Yeah, I know what you mean," she said. "And yeah, I do. Want to be friends, I mean."

As they walked down to St. Anastasius, he took up one of her hands just for a moment and squeezed it and felt her squeeze his back.

When they were directly in front of the church, they stopped. Mark saw a movement at the far corner of it. "Is that you, Mr. Arnold?" Zeena called out. A leathery black face emerged for a moment and then quickly disappeared. "You don't be yelling," Mark heard a voice say and a hand motioned. "Come 'round here."

They walked around the front of the church and into the parking lot.

"Taking a big chance doing this," Mr. Arnold said once they were out of sight of the street. "Big chance. You got the rest of the money?" He looked from Mark to Zeena with bright, inquisitive eyes.

"Right here," Zeena said, slapping the pocket of her jeans but making no attempt to take it out. "Eighty bucks."

Mr. Arnold smiled briefly, nodded, turned, and scuttled like a crippled spider through the parking lot almost to the end of the church. He stopped by a flight of concrete steps leading down to a very solid-looking steel door with three padlocks on it. Mark gazed up at the bell tower directly above them, but the clouds scudding behind it made him feel dizzy and he quickly looked down again.

"Yes, sir," Mr. Arnold repeated. "*Big* chance I'm taking."

"You got the keys to those locks?" Mark asked, and Mr. Arnold winked and patted a bunch that hung from his belt. Then he leaned on one of the pipe rails that ran out from the side of the church along both sides of the steps and looked pointedly at Zeena. She counted him out three twenties and two tens. Mr. Arnold licked his thumb and counted the bills again, folded them, put them carefully in his shirt pocket and buttoned it. Then, after looking theatrically in all directions, he hobbled down the steps. The three padlocks snapped open easily.

"All right, be quick now," he said, standing to one side. He glanced at his watch. "And I *ain't* going to wait on you two more than a half hour. A *half hour,* hear? You still in there, you be locked in there, understand?"

Mark walked down to the door and pulled on it. It too opened easily but to a wave of acrid, sour-smelling air. The firebombing, Mark remembered. It was pitch black inside. Mark got a flashlight from his backpack and checked his watch. "Okay," he said, "we'll be back here at 5:10. If we're done before then, we'll pound on the door."

"You don't be pounding on nothing," Mr. Arnold said. "I told you. It's a big chance I'm taking. Lose my job."

"You wouldn't ever have taken this kind of big chance with anyone else, would you?" Mark asked him. "You ever let anyone else in here?"

Mr. Arnold looked down at the three open padlocks he was holding and then up again, his eyes shrewd. "Go on with you," he said. "Only took *this* chance on account of Miss Zeena here."

She was still at the top of the steps, looking up at the bell tower, shading her eyes with one hand against the sun. She started when Mr. Arnold used her name and came quickly down. Mark stepped into the blackness and Zeena followed him. Just after the door slammed behind them Mark thought he could hear the padlocks being replaced but he couldn't be sure.

They were standing at the end of a long, bare room littered with paper, some books, and what looked to be piles of old clothes. At the far end of the room, there were a number of sinks against the wall and a lot of cabinets. The smell of charred wood blanketed everything. It was dead still.

"Over there," Mark said, playing his flashlight beam along a stairway directly across from where they were standing. The stairway led up and to the left. "That must be the way into the church."

They picked their way across the room to the stairs. At the top of them, they could see a closed wooden door.

"What if it's locked?" Zeena whispered.

Mark twisted his shoulders sharply so that his backpack clinked. "I got a couple of persuaders," he said, climbing just ahead of her.

"God, I bet there're rats in here," Zeena whispered again.

"I can handle that too," Mark said jauntily. He was exhilarated. The sour, burned smell of the church was pure oxygen to him.

At the top of the stairs the unlocked door opened into one end of a long, dusty hall, which seemed to run the whole length of the church. The left wall was of rough, dirty-looking plaster. A number of arched doorways, spaced at regular intervals, led off to the right. There were rustling sounds, scurryings, and then silence again.

"Damn, Mark. There *are* rats," Zeena said.

He took her hand, led her slowly down the hall to the first arched opening, and shone his flashlight through it straight into what had been the main body of the church, now no more than a vaulted empty space. All the pews had been removed and there was no other furnishing of any kind. To the right, they could see where the altar had been on a raised section of floor that curved to meet the semicircular rear wall. Small shafts of light, like a cross-hatch of laser beams, arrowed down to the floor through tiny gaps in the metal plates where the stained glass windows had been. St. Anastasius Church was nothing but a dusty floor, a lot of scorched plaster, and a webbing of arching black beams overhead.

"Wow!" Mark said, moving into the room, his voice echoing eerily. He raised both hands over his head as though to embrace something. In some strange way the church felt familiar to him, as though he'd been in it before.

And then his flashlight found the mural. It was on the wall above and to the right of the archway they had just come through, filling the whole of a space between two columns, thirty to forty feet apart.

Nothing in their reading had prepared them for the impact of what they were looking at. Even through the smoke stains and the great obliterating splotches of red and black paint, the energy of the painting was staggering. In the middle of it, though visible now only in outline, was the famous single eye—leering? glaring? suffering?—around which a host of images swirled and danced: human and partially human figures, strange beasts, things that looked like fish or insects or both.

Mark heard Zeena catch her breath, whether in awe or horror he couldn't tell.

For a while he just stared. Captured. Worked on. Then he began to move the beam of light over the painting.

"There," Zeena said, catching his wrist. "In that lower corner there. Hold the light where all that red and black paint is."

He kept the flashlight on the section of the painting she'd indicated, and she stepped forward toward the wall.

William E. Coles, Jr. · 163

She stood first to one side of the great smear of defacing paint and then to the other.

"This is it, Mark," Zeena said, her head slightly cocked, eyes on the wall above her. "I'm sure of it. That character in the monk's robe is pointing at—move the light just a little more to the right . . . There! Hold it right there!"

For a while she didn't speak.

"He's pointing at a *church*," she said after a time in a hoarse whisper. "It's . . . like a toy church, tilted on its side. If you hold the light right where it is, you can come up here and see. Turn your head to the side a little."

He moved to her and they stood together almost at the wall. "In fact it's *this* church," Zeena continued. "See the A on the side of it—and that square bell tower with those two slitted window openings? That tower's just like the one on this church. I saw it from the parking lot."

"So the next assignment's in here somewhere?"

"It's in the bell tower. Remember the verse clue:

```
Hooded Grief in the Gypsy's Mural
Shows the sweet that now is mute.
The middle brick there of the north side embrasures
Restarts the music with a different lute.
```

"It's the *bells* that were sweet but now they're mute. Lute is loot, money. So what we want is the brick that's in the middle of those two window openings up there, the two embrasures, that face north."

He must have looked uncomprehending.

"Look," she said, stooping to the floor. "Shine the light down here a minute." She drew in the dust with her finger. "Here are the two embrasures, okay? And here's the brick wall between them. So it's this brick," she rubbed the dust away, "that we want. Okay?"

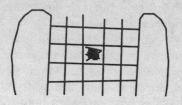

"Okay," Mark said, playing his light toward the rear of the church where the altar had been. "Then there's got to be a stairway up into the bell tower back there somewhere."

They made their way back to the semicircular wall at the rear of the church in the center of which was a massive wooden door set on a pair of huge wrought iron hinges. Where the knob should have been was a heavy metal ring. A padlocked chain ran through it over to another ring set into the stone wall.

Mark pulled on the chain, shaking it, and flakes of rust fell. The door moved outward about half an inch. He dropped to one knee to examine the padlock. Then he looked carefully at the screw plates holding the one ring to the door and the other to the wall.

"Here," he said handing Zeena the flashlight. He slipped his backpack to the floor and knelt to rummage in it. "We need the crow's-foot."

The crow's-foot was an oddly shaped tool about a foot long, part nail-puller, part hatchet, part hammer, and part pry bar. Still on his knees, Mark put the head of it between the doubled chain and took a half turn with it as though he were tightening a tourniquet. The chain pulled taut.

"Better step back," he said, standing up. "Something's going to give here. Keep the light on those rings." He heard her move away, but she kept the beam of light where he'd told her to.

Slowly, Mark tightened the chain, pulling the crow's-foot toward him, putting on more pressure, and more, and more. There was a grinding, and then suddenly a sound like a shot as the ring from the wall pulled loose and rocketed against the heavy wooden door. Mark fell to one knee. He got up quickly and took hold of the chain and the ring that was still attached to the door. "Okay," he said over his shoulder, "come help me open this thing."

She came up beside him and they pulled together. The door opened easily an inch or so but then it stuck fast. Mark drove the pry bar part of the crow's-foot between the edge of the door and its casing and levered. With a sharp snap, the door burst open, and light, and a roar of sound, drove both Mark and Zeena back coughing and sputtering in the midst of a shower of debris.

Zeena had dropped the flashlight, and Mark could see her scrabbling back into the church on all fours.

"It's only birds," he called back to her. "It's just pigeons."

Daylight from the top of the tower filtered down through a haze of dust and feathers. Bits of straw were still falling. High above were the sounds of peeping and cooing.

"The whole flock left at once, I bet," Mark said. "It's just the babies up there."

She came up beside him, and together they stepped through the doorway into the circular room at the bottom of the bell tower. It was filled with charred lumber piled as high as their heads, leaving them barely room to walk alongside the wall. The tower was open straight to the top where three blackened bells with chains dangling among them hung up at what looked to be the level of the embrasures. There were two such windows on each of the four sides of the belfry. They were sixty feet up at least. If there ever had been a stairway to the top of the bell tower, it had burned down. Mark dropped his eyes, feeling sick.

Zeena laughed, pointing up. "Told you, Mark. It's the middle brick of whatever pair of those windows . . . let's see," she said, stepping into the tower just past the doorway, turning, still pointing, "the sun's over here so . . . *those,*" she said happily. "That's got to be the north side."

Mark glanced quickly up to where she was pointing and then just as quickly looked down again. He leaned against the door frame.

"We're home free," Zeena said.

He looked up at her. "If we were pigeons, maybe. What do we do, levitate up there?"

"I'm going up the ladder," she said, whipping off her windbreaker. "Right up the north side too. Here, hold this. I'll need that pig's foot." Zeena's mood seemed to have shifted the moment there was natural light to work in.

"What ladder?"

"On the wall over there," she said over her shoulder as she went back inside the church. "And how much time have we got?"

Mark looked closely at the wall opposite the door and saw a series or iron rods bent into rectangles and set into the stone like half-inserted staples. Each was about three feet up from the one below it, and they did indeed make a kind of ladder all the way up to the belfry. The first rung, however, was ten or twelve feet up from the tower floor. Mark's palms began to sweat.

"How much time, Mark?" Zeena asked him again when she came back up behind him.

"You can't go up there, Zeena," he said firmly.

"You got us in the tower. Fair's fair. Besides, I don't weigh as much as you do. Come on over with me," she said, moving past him and working her way around the pile of charred wood. "I'm going to have to stand on your shoulders. What time is it?"

Mark held his watch up to catch the light from the top of the tower. "It's too late. We only have five or ten minutes left. Besides, those things may not be strong enough to hold you."

"They held somebody. Assignment Six is up there."

"Zeena, look—" he started, but she cut him off.

"Get over here," she said, sliding the crow's-foot inside the belt of her jeans. "You're going to have to boost me."

Mark hung Zeena's windbreaker from a nail sticking out of one of the fire-blackened beams and followed her around the wall. He moved woodenly, as though in someone else's body.

"Zeena, there isn't time," he said again.

"He won't leave us in here. Face the wall. Get down in a knee bend."

He did and felt Zeena step up on his shoulders. She was heavier than he expected. He came slowly up, shaking a bit, his good leg taking most of her weight. Suddenly, she was off him and he was showered with grit. He stepped back to see her chinning up with one hand to the first rung and reaching for the one above it, her sneakers scraping at the wall. Then she was at the third rung with her feet under her and climbing rapidly. He couldn't watch her past the start. Once he heard the screech of metal above him, and there was another shower of grit.

"Zeena!" he cried out to her, glancing up in spite of himself. "For God's sake be careful."

"Whooee!" she sang out in triumph above him. Head down, he leaned back against the charred lumber, his palms sweating. He felt as sick as though he himself were climbing.

The cooing and peeping grew louder and then there was the sound of wings again, like a lot of snapping towels. She had to be by the bells. "Sappear," her voice floated down to him.

"What," he called up, raising his head but keeping his eyes closed. "I can't hear you. What did you say?"

Her voice came down clearly then but with a sort of an echo, as though she were at the other end of a tunnel. "I said, there're a lot of nests up here, a lot of baby birds. I think I see the middle brick. Watch your eyes."

He risked a glance up, but then quickly shut his eyes and looked down again as a wave of nausea took him. He'd seen she was beside the bells. There was the sound of metal chinking on stone, a rain of dirt, and then he heard her call, "Look out!" Something solid thunked down onto the burned lumber off to his right. He drew his head down into his shoulders and squeezed his eyes shut as hard as he could.

"Bingo!" he heard her sing out. "It's here, Mark. It's a packet. I'm coming down."

He couldn't watch her descend, but he could hear her. And then he heard her stop.

He looked up. She was standing on the fourth rung or so from the bottom, about twenty feet above him, looking down. "What's wrong?" he asked.

"One of these things is loose. I felt it give on the way up. I'm not sure which one it was though."

"Wait a minute," Mark said, moving over until he was almost under her. "Test each one before you put your full weight on it. Easy now."

He watched as she eased herself down a rung. He checked behind him, made sure his feet were planted squarely, and held his arms at ready, out from his sides. There wasn't really any room between him and the pile of charred wood at his back.

"If you fall, don't worry, I'll catch you."

Zeena eased herself down another rung and then another. Not many to go now. Suddenly, he saw her sag and then twist away from the wall into the air. Mark caught her with both arms around the hips, but the force of her fall knocked him backwards into the pile of burned wood. There was a stab of pain in his bad knee, and he could taste charcoal. She was on top of him.

"Are you all right!" he cried, spitting and struggling to roll out from under her. "Are you all right!"

Zeena rolled off him onto her side. She began to laugh. "You should *see* yourself," she said. "You're absolutely filthy."

He stopped struggling and looked up at her. There was a great black smear on her face. He reached up, put his arm around her neck, and pulled her down and kissed her. He kissed her lightly but full on the lips. Then he smiled. "You're older than Africa," he said to her. And then she leaned down over him and took his face in both her hands and kissed him back, on his forehead first, and then on each of his eyes, and then lightly on the mouth. And then she kissed him firmly on the mouth, kissed him hard.

"It's *deeper* than Africa," she smiled.

"Deeper too," he said, putting both arms around her to draw her to him, but she pushed herself back up.

"We better get out of here," she whispered.

She got to her feet and helped him out of the lumber. They were almost half an hour past Mr. Arnold's 5:10

deadline. Quickly they gathered up their things, Mark limping slightly. "Where's the packet?" he asked, and Zeena patted her shirt as she was putting on her windbreaker. By the time they got back down to the basement door, it was 5:45.

18

Mark tapped on the door a couple of times with the flashlight and waited for Mr. Arnold to open it. When he didn't, Mark turned the knob and pushed. The door was unlocked and he opened it about halfway. As he started up the steps, he heard a voice from above and behind him. When he turned to look up, he was conscious only of a great bursting light and then of nothing at all.

He came to sitting in the well at the bottom of the steps, propped up against the wall. Zeena was crouched beside him, holding his head in her hands, just as she had when she kissed him. But her eyes were wide with fear. He reached out to her shoulder and tried to get up, but a jolt of pain under his arm made him drop back with a groan.

"Mark," Zeena said. "Just stay down. I'm going to go get an ambulance."

He took hold of her forearm and tried again to push himself up. His lips were puffed and he could taste blood.

"No," he said to her shaking his head. "Just help nee." But shaking his head filled it with fire. "Ut hattened?" he mumbled at her. "Ut hattened?" His mouth felt pillowy.

She stood up and pushed down on his shoulders. "Somebody hit you in the face with a bottle. This one."

She picked up a heavy-looking, green bottle with a deep indentation in the bottom of it. "Why it didn't break I don't know, but it didn't. You fell and your head's cut. I don't know how bad, but you could have a concussion. Now *sit*. I'll be right back." In two jumps she was at the top of the steps and away.

Mark felt strangely peaceful waiting for her. He knew that blood must be trickling from his head still because he could feel something dripping from his ear, and his tongue made him aware that one of his front teeth was broken off. But he was in no pain.

Zeena was back alongside him and with her a couple of men who looked down at him from the rail at the top of the steps. "Jesus," Mark heard one of them say. The other didn't say anything. Again Mark tried to get up and couldn't, and again Zeena told him to stay still.

"How doubt you?" Mark asked her through his smashed mouth. "You okay?"

She nodded. "Whoever did it just threw the bottle and took off."

"Who did it?" he asked her. "Silk?"

"No," she said scornfully. "Of course not. Silk wouldn't do anything like this."

"Who us it then?" he asked her after a time.

"Mark, please don't try to talk right now, okay? I didn't see who it was. I told you that whoever did it ran."

He sucked on his broken tooth and a sharp pain jolted him. He glanced up at the men leaning over the rail above him, four of them now, and then pulled Zeena toward him. "Ee eren't in there, all right? Ee ere just looking around out here. Understand?"

She stared at him.

"I *nean* it," he said, squeezing her forearm. "The kest . . . No trottle."

"What," she said. "Oh. The quest, you mean. No trouble. Well—"

He shook her forearm and pointed to two open padlocks lying in the corner of the cement stair well. "Ut ack the adlocks. Ere's the third?"

Zeena had just put the two padlocks back into place on the basement door, the third was under Mark's legs, when the ambulance arrived, screaming into the parking lot. Mark protested the stretcher, but the paramedics made him lie down on it anyway, and he was carried to the ambulance through a crowd of blacks. Zeena rode with him to the emergency ward of Shadyside Hospital, holding his hand.

"Tlease," Mark said to her on the way to the hospital. "Ee eren't in there, okay?" Zeena glanced over at the paramedic riding with them and then reluctantly nodded.

"How nuch?" Mark asked her forcing a grin, but again she looked at the paramedic and this time just shook her head.

His nose was broken, his ribs bruised, and he had a slight concussion. They could do nothing about his broken tooth, but they taped his chest and face and stitched the wound in his head. He'd begged the hospital not to call his mother, but they had anyway, and she arrived, ashen, grim-looking. Zeena did the talking for them, both with the people at the hospital and also with the police. Mark heard her say only that they'd read about Vlastos's mural and had gone down to St. Anastasius just out of curiosity, just to look around.

"I noove like Ister Arnold," Mark said to Zeena as he limped from the hospital wheelchair to his mother's car. They'd given him a shot and he felt very peaceful again, very floaty.

"Call nee," he said to Zeena, when his mother let her out at the corner of Rural Street. "Call nee tonight, okay?"

She nodded.

"Mark, what's going on?" his mother asked him as they pulled away from the curb. "Why wouldn't she let me take her home, and what were you doing at that church with her?" She was frightened as well as angry.

"Not now, okay?" he said, turning his head away. "Not now."

At home that night, he moved the phone from his desk to beside his bed. The shot wore off and he began to ache all over. He was glad for the pain pills they'd prescribed for him. When the phone rang, he answered it immediately.

"It's me," Zeena said. "How are you?"

"I'm okay. How nuch us there?"

"Mark, you're not going to believe this. There were seventeen one-hundred-dollar bills with the assignment! *Seventeen* of them!"

"Ow! Ut's the assignment?"

"It's another doozy."

"Read it to nee."

Assignment 6

The planet Pluto, Children, furthest from the sun and smallest of the nine, the coldest, darkest, and most mysterious, was not seen by astronomers until some years after mathematicians had determined it must be there. Certain orbital irregularities in the giants of our solar system, Neptune and Uranus, led them to this conclusion.

Similarly, if we examine the behavior of a capitalistic giant like Andrew Carnegie, certain anomalies appear. The duty of a millionaire, he declared early in his life, was ''to labor not for self, but for others—'' and by the time of his death in 1919, he had succeeded in giving away (Alexander Berkman, of course, would have called it giving back) over three hundred and fifty of the four hundred million dollars his factories had amassed for him in Pittsburgh. An orbital irregularity to say the least, would you not agree, Children?

What sort of thing then is tiny Pluto in being responsible for such an unlikely perturbation?

Let us do what we can to examine the phenome-nology here by considering a simpler example of it.

> The Pennyman did for his best friend
> What the Geats did for the Dane.
> Questers! locate and read his attempt
> To transmogrify his pain.
>
> Guilt or Fear or Greed or Lust
> Is tiny Pluto's real name—
> At least that is the judgment of the world,
> Would your judgment be the same?

19

Even if the doctor hadn't ordered it, Mark would have needed no urging to stay home from school on Thursday and Friday. He hadn't even been out of bed except for the visit to the dentist to have his tooth capped. His mouth had stopped hurting, but his head ached constantly, and he felt as if he'd been kicked in the chest by a horse. Under the influence of the pain medication, he'd slept most of the two days away.

On Saturday, about noon, Merial appeared with Mark's mother at the door of his bedroom, and his heart sank over the prospect of what he was in for. He'd talked to her only once since he'd been hurt, late Thursday afternoon, when she called to see why he hadn't been in school. He'd given her only a very general account of what had happened—and without mentioning Zeena. But he had the feeling she already knew everything he told her— as well as that Zeena had been with him.

"My God," Merial said, stopping short at his doorway, one hand at her mouth.

Mark was grateful for how bad he knew he looked. His eyes had blackened, and though his lips no longer looked like raw liver, his taped nose was still swollen. The bandage for the wound in his scalp, which was really only superficial, covered his entire head from the ears up.

"It's not as bad as it looks," Mark said, smiling what he hoped would look like a brave smile. "But you can see why I didn't feel like talking."

Merial walked over to his bed. "I'm sorry you're hurt. I really am."

He nodded. "Thanks. I was pretty lucky, I guess. The doctor said that if that bottle had hit me in the temple, I could have bought it."

For a while no one said anything. Then Merial sat down stiffly on the edge of his bed. She had on a new sweater he saw and was wearing the garnet bracelet he'd bought her for Valentine's Day.

"You were down there because of your honors English project?" Merial asked flatly. Mark glanced at his mother still standing in the doorway. He was certain she'd talked to Merial; he could imagine what she'd said.

"In a way," Mark said, struggling to sit up. His mother came forward and put some pillows behind him. "You've heard all this," he said pointedly to his mother once he was propped up, but she made no move to leave the room.

There was an uncomfortable silence. "Do you mind if Merial and I talk, Mom?" Mark asked with some exasper-ation. "Jeeze."

"Oh," she said brightly. "Sorry. Of course." She smiled at Merial. "I'll go make some tea." She left Mark's bedroom and went downstairs.

Mark leaned back and closed his eyes. He didn't want to look at Merial. He didn't want to have to talk to her either.

"So what were you doing down there with Zeena Curry?"

Mark then told her about Stefan Vlastos, told her in

such a way as to emphasize his Hungarian nationality. Maybe Merial's family remembered the events or knew the church? Maybe she herself knew about Vlastos?

Merial didn't look at him while he was talking, but she didn't respond to any of his attempts to change the subject either. When he finished, she looked him full in the eyes and said, "You're a liar, Mark."

He was ashamed and angry. "What do you mean by that?" he blustered.

"You know damned well what I mean," she said, her voice ominously matter of fact. "I don't care what you want to *call* what you and Zeena are doing. You're going with her now, not with me. You're just not man enough to admit it."

"That's not true," he blazed. "It's something else with her."

She smiled and rose from the bed. It was a ghastly smile. "I'll bet it's something else," she said, looking off and smoothing her sweater over her breasts with a gesture that made his heart catch in his throat. "What, are you sleeping with her, Mark?" she asked with the same terrible bone-white smile. "Is that it? Does she let you sleep with her when you know I won't?"

"No!" he exclaimed, shocked. "That isn't it." The unfairness of the accusation made him furious. "And it's a lousy thing to say!"

"Really?" she said in a way that shriveled him. "Really?"

He looked away from her, beaten. He could feel her staring down at him.

"You're a bastard, Mark," she said evenly after a time, and then he heard her walking down the stairs. He heard her in the hall and heard the front door open and then close again. And then he heard her car start up and drive away. He looked to the photograph of Merial in a stand-

William E. Coles, Jr. · 179

up frame on the table beside his bed. It was a picture of her laughing, her hair blown across her mouth. She was hugging a snowman.

There wasn't a sound in the house but Mark knew that in a few moments his mother would come up to him. He pushed all the pillows onto the floor and lay flat on his bed, his face to the wall. After a time he heard one of the stairs creak. He knew his mother was at the doorway of his room looking at him.

"Mark?" she called softly. "I made you a cup of tea."

He didn't move, didn't respond.

"Mark," she called again. "I know you're awake. What happened? You two have a fight?"

He heard her cross the room and put the cup of tea down on his bedside table. He kept his eyes closed, his breathing regular. "Maybe you'll feel like talking later," she said finally, and he heard her go down the stairs again.

After a time, and as quietly as he could, he took up his bottle of pain pills from the table by his bed. He was to take only one every four hours. There were two left, and he took them both and then lay down again facing the wall. He thought of Merial at their dinner together, of the light shining in her eyes, and of the stab of love he'd felt for her. And then he remembered the way Zeena had held his face, the coolness of her hands when she kissed him, kissed him once, twice, and then again and again. He squeezed his eyes shut as hard as he could against all of it. And then, out of nowhere, into his head came the word "Daddy." He said it inside his head and it made his closed eyes feel hot. And then he said it again, said it softly but aloud, "Daddy." And from under his fast-shut eyes tears came, and after a while he slept.

20

Mark took off the sunglasses he'd worn for a week to hide his black eyes, but even without them the far side of the reservoir remained curtained by the drizzly April rain. Joggers, more of them than he thought there would be on such a day, moved through the mist like ghosts. He made Zeena out as soon as she materialized, all legs in her black tights, moving in a kind of slow motion lope. She was running the reservoir in a different direction from almost everybody else, Mark noticed. He turned his back to the rail and leaned against it, waiting for her.

"Hey, Zeen," he called. She'd have run right by him if he hadn't spoken. She lurched to a stop, eyes wide as though she'd been shaken from sleep. For a moment she just stood looking at him, chest heaving. And then, with her hands on her hips, elbows jutted out behind her, she walked slowly over to where he was standing. She had on a black sweatband. Her face was high with color and streaked with sweat and rain.

"Hi," he said softly, suddenly embarrassed. "I had a feeling you'd be up here. I just wondered . . . how you're doing." He put his sunglasses back on.

She nodded without saying anything, catching her breath.

For a week she'd put him off about working on Assignment 6. Because they'd kissed the way they had? Because he'd been hurt? Because he'd told her he and Merial had broken up? Whatever, she wanted "space" she gave Mark to understand, and something told him not to push things. Until today he hadn't.

They leaned on the rail together, looking out into the grey mist over the water. Zeena took off her terry cloth sweatband and squeezed it, dripping a stream down onto the concrete curb beyond the railing. She sweat heavily, just the way he did, he realized, and he thought of the feel of her hands on his face and the smell of her hair and of her body slick and slippery in her tights.

"I miss you," he heard himself say to her.

She put her hand on his arm and patted it lightly. "Take your sunglasses off," she said, sending jolts through him.

He did and she peered at his eyes.

"I'm all healed if that's what you're wondering."

She nodded. "It really wasn't Silk—or anybody connected with him—at the church. I know that for a fact."

"Okay," he said, wondering how she could know it for a fact.

"Look," she said. "How about we meet at the Carnegie this Saturday morning? We'll go back to work."

"Only if you're ready," he said. "It's okay if you're not."

"Oh, I'm ready for *that*," she said easily. "It's . . . everything else, if you know what I mean."

No, he thought to himself, he didn't know what she meant. But he didn't have the courage to ask about it.

She shivered slightly and then zipped up her partially open windbreaker. "Let's walk," she said, turning from the rail and putting her hands in her jacket pockets. "I don't want to catch cold."

He fell in beside her, and they walked for a time in silence.

"What makes you so sure Silk wasn't involved in what happened to me?"

She shrugged. "I asked him. How else?" And then she added, "Which he didn't exactly appreciate."

He stopped her from walking with a hand on her arm.

"What is it with you two anyway? Are you going with the guy or not?"

She didn't respond immediately. Then she nodded and said, "Okay. It's a fair question. But I'd like you to tell me something, too. I want to know *how* you and Merial broke up. I mean how exactly—and *don't* say there's nothing to tell. This is important."

He nodded, not knowing whether she meant he was to go first or not, but he spoke anyway. "She came over to my house last Saturday; I told you that. I didn't ask her over, she just came. The first thing she asked was what was I doing at the church with you."

"How'd she know we were together?"

"I'm not sure. I know I didn't tell her. Maybe my mom did, but I have a feeling she knew even before she was at my house."

"Okay, then what?"

"I talked about Vlastos. It was just smoke and she knew it. She called me a liar. She said I was . . . that I was going with you now. Then she called me a bastard and left."

Zeena took a deep breath and then audibly let it out again. She went to the rail of the reservoir and gazed out over the smoky-looking water. Mark came up beside her

"I didn't say a word about the quest," he said. "Not a word."

"And you haven't talked to each other since? Either on the phone or face to face?"

He shook his head. "What for?" What was she trying to put together?

"What *exactly* did Merial say she thought was going on with us? Did she ask you whether you were having sex with me?"

It shocked him the same way Merial's question had, and he was tempted to lie but didn't. "Yeah, she did—and I told her no—and I told her it was a lousy question too."

Zeena compressed her lips into a line. "Did she . . . say anything about me? Or ask anything else?"

"No," he said. And then he added deliberately, "Not then she didn't."

She looked up quickly. "When then? What'd she say?"

"The night we had dinner she said you didn't know what you wanted."

Zeena chewed her lower lip for a moment and then looked off, smiling wryly. "She's got a point."

When she didn't go on, Mark said, "I have some questions, too, remember?"

Zeena took one of his hands and half turning from him pointed down the path. "Let's sit down for a minute, okay."

Mark felt the wet of the bench through his jeans the moment they sat. She hadn't, he was acutely conscious, dropped his hand. In fact, she covered it with her other hand.

"See," she said, with the same self-deprecating smile he'd seen her father use. "I'm not even supposed to be here still, in Pittsburgh I mean. We were all supposed to go to Cincinnati together, me and Mom and Robbie and my dad. Our whole family. Dad got a big job at the University there, and we were all supposed to move together."

Then she did drop his hand. She raised her knees up under her chin and clasped them, resting her sneakers on the edge of the bench.

"My dad kind of . . . won it. He was head of this big research project at Pitt and, well, he and his team had this big breakthrough, after over a year of work. He had his picture in the paper, and they got a lot of awards and—" She stopped herself. After a time she went on, "There was this woman, see, a graduate student who worked on the project with my . . . with him, and he . . . well, he got involved with her."

She put her forehead down on her raised knees and rested it there a moment. Then she looked up and out over the reservoir. "I even knew her. Our whole family knew her. Dad used to bring her home to eat with us when they were working all those crazy hours, and she gave us Christmas presents . . ."

Zeena's mouth tightened.

"My mother made that bitch meals. She was married, too. And she was white, and I thought she was wonderful, can you imagine? Just wonderful. I really did. I even fixed her stuff to eat sometimes."

She stopped, though Mark knew she wasn't finished.

"You know how my mom found out? She didn't find out herself. My dad told her. *Told* her, can you believe that?—and how the whole thing with the woman was all over now, and how sorry he was now. Mom made him leave the same day, the day after Christmas it was that he moved out, and the next fall he left for Cincinnati. He wanted me to come with him, and for a while . . ." she made a strange gesture with one hand as though to ward something off. Then she went on. "Anyway, right in here is where things get kind of crazy. Mom was doing all this stuff with the Coalition. I mean she still does, but she was really into it then, and there were always a lot of people around the house, night and day, and one of them was Silk. I knew who he was from school, of course, but . . . see, he was putting the Black Action Society together then, and Mom was helping him. She likes Silk, likes the way he thinks about the black community and stuff like that."

Zeena put her legs down and hunched forward, resting her forearms on her knees. It had begun to rain a little harder, softly, but a little harder.

"Actually," she said, "I like the way he thinks too."

She took another deep breath.

"Anyway, I started to get involved with this guy who was always around the house, not Silk, somebody else, a guy who was older, and Mom got worried and so she asked him, Silk, I mean, to . . . sort of look after me."

She looked over at Mark, her face working. "But I didn't know that, see? Mom never told me. So when I met him up here, and we talked, I didn't know he was just . . . I didn't know that all he was doing was keeping the honey bees off me." She paused. "Like a babysitter or something."

Mark waited for her to go on, but she didn't. He didn't want to ask, but he felt he had to. "So you were . . . in love with him then?"

She didn't answer right away. "I guess I was," she said simply after a time. No tone. No feeling.

He took her by the wrist and said, "Is there a chance for you and me? That's . . . that would be enough. I want there to be a chance for you and me."

She dropped her head. The rain began to fall harder, making the reservoir sound as though it were starting to boil. "Oh God, Mark," she said. "Look—"

"I'm not just a . . . honey bee," he interrupted. "I want

another kind of Monday too, just the way you said in your poem. But I want it with you. *With* you."

"Oh, I know you're not a honey bee," she said, looking up quickly. "I know that." And then she smiled though her eyes were filled with tears. "Really," she said. "I do know that."

"All right then," he said, drawing her to him. "That's enough for now then."

21

Behind the small black aide who led him, the Pennyman rolled down the length of the visitor's lounge like a balloon filled with water. He was a huge man, hairless as an egg. His maroon and white seersucker bathrobe hung around him like a carnival tent.

"These are some of your children, Harry," the aide said as she steered him into a chair opposite Mark and Zeena. "Ain't that nice?" She herself did not sit down.

The aide said "chillen" for "children" and "dat" for "that." She was small but very alert. Her sleek, dark head reminded Mark of an otter's. She could have been thirty; she could have been fifty-five.

Mark and Zeena were at Hawthorne Psychiatric Hospital, a long-term commitment facility located about twenty miles outside Pittsburgh. They'd been ushered through two locked doors to a small oval table by a bored-looking but muscular male attendant who seemed to move away from them as soon as they were seated. But he hadn't moved very far, Mark noticed, and he was only one of several such men leaning against the walls of the lounge. A number of patients and visitors were sitting at the tables, all of which were surrounded by gaily-colored, molded plastic chairs. The chairs were moveable; the tables were bolted to the floor. A row of wire-meshed windows ran along the outside wall of the lounge, but too high up for anyone to see out of.

The Pennyman had been in Hawthorne for six years. Like everyone else in his part of the hospital, he was probably going to be there for life. He dug elaborately into his bathrobe pocket, extracted a penny and held it out to Zeena, smiling the sweet toothless smile of a baby. She took it with one hand and put it on the open palm of the other, where it lay shining like red gold. And then the Pennyman gave Mark a penny too.

"Harry polishes those all by hisself, don't you, Harry?" the aide said, smiling down at him. She was standing at his shoulder with one hand resting lightly on it. "Makes them all clean and shiny for his friends."

The Pennyman turned his great moon face to look up at her. "Yes," he said, still smiling and nodding. "Pennies for the children." His voice was surprisingly clear and full. He dug another penny out of his bathrobe and handed it up to her. "You, too, 'Manda," he said.

"Why, thank you, Harry," she said, slipping the penny into the pocket of her uniform. Mark heard it clink very faintly and saw the aide smile at the attendant leaning against the wall.

"You knew Harry, did you?" she asked Mark and Zeena casually. But her eyes weren't casual at all.

"Well, no," Mark said, "not exactly." He took off his sunglasses and smiled. There were still black smudges under his eyes. "But we heard about him."

The aide looked down at the top of the Pennyman's smooth bald head and ran the back of one hand softly down his cheek. "Lots of people *heard* about Harry," she said. "He don't get company much though. Whachall want with him?"

The Pennyman paid no attention to the conversation. He sat gazing at the room beyond Mark and Zeena, his face as peaceful as a lake.

"My momma knew him," Zeena put in, "when she was little bitty."

The aide gave Zeena a quick, appraising look. "Where was that, honey?"

"Around East Liberty, Highland Park. By Carnegie School. Momma said he used to wait there by the crossing guard and pass out pennies to the children. Summer and winter, she said."

It was true what Zeena was saying about the Pennyman and her mother. Indeed, it was Zeena's mother, asked only out of frustration, who'd identified him for her daughter after Zeena and Mark had spent more than a week trying to run down who the Pennyman was from the verse clue of Assignment 6:

> The Pennyman did for his best friend
> What the Geats did for the Dane.
> Questers! locate and read his attempt
> To transmogrify his pain.
>
> Guilt or Fear or Greed or Lust
> Is tiny Pluto's real name—
> At least that is the judgment of the world,
> Would your judgment be the same?

Their way into things finally had been with the line "What the Geats did for the Dane." Mrs. Harbinger had been no help with it, but their English teacher had. Ms. Hunter told Zeena that the famous old English epic poem *Beowulf*—there had been a reference to it in Assignment 2, Mark remembered—had both Geats and Danes in it and suggested that "the Dane" might be a reference to Beowulf himself, the poem's hero. It was, as Zeena discovered in her reading of the poem, and what the Geats had done for him was to erect a barrow to his memory. "Barrow," the dictionary defined as "a heap of earth or rocks serving as a monument to mark a grave."

Okay then. The Pennyman had to be the nickname of somebody from Pittsburgh the way Frick had been known as The Coke King. What Mark and Zeena had to find was the monument this figure had erected to the memory of his best friend. Once they knew that, they'd have a way to Assignment 7.

Except that they could find no Pittsburgh figure, public or private, known as the Pennyman. No librarian they talked to had ever heard of such a person, nor had anyone at either of the two historical societies in the city. But Zeena's mother not only knew who he was, she remembered him waiting for the children to be let out of school. Even in the rain he'd wait, she said, dripping water as unself-consciously as a tree. Big as a mountain he'd seemed. Reliable as God.

Still alive? Oh, no, Zeena's mother said, shaking her head. She was afraid not. An awful thing had happened, seven years ago, eight was it? A terrible thing. One night in the winter, while sleeping by a dumpster in the center of East Liberty, the Pennyman had been set afire. That was what had killed him.

But it was from the East Liberty police that Mark and Zeena learned the Pennyman had survived—and also that he'd been sent out to Hawthorne under the name of Harry Smith. No one seemed to know his real name, not even the Pennyman himself.

"You momma went to Carnegie School?" exclaimed the

aide, instantly animated. "Shoot. *I* went to Carnegie. How's you momma called?"

"Dora. Dora Neale."

"Why shoot," Amanda said laughing. "You *Dora's* girl? I know you momma. How's she taking herself?"

"Just fine, thank you," Zeena replied, smiling, her face coloring slightly. "Just fine."

"Well, you tell her Amanda Gates asked for her. She still up there in Highland Park?"

"No, Miss Amanda, we're on Rural Street now, in East Liberty."

"She was real smart, you momma. Set on college even back then. Full of fire. She get to be a doctor, like she wanted?"

"No, but she did go to college. She went to Pitt. She works for the East Liberty Coalition now."

"Well!" Amanda said delightedly. "Well, now! This here's Dora's girl," she said to the Pennyman, giving his shoulder a little shake. "You used to give us pennies outside Carnegie School way back. What do you think of that?"

The Pennyman turned again to smile up at her and again dug out and reached her up a penny. She dropped it in her pocket. Then he gave Mark and Zeena pennies too. "Pennies for the children," he said solemnly, "pennies for candy," and he went back behind his mild, grey eyes.

"He don't remember nothing, really. Poor man don't even know his real name. Used to beg his pennies all morning, shine them up real nice with steel wool, and give them away in the afternoon to the children." She patted Harry's shoulder. "He just a child hisself really. Not a mean bone in him. Never hurt nobody, but they burned him anyway. Just look here." She moved the Pennyman's bathrobe down off his neck. "See that?" she said, nodding her head at the mass of scar tissue. "He like that most all over. He just asleep there, and they douse him with gasoline and burn him for fun. Burn him for meanness. But we take real good care of him, don't we, Harry?"

The Pennyman smiled while continuing to look into the distance.

Zeena shook her head. "I can't understand how anybody'd do a thing like that."

Amanda shrugged. "Ain't never no reason for meanness."

"The police said they never found out who did it," Mark said.

Amanda shook her head. "Could have been anybody. Lot of riff-raff in East Liberty, and everybody know Harry sleep by that dumpster all winter. He live on scraps out of the bakery. Man stuff his pockets with scraps every morning for him and his dogs."

"He had a friend, too, didn't he?" Mark asked. "He must have had a friend."

"Naw. Harry all alone. Just hisself. Didn't have no friends. Just his dogs."

"What do you mean, his dogs?"

"Dogs in the holler, down by the zoo. They wasn't really *his* dogs. They was wile dogs, really, but they Harry's friends till the police shot 'em," Amanda said. She rubbed the Pennyman's shoulder. "They you friends, wasn't they, Harry?"

The killing of wild dogs in the hollow Mark could remember. He'd had bad dreams about it when he was in elementary school. "Wolf was my friend," the Pennyman said, turning to look up at Amanda. "My best friend."

Mark looked quickly at Zeena. "*Wolf* was his best friend," he said to her in a low but excited voice. "Wolf, like Beowulf. Maybe he made a barrow for that dog somewhere."

"Did Wolf . . . did your best friend . . . did he die?" Mark asked the Pennyman. "And did you . . . bury him, or anything like that?"

"Wolf was my best friend," the Pennyman said gravely. "Wolf's in church."

"In what church?" Mark asked, leaning across the small table and taking the Pennyman by the arm. "Did you *put* him in a church somewhere? Did you build him a church?"

The Pennyman looked down at Mark's hand on his arm and then up at Mark again. He began drawing himself back in his chair, his mouth opening, a look of fear in his eyes.

"Mark, let go," Zeena said, taking his elbow, and Mark did.

"Don't be grabbing Harry," Amanda said sharply, taking a step in Mark's direction. "He don't like it. Whachoo two want here anyway?" The attendant who had shown them in straightened up attentively.

"It's for . . . for a project in local history, Miss Amanda," Zeena said. "Around in Highland Park and East Liberty? The whole East End. I'm sorry if we upset Harry. See, he's sort of a . . . like a legend in East Liberty, but nobody knows anything about him for sure. Momma thought he was dead. Do you know . . . where he came from, or anything like that?"

"I told you. Harry don't even know his name his own self," Amanda said. "He don't live nowhere except by the dumpsters and in the holler with the dogs. That's how he be here. He got no home. No name, no home."

Zeena opened her hand and held out her two bright

pennies to the Pennyman. "Thank you for my pennies, Harry," she said, smiling at him. "They're beautiful."

"Pennies for candy," The Pennyman said with great seriousness.

"Did you make pennies for Wolf, too?" Zeena asked him.

"No," the Pennyman said, shaking his head. "I made a church."

"You *made* a church?" Mark said. "Did you build Wolf a church somewhere? In the hollow? Down by the zoo?"

"A church for Wolf," The Pennyman said. "Wolf was my best friend." He dropped his great, hairless head onto his chest, took a deep, deep breath, and then groaned it out in a long heartbreaking moan. And then he began to cry, silently at first, his body shaking, but in a moment with a kind of a wail, like a child.

"Hush, now," Amanda said, sinking to her knees beside him and putting her arm around his huge convulsing shoulders. "Hush, now, Harry. They be going now. We get you some more pennies to shine."

But the Pennyman paid no attention. He looked up straight at Zeena, and his mouth formed itself into a large round O. "Ohwaa!" he wailed, and then again, more drawn out and even louder, "Ohwaaaaa!"

As the attendant moved smoothly from the wall to the Pennyman's side, a number of other people in the room turned to look. Zeena and Mark came to their feet. "It's all right, Harry," Zeena said. "Please don't cry."

Abruptly, the Pennyman stopped crying and looked straight at Zeena. And then, as if in some way cued, he took a deep breath, threw back his enormous head, and howled again, but it was no longer the cry of a child. It was a pure animal sound and it went through the visitors' lounge like a siren, driving Mark and Zeena back from their chairs.

"See?" Amanda hissed at them. Both she and the attendant had their arms around the Pennyman. "See what you done?"

There were loud voices in the lounge and a sudden shriek of terror. A woman in a wheelchair swiveled around from one of the tables near them and rolled herself up to Mark and Zeena. She was sitting, Mark thought at first, cross-legged, but then he realized that she had no legs. "Liars!" she cried to Mark and Zeena. "Liars!"

And then the Pennyman put back his head and howled once more, an even longer cry this time and of incredible force.

"Liars!" the legless woman cried out again, and to the right of her Mark saw a man in a bathrobe fall, twisting to the floor. There was more shouting, and two additional male attendants came bursting through a door at the far end of the lounge and hurried toward them.

"You two *git*!" Amanda roared at Mark and Zeena from her knees. She was still holding tight to the Pennyman. "Just git out of here! Go!"

22

The hollow dividing Highland Park from Morningside was like an enormous funnel, the mouth of which had been turned into a huge asphalt parking lot for the Pittsburgh Zoo. Mark drove through the almost empty lot and parked at its narrow end by a chain-link fence topped with strands of barbed wire. Behind the fence was a vast unpaved yard owned by the city and filled with what looked like highway maintenance material: piles of sand and gravel, rows of massive concrete bumpers, heaps of cobblestones. On its far side the yard ended at the edge of a wood.

"In there," Mark said, pointing at the trees. "He must have lived back in there."

He and Zeena wormed around the edge of the fence closest to them and then picked their way across the heavily rutted maintenance yard. At the wood they stopped. Up close it looked as impenetrable as a wall.

"How far back in do you think this goes?" Zeena asked, peering up at the wrist-thick vines. Her hands were jammed tight into her windbreaker pockets.

"Can't be that far. We're almost at the end of the hollow."

"And you really think there's . . . a barrow in there?"

Mark shrugged. "We know this is where the dogs were killed. We're just going to have to go in and see." He said it with a lot more nonchalance than he felt. The newspaper pictures of the wild dogs the police had trapped and shot in the hollow had given him nightmares. They were pitiful-looking creatures in a way, gaunt and mangy, but even in death their bared teeth had been as menacing to him as drawn swords.

"How'd he get in there, do you think? He's a big man. Maybe he came down the hill the other side of this stuff."

"It'd be too much of a drop. Too much of a climb up too. He had to go in and out along here somewhere. There has to be a path." Mark walked off to his right. "Look along that edge," he said to her.

"But won't a path be overgrown by now?" he heard her call, and he turned to see she was still standing where he'd left her. "He's been out at Hawthorne six years, Mark."

He bit back the impulse to tell her to get moving. "Well," he said, "we won't know till we look, will we?" And he turned from her and continued walking. Merial wouldn't have acted the way she was acting, he couldn't help thinking.

There was again some kind of distance between him and Zeena that he didn't understand. It had started the night they'd seen the Pennyman. Was it that she blamed him for what had happened? She said not, but since their trip to Hawthorne, Mark hadn't been able to bring himself to so much as hold her hand.

He kicked irritably at the dead weeds he was walking through. High up on the hill to his right he could see the houses of Morningside, gleaming like new toys in the bright April sunshine, but none of the light seemed to come down into the hollow. He'd seen nothing like a path. When he turned, he saw Zeena crouched, hands still in her windbreaker pockets, looking into the wood. She was almost at the far side of the hollow where the trees met the cliff face that rose to the zoo far above.

"Anything?" he yelled.

"I'm not sure," she called back.

He ran over to her. She'd gone to her knees and was pointing into the undergrowth.

It was more a tunnel than a path, and not much beyond a suggestion of that. A number of thick vines had been hacked off about three feet above the ground so as to make a kind of passageway that ran straight in for a space of perhaps ten yards, and then seemed to bend sharply to the right. The cut vines had been seized and bridged by a number of new ones. To one side of the passageway, not very far into the woods, was a mound covered with leaves.

"The barrow!" Mark exclaimed. "*Has* to be!"

Zeena looked up to the vine-covered trees towering above them. "I'll bet that's all poison ivy," she said.

Mark shrugged. "Some of it probably is. So we'll wash." He dropped to all fours and crawled into the tunnel.

It was hard going. The new vines were as tough as rope and kept catching on his backpack, but he wormed his way to the mound and cleared away the leaves. It was nothing but a pile of rusty tin cans, all of them mashed and torn as though they'd burst at the center. Then Mark looked closely at several of them and realized what he was seeing. The cans hadn't exploded open; they'd been chewed open.

"Is it the barrow?" Zeena called in to him. Lying on his side, he could see her face just past his feet.

"No," he said, "it's just trash." He took his knife from the backpack and continued crawling through the tunnel.

In his mind's eye he could still see the Pennyman's white moon face baying at the ceiling.

At the bend, suddenly, there was room to stand, and Mark rose into what felt like an enormous grotto. So thickly intertwined were the vines and tree branches above him that even this early in the spring they shut out virtually all direct light. There was almost no underbrush. What looked like a path stretched out before him.

He heard Zeena in the underbrush, and in a few moments they were standing together.

"What about the poison ivy?" he asked her.

"We'll wash," she said, but with what tone he couldn't be sure.

For a few moments they just stood together in the strange filtered light, and then Mark started down the path and she followed. After twisting about for maybe fifty yards, it ended in a small clearing.

"What's that?" Mark said, pointing off to the left.

Even under the vines and dead leaves that had almost buried it, they could make out the rectangular structure of cobblestones, piled as a child might build with blocks. The top was tapered, suggesting a peaked roof. Wolf's church. Mark and Zeena walked over to it.

Up close, they could see that part of the roof had fallen over. There was a scattering of cobbles on the ground by one end of the structure and, lying among them, a star of two triangles made of sticks and held together with wire. It fell to pieces when Mark picked it up.

Zeena sank to her knees and Mark knelt beside her. The cobble he picked up was about twice the size of a brick and was surprisingly heavy. One face was worn smooth as though the stone had been polished by years of flowing water.

"He must have brought these in from the yard," Mark said. "I saw a big pile of cobbles out there."

Zeena sat on her heels and looked at the structure. "Must have taken a lot of trips."

Neither of them spoke for a while.

"I'm sorry we upset him, Mark," Zeena said after a time. "I mean I'm really sorry."

He nodded without looking at her. "I am too."

"Let me ask you something," she said after a moment. "If you'd *known* we were going to upset him, I mean the way we did; if you'd known we were going to *have* to do that to . . . to go on with the quest, would you have done it anyway?"

He sat down and drew his knees to his chest. Then he put his arms around them and leaned his forehead on his knees. "I guess so," he said after a time.

"Me, too," she said grimly. "It's like somebody's seeing just how much we'll do for money."

Was it that she saw them as grave robbing? Was that what was wrong? He looked up and cleared his throat. "Okay," he said, "what do you say to this? We'll take the stones off one layer at a time and put them back exactly the way they were. If we come to . . . bones, or anything like that . . . well . . ." Then he pointed at the scattered cobbles, off to one side of the crudely built church. "I think that some of those stones over there once made like a steeple or a bell tower. I'll put it back when we're done, so it'll be like it was when he made it." After a time he added, "And I'll make a new star too. Or a cross."

For a moment she just stared at the barrow. And then she nodded.

They brushed off the dead leaves. Then, gently, they lifted off the vines that had grown over the cobbles and began to remove the stones, layer by layer, arranging them in order so that they could replace them exactly. There were three layers of cobblestones, laid end to end, making the peaked roof, one stone on top of two on top of three; the body of the structure was five cobbles wide and six deep. Two layers down, in about the middle of the structure, was the black plastic packet. It was heavy and felt hard, as though it contained a stone.

"Let's fix the church first," Mark said, and they did. The church had indeed had a kind of bell tower, which Mark topped with a cross of two green sticks tied together with a bit of his shoelace. Then he and Zeena carefully replaced the vines over everything.

"There," he said from his knees. "I hope that's okay with . . . both of them."

Zeena had gotten to her feet beside him. She put her hand on his shoulder. He wanted to reach out to her, to take her hand, but didn't.

"You know," he said, "we could . . . maybe take a box of pennies out to the hospital with some steel wool. We could leave them for Amanda with a note, saying . . . we were sorry."

She withdrew her hand from his shoulder and for a moment didn't say anything. "Yes," she said after a time. "Let's do that."

He got to his feet and picked up the plastic-wrapped packet and hefted it. "Maybe we better get out of here. You're probably right about the poison ivy."

Zeena was about to respond when a sound froze them both. Deep and full, it filled the whole of the hollow. It was as though the hollow itself had moaned.

"My God!" Mark heard himself exclaim, his skin crawling. "Did you hear that?"

Zeena smiled at him. "It's the tigers I wrote about. From the zoo."

They stood waiting, waiting. But the sound was not repeated.

"It's like that sometimes," Zeena said. "Sometimes it's only once they roar—or that one does. I don't know why." She knelt again. "Let's read the assignment here, all right?"

He sat down next to her and handed her the packet. Then he gave her his knife. "You open it."

There were two envelopes, one of them taped to a rectangular piece of pale white stone. Embedded in one face of the stone were what looked to Mark like small animal teeth or perhaps bone fragments. Either by chance or design, they formed a rough circle with radiating lines suggesting a sun. The assignment was in the taped envelope. They read it together in the twilight of the woods, she holding it, he looking over her shoulder:

Assignment 7

So far out is Pluto, so far out at the rim of everything, mere flotsam in space you might say, Children, of origin unknown, of composition uncertain, maverick in its inclination, eccentric of orbit, not even visible except under very special conditions—no wonder it has been doubted as there at all, let alone imagined as counting for very much.

What do you think, though, Children? What would you say? Does the Pennyman matter? And what is in him: What does it count for?

Perhaps the perspective of time can help.

Full fathom five this life form lay,
Or rather a fifth that measure squared,

Before the Brilliant Cut that day
Evolution's story shared.

In what the famous eyes became,
The coral bones of its colleagues hide
The way to the end of this journey, Friends—
And to a view of the other side.

"Well," Mark said, "we're almost done, Zeen. 'The way to the end of this journey, Friends.' Open the other envelope."

Zeena did and counted out the hundred-dollar bills onto the ground between them—all of them brand new as always, and as always with consecutive serial numbers that ran up from those on the bills they'd already been given. There were twenty-four of them.

Mark breathed a low whistle. "This is serious money."

Zeena picked up the piece of stone the assignment had been taped to and peered at it. "What is this thing?" she asked. "A fossil?"

"Something like that. Looks like we have to find out where it came from." He got to his feet, but she did not.

"What do you think's going on here?" she said to him without looking up. "I mean what do you think's *really* going on?"

There were several things she might mean. He knelt beside her. "What are you getting at?"

"Why such a funny amount, for one thing—twenty-four hundred dollars; seventeen last time. Not some round number like five or ten. And why so much? Two thousand four hundred dollars is a little scary, don't you think?"

Mark picked up the sheaf of bills and riffled the money with his thumb, once, twice, three times. Then he put the bills back on the ground. "You know what I thought once? I thought maybe it was my father setting up the quest." He smiled briefly. "It's not though. I know it isn't."

She didn't say anything, but he could feel her looking at him.

"What I mean," he said, turning to her, "is that I'm not a sucker for this guy the way I was. We're not his children. We're not his friends either."

"You don't think he's out to . . . hurt us, or anything, do you?"

He thought for quite a while before he answered.

"I don't know what he's doing, why he gives us the amounts of money he does, what he's getting at with all this stuff about the stars. The whole thing about the quest I don't understand. I don't know what we're supposed to be learning or seeing. But I think what really matters is that we're almost at the end, and he promised us a payoff. And so far he's always come through."

23

"Mark," his mother said to him that night at dinner in a tone that made him pause with his fork and look up at her, "I . . . we have something to . . . something we want to tell you."

Mark glanced quickly at Guy who was watching his mother and then looked back to her. She was looking down, her hands resting on the table on either side of her plate. She'd only picked at her shrimp casserole, he noticed, but Guy had finished his. Somehow, Mark knew exactly what it was she was going to say.

"Guy and I have decided to get married this summer."

"Hey, great," Mark heard himself say. He could feel both Guy and his mother looking at him. "I mean it," he repeated, putting down his fork. "I think it's really great. I hope you'll be very happy."

"We . . . wanted to tell you together," his mother said, putting her hand over his and squeezing it.

"Yes," he said, nodding. "I can see that." He looked down at his mother's hand on his. "I hope you'll be very happy."

"Thank you, Mark," Guy said.

"Yes, love," his mother echoed, squeezing his hand again. "Thank you."

For a while no one spoke.

Guy cleared his throat. "It's probably something of a shock," he said.

"Well," Mark said. "Maybe." And then he added, "But not really, I guess." He thought gratefully of the money hidden in the bottom drawer of his desk.

Mark's mother removed her hand from his and straightened the unused silverware by her place. "We thought July," she said. "Both of you will be out of school—" she laughed nervously, "both my men—and we thought we'd have it here. At home. Out on the deck maybe, if the weather's warm."

Mark looked out the dining room window at the deck his father had built and thought of the heat of August, locusts singing, iced tea. "You're going to get married on the deck?"

"Well, yes," his mother said, sliding her gold bracelet up onto her forearm. "That would be nice, don't you think?"

"It's going to be a very small wedding, Mark," Guy put in.

"Oh, very small," Mark's mother said. "Just a few friends, but we'd like to have Merial, of course. There'll be plenty of room for the wedding. The living space problem we can take care of later."

Mark looked at her. "What do you mean, the living space problem?"

"Ev—" Guy started, but Mark interrupted him.

"What do you mean?" he repeated, looking steadily at his mother.

"Well," his mother said sunnily, "another nice thing is that we were thinking of getting a new house, a bigger one with a bigger yard. This is the main selling season you know, spring and summer, and there're going to be some really nice places coming on the market soon."

"You mean we're going to *move?*"

"Not that way, Mark," Guy said. "We want to get something in this same area—close to Pitt—and we want all three of us to look at places together."

"Of course you wouldn't *have* to live with us at all if . . . if you'd rather live down at Pitt next fall," Mark's mother said. "We could swing that I think, financially I mean, if it's what you wanted. You could . . . we could even see about you getting an apartment."

"But we'd like you to live with us, Mark," Guy said.

"Oh, yes, of course," his mother added quickly. "Your home'll always be with us."

Mark glanced again at the deck outside the dining room windows. "Well," he said off-handedly, "I'm going to get my own apartment all right, but I don't know about Pitt in the fall. I may just work for a while, do something besides school for a change." He knew he had spoken heresy so far as his mother was concerned.

"But you're already accepted at Pitt for the fall."

"Look, all I said was I'm not sure yet what I'm going to do. I can pay you back the deposit, if that's what you're worried about. I can pay for my apartment myself too."

"Ev," Guy said, "I think you better tell Mark about the money that's being held in trust for him."

Mark's mother's face went chalky. She stared at Guy with wide, frightened eyes.

"Come on, Ev," Guy said, his voice calm but firm. "He's going to know anyway. He has a right to know now. We agreed, remember?"

Mark felt a prickling at the base of his spine. He watched as his mother took a sip of water and then set her glass down carefully.

"Your father's sent money for you," she said without meeting his eyes. "Not to me, to a lawyer downtown. It's being held in trust for you. It's . . . enough for you to go to Pitt for four years."

For a time Mark could do nothing but stare. There was a ringing in his ears. "When did he do this?" he heard himself ask. His mother remained quite still, but Mark had the sense she was twisting inside her skin.

"Well, for a while."

"For a while? What do you mean, 'for a while'?"

Mark's mother continued to look down at the table in front of her. She did not respond. Guy cleared his throat and then said, "Mark, your father's sent money for you ever since he left Pittsburgh. Every month. He never missed. Part of it was child support ordered by the court. That went—" he nodded at Mark's mother—"directly to Ev through your father's lawyer. But for the last five or six years your father's been sending extra money to the lawyer for you. It's being held in trust for you, this was your father's stipulation, until you graduate from high school."

Guy glanced at Mark's mother and then looked back at Mark.

"It's important you understand that this money is yours to do with whatever you want. No strings attached. It's a good sum, too. Forty or fifty thousand dollars by this time."

Mark had no way of placing anything he'd heard. "You never told me you got child support money for me," he said to his mother.

"I . . . I assumed you knew," Mark's mother said helplessly.

"No," Mark said after a space of time. "No, you didn't. You just plain lied. You let me think he never sent you anything. That's what you wanted me to think, wasn't it?"

"I . . . I don't know. I don't know."

"Why didn't you let me know?"

She dropped her head and shook it slowly without speaking.

"Damn it all, *why?*" Mark barked, slapping the table with his hand at the same time. Both his mother and Guy jumped at the sound.

"Ev," Guy said, "please remember we agreed that Mark ought to know now."

It infuriated Mark. "Don't talk about me like that!" he said to Guy savagely. "As though I wasn't here!"

"I was afraid, Mark!" his mother cried. "I was afraid." Her eyes had filled with tears.

"Of what?"

"I don't know. Of losing you, I guess."

Again, there was silence at the table.

"Did *he* want me to know?"

"No. That is, he never said so. His lawyer never said so. If he'd said he wanted you to know, I'd have told you."

"And he still sends money every month?"

"He still puts money in your trust every month. I haven't got any since your eighteenth birthday."

He nodded.

"You still should have told me, Mother," Mark said after a while.

"Maybe I should have, Mark. Maybe I should have."

"I have a right to know."

She looked down and nodded without saying anything.

Mark rose from the table and stood at his place. He looked down at his unfinished dinner, then at Guy, then at his mother. He felt bigger than the two of them. He felt strong.

"I want to know something else," he said. "I want to know why my father left us—and I *don't* want to hear that he just couldn't handle having a family."

For a while his mother just stared at him. There were tears on her cheeks, but her expression he couldn't read. All of a sudden, her mouth twisted and she looked out the window. "I don't think that's what I said."

"Yeah, it is," Mark said to her. "And that's all you'd say. I want to know all of it. And I want to know the truth."

At first his mother, continuing to look out the window, didn't move, didn't speak. And then she turned and looked directly up at Mark. "He thought I'd taken up with another man," she said. She held up one hand palm outward as though commanding something to stop, and added, "I hadn't, of course, but he wouldn't believe me."

Mark and his mother stared at one another.

"Who?" he asked her.

"Who?" she echoed, gesturing in puzzlement. "Your father."

"I mean who was the other man?"

"What difference does it make? A man he worked with. Nobody you know—or have ever heard of. He and his wife were our friends."

"What was his name, Mother?" He had no idea why he was pushing her as he was. What difference *did* it make who the man was?

"Mark, please," she said, her eyes filling with tears again. "His name was Ed."

"Ed who, goddamn it!" Mark ripped out at her, slamming his palm down on the table again.

"Ed MacAlster was his name. Are you satisfied?"

Again Mark and his mother stared at each other.

"So . . . why'd he think that, Mother? Why'd my father think you were . . . sleeping with this guy?" He could not believe he was talking as he was.

She looked down and shook her head. "Mark, don't,"

she said, her voice breaking. "Please don't. It wasn't true. It wasn't true."

"Mark," Guy tried, but Mark turned his back to him.

"So . . . he just left, is that it?" he went on.

She nodded, her head still down. "He just left," she said, sobbing. "Took his clothes and the car and left."

He looked down at his mother's heaving shoulders, at her thick, dark hair, dark as a raven's wing, and into his mind came an image of her naked in a bed, moaning with pleasure. He shivered as though with a chill.

"Why . . . why didn't he ever want to see me again?" Mark asked her in a voice that didn't sound to him like his voice at all. His mother glanced up at him quickly and leaned forward to take his hand. He pulled it away as though it had been burned. "Why?" he asked again.

"Now listen to me, Mark," his mother said firmly. "All I know is it had nothing to do with you. Nothing. It was *me* he didn't ever want to see again."

"Where is he?"

"I don't know. I honest to God *do not know*. He went to Alaska from here. I found that out from the electric company. But that was years ago."

"And you've never heard from him?"

She shook her head. "Never. That's the truth."

"Was there . . . did he ever send, like a note for me, or anything like that?"

"No. Anything like that I'd have told you about."

"Maybe he sent something to the lawyer?"

She shook her head.

"Did he ever?—" Mark started, but then he stopped himself with a brief contemptuous laugh. "Forget it," he said. "It was a stupid question." He turned as if to leave the table but then turned abruptly back. "You can tell him to shove his fifty thousand dollars, by the way. I don't need it and I don't need him." He glanced from his mother to Guy. They looked at him like a pair of dolls. "And I don't need you two either," he said and went up to his room.

For a while Mark simply sat at his desk staring at nothing. After a time, he telephoned Zeena. "You get a shower?" he asked her. "For the poison ivy?" She said she had. Then he asked her whether she had any ideas for the next assignment, which she said she hadn't. Then he didn't know what else to say to her.

"What's wrong?" she asked after a silence. "Is there something wrong?"

He told her what he'd learned at dinner, the whole of what he'd learned and what he'd said. She didn't respond for a time. And then she said, "You like Guy too, don't you?" and he said he did. He heard her breathe out a long deep breath. "Yeah," she said. "I like Corinne too. Why that makes it harder, I don't know, but it does." It made him feel better for some reason. He thanked her for listening and they hung up.

Again, he just sat at his desk for a while. Then from the envelope under the assignments and money in the bottom desk drawer, he took out the photograph of his father sitting with him on the deck. From his top desk drawer he took out the photograph of Merial with the snowman. He held the two pictures up alongside each other. Very deliberately he tore the picture of him with his father in half, and then those halves into further halves, and then those into pieces that were too small to tear up any further. He did the same with the picture of Merial, and then he mixed the piles of pieces, and carried them all to the bathroom where he flushed them out of his life forever.

24

"Well," Zeena said, leaning up against the huge block of limestone she'd been working on, "either it's too well hidden or it's gone or we've missed something. Let's take a look at the clue again."

Mark scrambled over to her, digging the folded copy of Assignment 7 out of his back pocket for her as he did so. He sat down next to her and shoved his feet irritably into the crushed shale that blanketed everything. His sneakers were buried immediately.

It was late Friday afternoon and though only mid-May, felt like midsummer. It was hot and still. The sounds of rush hour at the heavily trafficked intersection of Washington and Allegheny River Boulevards, almost a hundred yards straight down from where they were sitting, were muffled by the trees to nothing more than a pleasant swish. Far off to the right was the river, swollen and muddy with spring rain, moving grandly down to the city. The cliff behind them trickled water. From time to time, small pieces of stone fell from it, clicking pleasantly on top of the house-sized block of limestone they were leaning up against.

Mark took off his sneakers to shake out the tiny splinters of stone. Zeena, he saw, had had the foresight to wear high-topped workshoes this trip. "Damned stuff is worse to get around in than broken glass," he grumbled. She patted his thigh lightly and rested her hand there while continuing to study the assignment. The casualness of the gesture made his heart jump. A plan had been forming in Mark's head. What if they got an apartment together right after they graduated in June? Or, at least, they could get apartments near each other, in Oakland where Pitt was, or in Shadyside—somewhere away from where they lived now in any case. They'd be free then to live any way they wanted, and with no one else to have to answer to.

Of course, the absolutely essential ingredient for the realization of this dream was their coming into their Great Expectations.

Mark picked up a piece of shale and threw it in the direction of the old, rusted railroad track which ran in front of them about twenty-five yards down the slope from where they were sitting.

"I *hate* being stopped this close to the end," he said. "I thought after Dr. Harkness we were home free." He leaned back to look at the verse clue of the assignment again:

> Full fathom five this life form lay,
> Or rather a fifth that measure squared,
> Before the Brilliant Cut that day
> Evolution's story shared.
>
> In what the famous eyes became,
> The coral bones of its colleagues hide
> The way to the end of this journey, Friends—
> And to a view of the other side.

It was some lines from Shakespeare's *The Tempest* that were being played with they discovered:

Full fathom five thy father lies;
Of his bones are coral made;
Those are pearls that were his eyes;
Nothing of him that doth fade,
But doth suffer a sea-change
Into something rich and strange.

"So all we need," Zeena said, "is to know where that fossil came from. It's other fossils just like the one we have that are going to be hiding Assignment Eight—and hiding it in something that's . . . that's like a pearl? or pearl-colored? that's connected with pearls anyway."

The next afternoon a couple of telephone calls had gotten Mark and Zeena to Dr. Edward Harkness of the Department of Geology at the University of Pittsburgh. He told them to bring the specimen to his office Wednesday afternoon. Four o'clock sharp.

"Come to me, dear," Dr. Harkness sang out cheerily, wriggling his stubby fingers the moment he saw the stone emerge from Mark's backpack. He was a dwarf, no more than three feet high. He peered down at the embedded fragments of the fossil for a few moments and then looked back up at Mark and Zeena, grinning. "Hot diggity," he rapped out. "That's Ames, no mistake, and those are deltodus teeth, bet a cookie." He scuttled quickly to his desk and picked up a magnifying glass with which he looked at the fossil again. "Yes! Yes! Yes!" he cried. "Deltodus for win. Petalodus for place and show." Then he whipped around the back of his desk to the bookcase filling an entire wall of his office. "Where are you, dear," he warbled, his head moving along the shelves like the carriage of a typewriter. "Ah," he said. He scooted a small wheeled stepladder from the corner to about the middle of the bookcase, snapped some kind of brake on it, and climbing to the very top, extracted a book.

"Take this," he said to Mark, gesturing with the fossil, but when Mark made as if to return it to his backpack he was told "No, no, no, no. Hold it *up*." Mark held the fossil on about a level with his forehead as Dr. Harkness turned pages, peering alternately at them and the stone.

"Hot diggity," he said after a time. "Petalodus and *not* deltodus. Always hedge your bets, my dears. Always hedge your bets."

Location? Well, the remains of petalodi, a species of shark extinct for millions and millions of years, could be found only in *marine* limestone, in Ames limestone. But there were outcroppings of Ames all over the Pittsburgh area, in road cuts, along streams and rivers, everywhere. Chances were, though, if the fossil was from the city, that it came from Brilliant Cut. "Nice piece of Ames to work on there."

Both Mark and Zeena had jumped at the name. "Brilliant Cut's a *place*, then!" Mark exclaimed.

It was, indeed, the name of a railroad cut around a cliff that had exposed three hundred million years of geological record. In fact, the Department of Geology often took students on field trips there. The "nice piece of Ames" Dr. Harkness spoke of was a bungalow-sized chunk of rock that, in 1941, had broken off near the top of the cliff and derailed a train. Dr. Harkness showed them on a topographical map where Brilliant Cut was at the foot of Washington Boulevard. In spite of having driven by the area thousands of times, neither Mark nor Zeena had ever noticed the two-hundred-foot cliff.

"You wouldn't," Dr. Harkness said. "Hidden by trees. Have to know it's there."

"And you know that big piece of Ames he was talking about at the bottom of the cliff?" Mark said to Zeena just outside Dr. Harkness' office. "It's just about the right distance down from the top. A hundred and eighty feet."

"What do you mean?"

"The clue, remember?

```
Full fathom five this life form lay,
Or rather a fifth that measure squared,
```

Okay. A fathom is six feet. So five fathoms is thirty feet. Square thirty and you get nine hundred. And one-fifth of nine hundred is a hundred and eighty feet."

Except that for the second afternoon that week they'd combed the fallen block of Ames limestone, sides and top and as far under the edges of it buried in the shale as they could reach, and they hadn't found a thing. No pearl-covered or pearl-shaped anything. Nothing.

Zeena got to her feet and worked her way along the block of Ames limestone until she could look up to the top of Brilliant Cut cliff. For quite a while she stood looking up, shading her eyes with one hand. Then she studied the assignment again, and again looked up, this time shading her eyes with the paper.

"Come over here, Mark," she said still looking up. "I think we're in the wrong place. Come look at this."

He made his way over to her and looked high up on the cliff to where she was pointing. He looked up and then down again quickly as his stomach lurched. The cliff was twenty to twenty-five stories high and edged at the top with trees, most of them with their roots exposed by erosion. Several such trees, big ones, had tumbled to the bottom of the cliff where they lay with their dead black roots reaching upward. The cliff wasn't the kind of thing even to stand near.

"See that belt of white stone up there?" Zeena said. "That's what this thing," she patted the block of limestone, "broke off of, right?"

"So?"

"So that's where I think Assignment Eight's going to be. Like in the bell tower. It's not in *this* piece of Ames," she said, kicking at the block of limestone they'd been working on. "It's in that belt of Ames up there."

He looked at her incredulously and then glanced up at the cliff again. The face of it was ragged with protruding pieces of shale. It looked about as stable as a stack of coins.

"What do you mean it's in that belt up there?" he asked. She was looking up again. She pointed. "There's like crevices in the limestone up there. Little caves. See?"

He didn't even bother looking up. "Zeena," he said, "there's no *way* we could climb that cliff. And besides, the distance is wrong. That belt up there isn't a hundred and eighty feet *down* from the top. It's more like a hundred and eighty feet *up*."

"I know. That's what stumped me. But look at these two lines again:

> Full fathom five this life form lay,
> Or rather a fifth that measure squared.

Now, five fathoms is thirty feet you said. Okay. But suppose you take a fifth of thirty feet *first*. That's six feet, right? And then square *that*. You get thirty-six feet. A fifth of five *fathoms* squared. You could read the lines that way too, couldn't you?" She looked up at the cliff again. "And

I figure that belt of Ames up there is just about thirty-six feet *down* from the top." She looked back at him and smiled. "What do you think?"

Mark just stared at her. She was right, of course.

"And I know we can't *climb* the cliff," she went on, "but we could climb up the other side of it and then go down the cliff on a rope tied to one of those trees up there, couldn't we?"

He risked another glance up but couldn't hold it. He just shook his head, not speaking.

"No other way I can see," she added.

"Forget it, Zeen. It's just too damned dangerous. It would be too dangerous even if we knew Assignment Eight was up there somewhere—and we don't."

She put a hand on his arm. "Yes, we do. The assignment's up there. I just feel it. You feel it too, don't you?" There were spots of red at her cheekbones.

He turned his back to her and with one arm above his head leaned on the block of Ames.

"I think what's really bothering you is the height," she said from behind him after a while. "But see, heights don't bother me at all."

"It's my turn," he said sullenly without turning around. "You went up the bell tower."

"Yeah, right, Mark," she said. "And how much do you weigh? I'm supposed to lower *you* and then haul *you* back up to the top of that cliff? Give me a break, will you?"

He whirled to face her. "What if I *can't* haul you back up?" he asked fiercely. "You ever think of that?"

She grinned at him. "Then I'll climb, baby. I'll climb." She kissed him, lightly, but full on the mouth. "Pick me up tomorrow morning at eight. Same place. Bring rope— and our old friend the pig's-foot. I have to be at work by noon, remember."

25

Mark knelt over his backpack, took out the coil of yellow plastic rope, and for a time just looked down at it. "It isn't right that you're the one going down there," he said.

"Look, Mark," she said. "We already settled that. There's just no other way." She picked up the coil of rope and got to her feet. "Besides, somebody *put* Assignment Eight down there, like in the church. It can't be all that impossible." She turned her back to him, tucked the coil of rope under one arm, and began looking around at the trees.

It was Saturday, almost midmorning. They were at the top of the cliff at Brilliant Cut, about ten feet back from the edge. It had taken them almost an hour of climbing to get there. The way was almost straight up in places and was pathless. Only just before the cliff edge, a sheer plunge into space, did the ground level off. Far below them, though Mark took Zeena's word for it, was the giant block of Ames they'd worked on. It looked about the size of a cinder block Zeena said. Mark had no trouble with the view straight ahead, however. He saw the two kidney-shaped lakes of Highland Park Reservoir gleaming like mirrors in the near distance, and beyond them, where the Allegheny River joined the Monongahela to make the three rivers of Pittsburgh, the downtown skyline.

Mark came up behind Zeena who was studying an oak tree about three feet in diameter.

"What did you mean, when you said yesterday that I can't deal with heights?" He'd been thinking of her comment ever since she'd made it.

She looked at him over one shoulder. "What do you mean what do I mean? You turn green when you look down a flight of stairs. Show me how we rig this thing?"

He smiled in spite of himself.

"I just don't know what it is," he said ruefully.

"Would it matter if you did?" she said without turning around. "What do you think of this tree as anchor? Do we have enough rope?"

Mark glanced back at the cliff edge, about twenty-five feet away.

"We only got sixty feet." Mark had measured the length of the rope in his father's workroom the night before. "How about that tree over there?" He pointed to another oak, about a foot in diameter but ten or fifteen feet closer to the drop-off.

Zeena watched Mark measure off enough rope to tie several times around the tree. Then he began tying knots in the rest of it at two-foot intervals.

"What are you doing?" she asked.

"Making handholds," he said. He had worked it all out in his head the night before.

When he'd finished knotting the full length of rope, he wound one end of it several times around the tree and tied it with a bowline. The other end he tied with the same knot around Zeena's waist.

"You're not going to lower me down tied like this, are you?" she asked. "I thought maybe I'd sit in something."

"You will," Mark said. "This is just for added safety."

Then he made a sling just above the section he'd tied

around Zeena's waist and held it out for her to step into. He could feel the firmness of her hips as he placed the sling under her.

"Now, you hold on here, see?" he said, putting her hands on the knot just above the one that made the sling.

Zeena looked at the section of rope around her waist. "And these aren't slip knots or anything, right?" she grinned at him.

"Don't get cute," Mark said firmly. "That rope's strong enough to lift an elephant by the way. It's nylon."

"I better take the pig's-foot," Zeena said, and Mark got the crow's-foot for her out of his backpack. He watched her tuck it in the belt of her jeans. They stood facing each other.

"I still don't feel right about this," he said.

"No," she said, smiling. "You wouldn't. Silk wouldn't either. But I don't need a hero, remember? I want another kind of Monday."

What'd she have to mention Silk for? he thought but he didn't say anything.

Zeena walked toward the cliff and about eight feet from it dropped to all fours and started to edge herself sideways.

"Wait a minute for God's sake," Mark called racing to the far side of the tree the rope was tied to. She stopped moving until he'd sat down, braced his feet on the tree, and taken up the slack on the knotted rope that stretched between them. "Okay," he called. "Easy now. I'm going to give you line. Try to keep it taut between us." She moved crablike toward the cliff edge as he paid out the rope.

Suddenly, there was a ghastly crashing sound, a scream and Zeena was gone. Mark felt himself slammed up against the tree and the knotted rope tore loose from his grasp and ran burning through his hands like a red-hot wire. There was another crashing sound from the other side of the cliff. The rope was stretched tight between the tree and the bottom of a U-shaped depression in the cliff edge where the rim had given way.

"Zeena!" Mark screamed, scrambling up onto all fours. Pain stabbed at his side. His ribs felt like they'd been broken this time, or bruised all over again. "Zeena!" he cried once more.

For a moment there was nothing but the sound of stones falling on the shale below, which came up to Mark like the sound of heavy rain.

And then he heard her voice. "Wow," she called up with a muffled-sounding laugh. "That was some trip down."

"Are you okay?" he bellowed as loud as he could.

"Okay," he heard from below. "You were right about the rope. And the knots too. I'm too low though. You'll have to pull me up some."

"Oh, thank God," he said in a low voice to himself. "Thank you. Thank you."

The palm of his left hand was raw and bleeding. He positioned himself behind the tree again and grabbed a knot in the rope on the far side of it. Bracing his feet and grimacing with pain in his hand and ribs both, he pulled with all his strength. More stones broke loose at the cliff edge as the knotted rope dragged through it, but Zeena came up a couple of feet.

"Hey," he heard her yell. "Stop."

He stopped, holding her weight.

"What do you want me to do?" he roared at her. For a moment she didn't answer, and he could feel movement at the end of the rope. His side throbbed and the strain was beginning to tell on his arms.

"You'll have to pull me up a little higher," he heard float up to him, "but not yet. I'll tell you when." There was more movement and again the sound of falling stones. "Okay," she said, "take me up now."

Mark twisted his right leg, his strong leg, around the rope several times, and then bracing his bad knee against the tree, he pulled up on the rope with his leg and arms both. Holding the rope with his leg and one arm, he wrapped the slack around his shoulders. Several times he repeated the maneuver, using his body as a fulcrum. His ribs were still on fire, but he began to breathe more easily.

"Okay, stop," she called out. "I'm by the Ames."

Suddenly, the rope went slack and then tightened again, but not with Zeena's full weight. Again Mark yelled out her name.

"Relax," he heard after a moment. "There's a ledge. Don't let me go, though. I don't trust it."

"I got you," he yelled.

The rope remained taut between them but had no real weight on it. It began to move slowly to the right side of the U-shaped depression at the cliff edge. But then it caught on something.

"I need some slack," she called up.

"Okay," he hollered. "But wait a minute. The rope's stuck."

"There's like a little cave here. I think there's something in it."

"Okay. Wait till I tell you to pull again though." He unwound a length of rope from around his shoulders and then another, and let the rope between him and where it was caught at the cliff edge go slack. Then he flapped the rope in the air to dislodge it, but it stayed wedged between some stones. He flapped it again, harder this time, and the rope bounced free. "Try it now," he yelled.

The rope went taut again and Mark began slowly to pay out the line he'd unwound. Then once more the rope went slack. She seemed to have stopped moving.

"Okay?" he called out. There was no response. Mark listened for the sound of metal on stone, but there was nothing. "Okay?" he roared loudly, more anxiously.

"Bring me up," he heard her sing out in triumph. "I got the bacon."

Mark had no more than wound his leg around the rope to prepare for the heavy hauling when Zeena's full weight again slammed him violently against the tree. There was a heavy crash from the shale below the cliff.

"All right, Zeena?" he yelled out into the air, pushing himself back from the tree. The rope seemed to be swaying, as though she were swinging freely in the air.

"Whooee!" he heard her sing out. "Told you I didn't trust that ledge. You pull up, I'll climb."

In a few moments he saw her head appear in the bottom of the depression, and then the weight went off his arms and shoulders altogether. When he saw her crawling, he turned over and lay on his back. She came up to where he was and turned over to lie face up on the ground by the tree with him.

"Wow," she said, and Mark knew she'd been a lot more frightened than she'd let on. "You wouldn't by chance have a cigarette with you, would you, baby? I could *really* go for a cigarette now." She laughed briefly. "I lost the pig's-foot," she said, "but look." She sat up and took a slim, beautifully-figured box from inside her shirt. Smiling, she held it out to him. It was about the size of a small candy box, pearl-colored, and shone iridescently in the morning sunlight. He too sat up and turned it in his hands.

"It's made of . . . mother-of-pearl? Some kind of shell, I think," Zeena said.

Mark looked at her. She was sweaty and her hair and face were filthy. There was a cut across the back of one of her hands. He put down the box, took her cut hand in his, and carried it to his face and kissed it. Then he eased her down onto her back and kissed her as she had him in the bell tower, forehead, eyes, cheeks. The skin of her face was wet but cool.

"Thank God you're okay." He breathed into her neck. "Just thank God you're okay."

After a time she sat up and said, "Let's see what's here. This may be the end."

"You open it," he said, sitting up with her, and she did. There was the same black plastic wrapper and two envelopes inside it. In one was the assignment. In the other there were twenty-three one-hundred-dollar bills.

Assignment 8

Did you notice the quiet, Children? The silence?

Once, for example, sitting where I suspect it is you are sitting now, I heard a hawk scream as he shredded clouds high above the cliff. That night, at the still point of the turning world, a fox barked with joy, and I saw the stars throw down their spears and water heaven with their tears.

But the next day, down below you there in the Valley of the Shadow of Death, I heard only the crunching of shale shards punctuating the silence as I walked. The remains of millennia it was I splintered beneath my feet: sigillaria, cordites, and crinoids, gone black and green;

fragments of bracheopods and coelenterata in
the limestone nodules, all of which once dia-
logued with sunlight, gladdened in rain.

What is real then, Children, music, or the silence it momentarily replaces? Our stories, or
the chaos from which we make them?

> In order to reach your Journey's End,
> You must the Doorway of No Wind seek.
> Ask Rose Tourette to point the way,
> To have your futures speak.

" 'In order to reach your Journey's End.' " Zeena said.
"This is the last assignment for sure, Mark."

He sat up and hugged his knees.

"Have you thought about how much we'll get?" he
asked her, looking out over the river to downtown Pittsburgh and then to the blue hills of western Pennsylvania,
rolling beyond the city into the misty distance.

"No," she said. "I haven't."

"Sure you have," he said, looking over at her and grinning. "We both have."

She sniffed a laugh. "Okay. So I've thought about it."

"And?"

"How will I spend it, you mean? To pay for college, I
guess. What about you?"

"I've been thinking about the things money can do."

"Oh, it can do things all right," she said, and her tone
made him look over at her. Her head was down. "Remember Pip in *Great Expectations*, though? The money he
got . . . cut him off from things. People he loved. People
that loved him."

He didn't speak for a while. "It wasn't money that broke
up me and Merial."

She didn't say anything. She didn't look at him either. The sound of a barge horn floated up from the river. Softened by distance, it was as small as a pitch pipe. The world felt far away to him, far away and insignificant. There was nothing but the two of them, just the two of them, above and outside everything.

"I want you to think about something," he said to her. "I want you just to *think* about it, okay? Don't say anything now. I want us to . . . be together this summer. When we finish the quest. After we graduate. I mean down in Oakland maybe, near Pitt, or in Shadyside."

Then she did look up at him, her face a mask. "Live together you mean?"

It sounded crude to him the way she said it. "No," he said. "Not just that way."

"What way then?"

He looked off into the distance and shook his head and sighed. "I love you, is what I want to say," he said finally. "I want us to look for another kind of Monday together. That's all I meant. Just think about it, okay?"

For a while they just sat together. And then she took his hand, as he had hers, and carried it to her face and kissed it. "Okay," she said. "I will."

26

The Doorway of No Wind turned out to be an ordinary row house on Pittsburgh's South Side: 1842 Cassandra Street, third down from the corner of Carson. PLEASE RING AND WALK IN read the sign inside the closely-curtained glass of the outer door, and it was signed ROSE TOURETTE. Mark pressed the bell. He heard no ring, but a couple of doors down on the other side of the street there was a rattle of chain and a pair of snaky-headed Dobermans on a stoop rose to look at him. He opened the outer door quickly, and he and Zeena stepped into a small vestibule four or five feet square from which a second door, this one solid and very sturdy looking, led into the house. Mounted on this second door in dull brass was what Mark thought at first was a face.

He looked at the symbol closely, but could make nothing of it.

To his great surprise, Mark had found Rose Tourette,

listed just that same way, in the Greater Pittsburgh Telephone Directory. He'd looked her up and called the same Saturday he and Zeena had been on top of the cliff at Brilliant Cut. A man answered. He had a deep full voice and at first sounded suspicious. What did he want with Rose Tourette? Mark's mention of the Doorway of No Wind turned him around immediately, however. "Oh yes," he said. "Come for your sitting a week from Monday at three o'clock," and then he repeated the address that was in the phone book. "What's a sitting?" Mark asked, at which there was a brief, deep chuckle. "Just bring yourselves—and the price of admission," the voice said. It wasn't until later that Mark picked up on the use of the word "yourselves." He'd never told the man that two of them were coming. The Monday of the appointment turned out to be a holiday, Memorial Day.

Mark knocked at the inner door of the vestibule, which pushed open to a long narrow hall, lighted by only a low wattage bulb screwed into a fixture on the ceiling. To the right at the far end of the hall was an open doorway.

The room they walked into had an unlived in but cluttered feel. The two windows facing the street were hung over with heavy black drapes, and the same material blocked off what looked to be a door to the left. In the middle of the room, surrounded by six straight-backed chairs, was a round table covered with a piece of dark-fringed cloth. A flared shade of stained glass with another dim bulb hung just above it. There were lots of other tables in the room too, small and highly ornamented, like fancy end tables. All of them were filled with framed photographs and knickknacks. The walls of the room, from floor to ceiling, were covered with pictures. Just across from where Mark and Zeena stood were three specimen cabinets with glass doors.

Mark raised his head a bit and sniffed. "What's that smell?" he whispered, but Zeena didn't answer. It was a sweet but faintly rotten odor, like decaying flowers. "Isn't it a great way to end the quest, though?" he whispered again. Still Zeena didn't say anything. Her hands were jammed down hard into her windbreaker pockets.

Mark walked over to a small claw-footed table standing in the corner of the room, just to the right of one of the draped windows. He leaned down, his hands on his knees. "Hey, come look at this, Zeen," he said after a moment.

She didn't move. Mark turned to see her staring at the specimen cabinets.

"Come over here," he said. "You're not going to believe this."

She came over and stood slightly behind him, looking down at the things on the table.

The groupings of gold-framed photographs made no sense, either individually or as a unit. In one picture a lot of rusty cogs had been photographed lying on top of a piece of bread. Another seemed to be a series of shots of an animal lying mangled on a highway, though in the dim light it was hard to be sure.

"What's this, do you think," Mark said, reaching out to take up a picture of a line of Xs.

Zeena caught his hand back. "It's stitches," she hissed in an undertone. "That's a stitched-up wound. Leave it alone."

"Jesus," he said softly, leaning over to look at the other things on the table.

There was a pile of filthy-looking white feathers and alongside it another pile of black grains, like seeds. An etched shot glass half filled with something dark and congealed lay just behind them and just behind it a fragment of what had to be a human jawbone because it contained several filled teeth. A small jointed puppet, blindfolded, sat beside an arrangement of needles laid point to point to form a circle. At the back of the table, almost covered by a gold cloth, was something dried or shriveled, like a piece of beef jerky. Mark reached carefully over the table to pick it up, and again Zeena caught back his arm. She held onto it this time, her fingers pressed hard.

"I mean it, Mark," she said in a harsh whisper. "Don't touch *anything*. This is some bad shit, here."

He looked at her grinning with surprise. He'd never heard her talk that way before. She started to say something else, but stopped herself, dropping her arm and taking a quick step back, her eyes on the wall behind him. Mark turned to see a grouping of oil paintings, but so blackened with age that he couldn't quite make out what they were paintings of. Shapes locked together, fighting, heaving, giving the impression of enormous energy.

"What are they?" he said.

"They're pictures of men and women, is what they are," Zeena said grimly. "Filthy. And those cabinets over there?"—she pulled his arm to turn him—"I think one of the shelves in there is full of human—"

They both saw her at the same time.

A woman was in the room with them, standing in front of the curtained doorway faced in their direction, but with her eyes downcast.

"I am Rose Tourette," the woman said. "I am of the company. I keep the watch." Her voice was the same one Mark had heard speaking on the telephone, the voice he'd taken for that of a man.

In appearance she was plain to the point of being nondescript. She wore wire-rimmed spectacles and was dressed like one of the older teachers at Moorland, in a plain blue, long-sleeved dress with small gold buttons down the front. Her shapeless, blocky body reminded Mark of a thousand other women he had seen, waiting at bus stops, moving up and down escalators, always with handbags and carrying packages. She looked like somebody else's grandmother, and except for her voice, was about as exotic as a box of cereal.

"What?" Mark said, taken aback. "What did you say?"

The woman smiled slightly and moved smoothly to the table where she pulled out one of the chairs and sat down. "Please," the man's voice said, and the woman gestured on both sides of her. She had not yet looked at either of them.

Zeena moved stiffly behind Mark, as though she were being dragged on a leash. He pulled out two chairs that were alongside each other and was about to sit down.

"On opposite sides of the table, please," the voice said.

Mark stepped around to the other side of the table, and sat down there. He waited for the woman to look up and acknowledge them, but she didn't. She just sat, hands in her lap, her head bowed slightly, and from the light over the table Mark could see that behind her glasses her eyes were closed. He looked up at Zeena still standing where he'd left her, her arms folded tightly across her chest. She was staring at the woman, her face set and tight. For some reason, Mark felt an impulse to laugh, which he smothered by clearing his throat. The sound seemed to trigger something in the woman. Slowly she raised her head. There was a whirring rasp, as in a clock about to strike, and then Mark realized that she was taking a breath. She turned her head first in Zeena's direction, then in Mark's. Her eyes were still closed.

"I am a Touretter," the woman said in her strange man's voice, "so I call myself Rose Tourette. I am Wild Rose to some, Gypsy Rose to others." She paused slightly. "Gypsy

Rose the Stripper," she added with a deep chuckle. "I am also known as Broker Rose, for I deal in futures." She placed both her hands palms up, cupped on the table in front of her. "How may I help you, Children?"

Children. Mark glanced at Zeena to see whether the word had struck her, but her attention was fully on the woman.

"Well," Mark said, "like I said on the phone, what we want is . . . to know about the Doorway of No Wind."

The woman didn't move at first, nor did she open her eyes. But it seemed to Mark as though something in her, like the Dobermans outside, had raised itself to look at him.

"Ahhh," the woman said, all in one low bell-like tone. She rose and went to the middle specimen cabinet. From behind one of the lower glass doors, she took out a manila envelope, returned to the table with it, and sat down again, putting the envelope in front of her.

Had she kept her eyes closed the whole time? Mark wondered, because they still weren't open.

"And now, Children," she said, smiling. "Both of you are to be seated—and I am to have fifty dollars."

"Better sit down, Zeena," Mark said, digging into the side pocket of his jeans. He'd brought a hundred and fifty dollars with him, not knowing what the price of admission was going to be. He laid two twenties and a ten on the table on top of the manila envelope. Zeena sank slowly onto the edge of one of the two pulled-out chairs opposite him, her eyes wide, her face frozen.

The woman removed her glasses and putting them to one side, her eyes still closed, she held out both hands to Mark, palms up. "And now your hand," she said. "I must have your left hand, please."

Mark put his left hand on top of the woman's right and

she covered it instantly with her other hand. For a moment both her hands were motionless. And then the hand on top of Mark's jerked as though rousing itself from sleep. It inched and hitched its way slowly up to his wrist, feeling, feeling as though looking for a pulse. Finally the woman's fingers locked themselves firmly around his wrist. Then she opened her eyes and looked at him.

It was like being hit hard in the face with something that at the same time drew Mark closer. He was barely conscious of the touch of the woman's fingers, but staring into her eyes was like being drawn into a pool of raw spinning energy. He could no more have looked or pulled away than he could have flown to the top of a building. There was a roar of noise in his head, shouting and crazy laughter. But it was not just noise he was hearing. It was words, phrases being yelled, whether at him or about him he couldn't be sure.

And then the face in front of him began to go to pieces, hunks of it lurching this way and that. It twitched and jumped, at first in small patches, under one eye, at the corner of the mouth, but then in larger and larger areas, more and more convulsively, across the forehead, up and down an entire cheek. Bones and muscles gnashed together, thrusting up into bulges and then flattening into hollows, ridging the nose, twisting the lips. The noise in Mark's head grew louder, more urgent.

"Mark!" he heard Zeena cry out as though from a great distance. "Mark! Let go! Let go!" But it was not a choice he had.

And then Mark realized the face was not going to pieces. It was changing, becoming another face, and drawing him into the process, making him a part of it. The clamor inside his head grew less, and then stilled, and finally there was absolute quiet. It was not the face of Rose Tourette he was looking at but his own face, his same forehead and mouth, his jaw and the angles of his cheekbones, but his own face as he had never seen it before, naked, and hideously repellent, as though some core of him, some core of absolute vileness, had been hauled up from the bottom of his being to become the whole of what he was. In shame, Mark tried to tear himself from the vision, to shut his eyes, turn his head, but he could not. He felt himself groaning but he could make no sound.

And then, as if acknowledging his recognition, the face in front of him slid slowly into a leering smile, a parody of his little boy grin. "How do you like us, Boy?" a new voice said. "Want to tell us what you see?"

He stared and stared, until suddenly there was noise again, a confusion of light and sound, and Mark felt himself spinning and falling, away from everything he knew, down and down and yet up at the same time, through stars, rocketed by some great force past the outer reaches of everything, into endless dark and ice and pain where he was to be alone forever, unloved, unloving, unlovable. The noise grew greater and greater, and then, somehow, there was Zeena clawing at his hand shrieking, "Let go, Mark! Let go! Let go!"

He was on his feet then, stumbling and choking, but still in the middle of the dark, surrounded by deep mocking laughter, where he heard the new voice saying, "I can show you more, Boy, I can show you more." And then there was light bursting, and he was stumbling, trying to run, and falling and getting up, and falling again and sobbing, crying for the world to come back please, *please*, come back, and finally the world reformed in the warm May sunshine with Zeena's arm around his shoulders and her saying "hush now" to him, saying "hush now, hush now, hush."

27

They had been walking on Carson Street for blocks. Several times they'd stopped to sit down, but Mark still had a searing headache. He could not bring himself to look Zeena in the eye.

"I'm okay now, really," he said, keeping his voice as even as he could. He nodded down at the torn-open manila envelope under Zeena's arm. "What's my half again?" he asked sarcastically. "Nineteen bucks?"

"I want you to read what he says, though," Zeena said. She pointed. "Let's sit down again. Over there."

They walked across the street to a low brick building that had a brief lawn, some small flower beds, and a few wooden benches. The South Side Branch of the Carnegie Library, the sign said, was closed because of Memorial Day. The library stood almost at the corner of the heavily trafficked turnoff from Carson Street onto the Birmingham Bridge over the Monongahela River.

They sat down on one of the benches and Zeena handed Mark the folded typewritten pages that had been in one of the two smaller envelopes inside the manila one. The other envelope had contained three ten dollar bills, a five, and three ones. None of the bills was new.

"I really don't want to read this guy now, Zeen," Mark said wearily. "I never understand him anyway."

"I know," she said. "But I want us to try."

Mark opened the pages and did his best to take them in:

Ave Atque Vale

Our revels now are ended, Children, leaving you at one threshold, me at another. Please consider yourselves free at this point to share anything of your experience with this quest with anyone you want to. Indeed, in a way that has been the point of it all. The end of this journey is the beginning of the real one.

A fitting stirrup cup would you call Rose Tourette? No Cumaean Sibyl she, of course, nor did our modest Rose ever aspire to oracular status; it was her idea to take her name from her affliction. But surely the window she opens—through which the musician may glimpse the whole of what is producing the music? through which the storyteller may see all of what is responsible for the story?—is the offering of a perspective you will wish to consider in responding to my story about the two of you with stories of your own.

For that is what I have been creating for myself with the quest, Children, and with my invention of the two of you to take it up: a story, a story about the importance of stories really, with you as my central characters. I invented you as two people who were strangers until I introduced you. I invented you as opposites that I bound together by insisting you discover the significance of decent common ground. I situated you, my characters, in the midst of a landscape, in the here and now of a place, this Pittsburgh, this western Pennsylvania, that like all places is no more than what its past and present and future can be made to mean. And I gave you the material, the stuff of story, with which to make that meaning and to make it whatever you wished.

And in this very particular but also cosmic landscape, you became my heroes, Children. I watched you, in my mind's eye, confronting a world you became increasingly aware is one of uncertainty, ugliness, and betrayal, filled with waste and vanity and shame—and yet which is shot through too with blazings of honesty, stunning courage, baffling fidelities, improbably acts of kindness and self-sacrifice.

And in your looking for some kind of lodestar to guide you in such a world, in your search for the still point of the turning wheel, for what shone only with its own authenticity, you moved steadily toward my Great Expectations for you: toward understanding that the importance of seeing one's life as a story is to see other ways in which the story may be told. And because you are my heroes, I saw you using this understanding to help one another look more closely at the stories the two of you are living, separately as well as together, revising them as necessary, and where possible. I watched you, in short—my characters, my heroes—growing up, and becoming friends.

I am well aware, of course, that nothing like this may have happened, that whoever found Assignment 1 may never have chosen a companion, or, if he or she did, that the money, never any more than a means to an end, may have become what really mattered—or worse, in becoming the only thing that mattered may have helped turn you into the very reverse of what I hoped for. No one knows better than I that there is no such thing as a legacy that cannot be misappropriated, an inheritance that cannot be squandered. I would be the first to admit that the two of you may exist as heroes only in my own imagination.

But life begins and ends in the imagination, Children, takes its shape from the stories we are able to construct for ourselves and others. It is dreams and fantasy, as Carl Jung has said, that create reality and not the other way around. My imagining you as I have, in other words, has given me much. I have no regrets.

Ave atque vale.

The phrase is Catullus's. Hail and Farewell. It is all there is left for me to say to you. Perhaps, it is the most anyone has to say to anyone.

In any case, ave atque vale—my co-creators, my fellow travelers, my friends.

Mark's impulse was to tear what he'd read to pieces, but he refolded the typewritten pages and handed them back to Zeena. "So?" he asked.

Zeena didn't respond right away. "Well," she said after a time. "At least we know we're not crazy. That's something."

"Oh, really?" he said mechanically, having no idea what she meant.

William E. Coles, Jr. · 241

"I'm talking about that woman. What her face did. What really happened. We weren't just seeing things."

Mark shook his head and smiled thinly. "I don't think you saw what I saw."

"What we saw was a woman with a disease, Mark. An affliction, he calls it. I bet if we look up Tourette we find it's some kind of condition."

"And that's what you wanted me to read his . . . his crap for? Because I don't get it. I *never* got what he was talking about."

For a while Zeena didn't speak. "Mark, you were a lot braver in that woman's house than I'd have been. I couldn't have let her touch me."

He knew she'd already decided she wasn't going to live with him. Even if the quest had paid off, she wouldn't have done it. "Look," he said, bitterly. "Quit just trying to make me feel better, will you?"

"Why don't you quit just thinking about yourself here for a minute," she retorted.

It brought his head up.

"I'm sorry," she said, looking off. "I wanted to talk about . . ." she gestured with the folded pages "about living a story. There's something I want to tell you."

"I'm the one who's sorry," he said. "Go ahead."

She didn't begin right away. "You know who Aretha Franklin is?" she asked him after a time.

He nodded. She was a singer Merial had made him listen to—and that he was glad he had. Aretha Franklin, the Queen of Soul.

"Yeah. Well, my mom and dad met each other at one of her concerts. I heard them tell it a thousand times. They were sitting next to each other—just by chance— and at the end of the concert my dad just sat there like he was in a coma or something. Mom couldn't get by him to get out, so she asked him if he was okay. Dad said he was just trying to work out whether he'd earned the right to love Aretha Franklin's singing as much as he did. Then my mom said she'd never known anybody white with enough sense to say a thing like that. They both got laughing, and they went to a diner and talked till morning."

She didn't continue immediately. Mark's eyes were riveted on her.

"My mom's family didn't want her with my dad, and his felt the same way, but of course that only pushed them closer together, into their own private world. It was them against the rest of the world, see, and within a couple of months they got an apartment together, and then they got married, and then they had me—"

She stopped, seeming to reflect on what she'd just said.

"Or maybe I was the reason they got married. I've never really been sure."

Zeena took hold of the seat of the bench with both hands and looked down at her knees.

"And you know that woman I told you my dad got mixed up with?"

"Yes," he said. "Corinne."

"No. *Not* Corinne. That's my point. Dad didn't meet Corinne until he was in Cincinnati. Marion was the other woman's name."

She looked up at him. "Do you remember I told you how they got involved?"

"You said they worked together."

"Day and night. Day and night they worked on that project—in their own private world." She glanced over at him. "And a year later my dad didn't even know where she lived."

Again she paused.

"And there's one other thing you should know," she

went on. "Marion looked just like Merial. Same blonde hair, same—" she thrust out one hand impatiently— "same everything."

He turned from her without saying anything, put his forearms on his knees, and stared down at the ground between them. Nothing she said was going to touch the fact that it was over. Everything was over.

"So," Zeena said, "want to hear what I want?"

"Sure," he said mechanically, without looking at her.

"Do you like movies?"

"What?" he said.

"Movies. Do you like them?"

"Yeah," he said. "I guess so. Sure."

"So why don't you ask me to a movie? You never asked me to a movie."

He sat up and looked at her, dumbfounded. She'd go out with him? She'd go on a date with him? She *wanted* him to ask her to go out with him?

"And want to know what else I want?"

He nodded, his throbbing head whirling.

"I want us to tell people about the quest. He says that that was the point of it. I think we ought to do it."

"Tell who?"

"Anybody we want. Anybody we think might want to hear about it."

Now he saw what she was trying to do. "You mean Merial, don't you?"

"I mean Merial, Silk, your mom, mine, Guy, my dad, maybe even your dad."

"Mine? I don't even know where he is!"

"You could try to find out."

"Why should I? He was never interested in me."

She widened her eyes. "Fifty thousand dollars put in trust for you might count as interest, don't you think? You aren't really just going to send that money back without even trying to talk to him, are you?"

He just stared at her.

She smiled. "You don't want to be that kind of a nasty ass, do you?"

It was what he'd said to her about her dealings with her father. It made him smile back at her in spite of his aching head, in spite of everything. Rose Tourette had torn him to pieces. The quest was over. Zeena was not going to ride with him into the sunset. Yet here he was, still with her, smiling at her. It made him laugh.

He stood up and she stood up with him. To their left loomed the superstructure of the Birmingham Bridge, a spiderish arrangement of cables and soaring lime-green girders. Above the steel and wires, floating behind a distant hill, was the topmost part of the Cathedral of Learning, center of the University of Pittsburgh. The whole of the downtown of the city, Mark knew, would be on view from the bridge in the other direction were he and Zeena there to see it.

"Let's walk the bridge," Mark said.

Zeena looked over her shoulder at the traffic on the bridge, three lanes each way, without even a median strip dividing them. "You sure you want to try?" she asked him. But some people on Carson Street showed them how to go down toward the river in order to find the stairs up to the walkway.

"Maybe we've had enough for one day," Zeena said doubtfully, looking at the five flights up, but Mark took the stairs running, two at a time. At the top, panting from the climb, he kept his eyes on the view. Behind him was the South Side, its houses marching across the side of Mount Washington like the squares of an unfinished crossword puzzle. He looked upriver to where the old J and L Steel Mill had once fired the night skies of Pittsburgh. The only thing left from it was a smokestack painted baby blue. Across the river, on the left bank, was a new-looking factory of some sort, brave with glass and steel, and just beyond it the skeletal beginning of still another new building, already as big as a town. And downriver was the city, brilliant with the high young sun of spring. Under bridge after bridge, the muddy Monongahela slid down to it, glistening, like a road paved with gold.

Mark had almost caught his breath by the time Zeena reached the top of the stairs.

"Did you know," he asked her, "that there are more bridges in Pittsburgh than there are in the city of Venice?"

She nodded and came over to stand beside him. He put his arm around her shoulders, and for a time they looked at the city together, squinting into the sun.

"That thirty-eight dollars," he said. "It wasn't just a joke, was it?"

"I don't think so. I think it was all he had left."

"So you think he's broke?"

"I think he's dead," she said. And then she added, "Of course, that's only a guess."

Suddenly, Mark withdrew his arm from her shoulders. "Give me the money, okay? The thirty-eight dollars. I want us to make like a sacrifice with it."

"A what?"

"I want to throw it down to the Monongahela, as a sort of . . . offering to everything. What do you think?"

She stared at him a moment and then took his arm for the walk the rest of the way across the bridge. "Now, let's not go crazy here, baby," she said, smiling.